The Savage Wil

The Savage Wilderness

Book 3 in the New World Series

By

Griff Hosker

The Savage Wilderness

Published by Sword Books Ltd 2019

Copyright © Griff Hosker First Edition 2019

The author has asserted their moral right under the Copyright, Designs and Patents Act, 1988, to be identified as the author of this work. All Rights reserved. No part of this publication may be reproduced, copied, stored in a retrieval system, or transmitted, in any form or by any means, without the prior written consent of the copyright holder, nor be otherwise circulated in any form of binding or cover other than that in which it is published and without a similar condition being imposed on the subsequent purchaser.

A CIP catalogue record for this title is available from the British Library.

Cover by Design for Writers

Dedication

To Roger, Steve and all the other readers who help in my research.

Contents

The Savage Wilderness 1
Dedication 3
Prologue 5
Chapter 1 7
Chapter 2 21
Chapter 3 34
Chapter 4 48
Chapter 5 62
Chapter 6 75
Chapter 7 85
Chapter 8 99
Chapter 9 111
Chapter 10 123
Chapter 11 134
Chapter 12 142
Chapter 13 152
Chapter 14 167
Chapter 15 179
Chapter 16 190
Chapter 17 203
Chapter 18 213
Fótr 224
Epilogue 230
Norse Calendar 234
Glossary 235
Historical Note 239
Other books by Griff Hosker 242

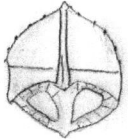

Prologue

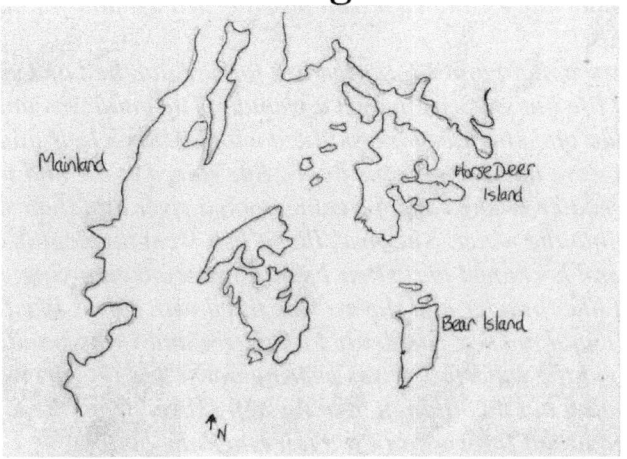

    I was born Erik Larsson but my people now call me Erik the Navigator for my skill in sailing. I am honoured that they do so for I am still young to captain a drekar. We are the Clan of the Fox and we were wanderers until we came across the seas from the land of ice and fire to find a new home far to the west. Our first years on the islands we now call home had been both fruitful and tragic. Encounters with animals, as well as the Skraelings, the barbarians who lived on what we thought of as the mainland, had taken men, women and children, but we were a hardy people. We came from Larswick which lay south of the Land of the Wolf and before that Orkneyjar and before that the fjords of the Norse. We could adapt and survive for it was in our blood.

    I had taken a woman. Ada was the widow of Dreng. Their son Dreng had been one of my ship's boys and he had died after discovering this new land in the west. We had grown very close but Ada knew that I would not marry her, for I had had a dream and a man ignored such dreams at his peril. When I closed my eyes at night, with Ada snuggling in my arms beneath my bear fur, I could still relive the dream. I had had the dream many times and it had changed a little since I had first dreamed it.

I sailed the seas. I saw the sun rising to my left, the east. We passed through islands and I saw a forest on the mainland. I was alone and I climbed a trail passing strange and wondrous animals.

I saw a maid and I followed her for she laughed and seemed full of life but she was not yet a woman. The maid was not of our clan and she was dark-skinned with jet black hair and eyes which were like deep purple pools. She stared at me and I followed her as she ran. We came upon a river and then she dived into the water. She rose, like a fish from the depths and her hand beckoned me. Then I saw a waterfall emptying with a sound like thunder and the air was filled with spray, like fog so that I could not see. Suddenly I could see and I was standing on top of the waterfall. I was peering down and the girl was beckoning me. I could not help myself. I dived from the top. I seemed to fall forever but I did not reach the bottom.

The first part was realised and we had passed through the islands. I had seen the forests but I had to, as yet, climb through them. Until I did so my spirit would be restless. It might be that Ada and I were meant to be together but, until I saw the waterfall and the Skraeling maiden then I would never know. Now that I had a son, Lars, I was tied closer to Ada but the dream still drew me to the mainland and I knew that one day, I would have to try to find this waterfall and the maid.

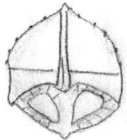

Chapter 1

When we had defeated the Skraeling, I had captured one of them. He had looked as though he was willing to sell his life dearly but when he saw the bear's teeth necklace around my neck he had meekly surrendered. I discovered that he thought I was a shaman, a Skraeling galdramenn. It had been the threads of the Norns! The youth had been lamed as had my uncle, Snorri Long Fingers. Gytha, his wife, was a volva and a powerful one at that. She had seen the webs of the Norns in all this and the Skraeling was given to Snorri so that he could teach him our words and we could learn his. I was a little selfish in all of this for I knew that I would wish to speak to the Skraeling maiden and I wanted the words to be able to do so.

Gytha and Snorri were kind. Since my cousin Tostig had married and left home they had an empty home and the Skraeling filled a void. Siggi, their eldest, had left home long ago. Snorri was keen for the boy to be able to speak our language while I wanted to learn his. None could pronounce his name as his people seemed to have sounds they made which were alien to us. We called him Bear Tooth as he seemed fascinated by my necklace and he seemed happy to answer to that name. That was our first breakthrough for when he kept pointing at it, Snorri told him the Norse word and he said the native word. It was then we learned that his people, his clan, were called Unamagi, or at least that was the sound he made. When we repeated it then he nodded. His tribe were part of a people called Mi'kmaq although, when we said, 'Micmac' he corrected us until we had the pronunciation right. That breakthrough enabled Snorri and me to make faster progress. Snorri was able to devote all of his time to the boy and they became close. I had other tasks such as fishing and hunting. I also had to spend time with Ada, our new child and foster children. I found myself disappointed that I could not understand as much as Snorri but I visited Gytha's home each day to learn a new word and see the progress which Snorri Long Fingers was making.

We learned that the bear was considered sacred to his people. They had holy men, shamans, and it was they who wore the teeth around their necks. He had thought I was such a shaman and it explained how I had been able to capture him relatively easily. He told us that his people would be far away from the coast when the days were short. It seemed they came to the coast in the summer to be away from the biting insects. They did not have permanent houses but they used beech saplings covered in bark; he called them a wigwam. The smaller ones might sleep ten or fifteen people while the larger ones fifteen to twenty. He told us that they would hunt the creature we called a horse deer but he called it a moos. He told us that they hunted them with dogs. They starved the dogs and then four or five men would track the animal. Their flint tipped arrows could not kill one and they relied on the animal tiring before they set their dogs upon it to finish it off. When I relayed that information to my brother Arne, he was interested because, if we had to fight them, and Arne was a warrior and expected to fight, then we knew the limitations of their weapons. The horse deer was vital to the tribe for they used every part of it. He also told us that his people had only recently come to this area for their natural home was further east and north. His tribe were aggressive and had driven the tribe which used to live there, the Penobscot, further south and west. His clan was part of a larger tribe and they had alliances and treaties with the tribes and clans around them. They had no kings and did not desire them; we had much in common!

The information took many months to gather for as we learned new words we went back over his story. He seemed to be happy to give us this information as we were from the land of the rising sun. He thought that made each of us special. He told us that the war chiefs of his people were concerned about our presence for we looked nothing like them. They thought we were evil spirits come from the east to devour them and had come to chase us away. I learned that his whole family were dead, for his mother and sisters had died when he was younger, and his father and two brothers had died on the raid on our camp. Arne worried that he might seek vengeance but Gytha would have none of that.

"We have given him a life and the Three Sisters sent him to us. Would you risk angering the Norns, Arne? Your brother's decision to save him was a good one and will be the salvation of the clan. Bear Tooth is happy here. He works in our longhouse and has made no attempt to escape. He is like a wolf we have tamed. Yes, we will watch him, but the first dogs which our people owned began as wolves; think on that!"

Arne would face any number of warriors but he would not face Gytha. He seemed to fear her for she had a power he did not understand and Arne was a warrior. After she had chastised him, he ceased to visit with her and seemed to ignore our captive. One evening, just before I returned home to Ada and Lars, Gytha and Snorri spoke with me. We did not know how many of our words Bear Tooth could understand but, to ensure that we were not overheard, Gytha sent him to fetch water from the stream which ran to the sea.

Snorri was the most thoughtful Viking I had ever known and when he spoke it was quietly and using words which he had considered deeply before he uttered them, "From what we have learned, Erik, Bear Tooth's people come back here each summer to fish and to gather the Mother's bounty, however, this is the furthest south that they come. There are other people further south and, from what Bear Tooth says, their language is not dissimilar to his. Gytha and I would have you sail further south to explore this land. Arne wishes to conquer the people on the mainland, Bear Tooth's people and those of us, who think, like you, know that is foolish. The people who live south of here may not be as aggressive. You have some words of the Skraeling. We know that they have some common words and one is '*friend*'. When you have learned more words, we would have you sail south when Harpa comes, for that is when the tribes will return to the coast. Try to make contact with them."

Gytha put her hand on my arm, "I know we ask a great deal of you for you now have a son and there is danger, but I also know of your dream. Inside you, the wolf gnaws at your heart and you cannot settle down with Ada until you have seen the waterfall and the maiden. Only then can you settle with your family. I do not know if you will see it on this voyage but you might. Consider my words. Do not answer yet for this needs careful thought."

When I got home, Ada had just put Lars, our son, to bed. He was a hungry little fellow and seemed to be feeding at every opportunity. He would be awake again, soon enough, and demanding more food. He was almost weaned for he was close to two but he still liked Ada's breast when he could! Ada, however, was content. Lars was a chance for her to raise a child with the knowledge gained from having had her first child more than fourteen years ago. There had been a gap and she doted on our son. It made me feel less guilty about the fact that I had not married her. Ebbe, her last son by Dreng, had his own sleeping compartment as did his sister, Egilleif. This was as alone as Ada and I would ever get. While she waited for Lars to give the sounds that showed he was soundly asleep she used her distaff.

"Gytha wants me to sail south and scout out the lands there. They lie to the south and west of us. I believe it is the mainland but it could be an island like the one we first landed upon."

Had Arne asked me then she might not have been happy but Gytha was the clan's mother and none would question a decision or a request made by her. Ada was something of a volva herself and she spun with the other volvas of the clan. "She hopes the tribes there will be less aggressive?"

I nodded. I was not surprised that Ada was privy to such information. The women shared all sorts of information when they wove, made cheese and beer or simply washed clothes at the stream. "The clan will need more land and if we can go to the mainland then we could spread out. No one likes being this close to their neighbours."

She was observant and said, "We were closer when we lived on the land of ice and fire."

"And that was why we left."

"And who will be your crew?"

It was an important question for the success of the voyage would depend upon my skill as a navigator and their skill as a crew. "I do not think that Fótr will wish to come. He and Reginleif are besotted with each other."

She laughed, "They are young, Reginleif is about the same age as I was when I bore Dreng."

I knew that Dreng would be at the forefront of her thoughts for he had perished on a voyage with me. Her husband, also called Dreng, had died fighting the enemies of the clan. Ada had sacrificed much already for the clan. "I will take young boys. The journey will not be hard and they need the experience of sailing. When Lars is old enough, I shall take him to sea too."

"And when will you sail?"

"Not until Harpa. That gives us time to make the snekke seaworthy."

When first we had come, we had used the snekke as a fishing boat but we now had dedicated boats which could work with others to land larger catches. The waters around the island teemed with fish and we found we could catch more by using numbers of boats to surround them. The snekke, *'Jötnar'*, would be needed for although we would not travel in the ocean, the waters off the mainland were unpredictable.

"You will be careful and come home? Lars needs a father." She laid down her distaff and ceased to spin. "Ebbe? He will want to come."

I nodded, "And I would take him but…"

"But you worry that I will forbid him. He will soon be a man and if he asks you then take him."

"But if he does not?"

She nodded, "Aye, Erik, I will be happy."

She came to me and kissed me; she was happy. I embraced her and we coupled. Such moments were, perforce, brief for Lars would wake at any time and demand his mother's attention. Once we had finished, Ada sighed with satisfaction for she was a woman and enjoyed a man.

The next morning, I spoke with Arne first and then Fótr. Arne, for he was jarl and Fótr, as I wished to give him the chance to come. If he refused, as I expected, then I could choose others to sail with me. Even as I woke, I felt excited as the chance to explore new waters and lands filled me with joy. This would be like my first voyage when I knew not if I would sail off the edge of the world except that now I knew that the world went on to the west. I could see the land to which I sailed. The excitement was about what I would find. Perhaps I would spy the waterfall and then the maid.

Arne was unconcerned about the native peoples who lived further south. "We can defeat them for they have poor weapons. They only took Benni and his family because of surprise. When we faced them, man to man, we defeated them."

I shook my head, "We are still few. I now have a son. You have children but we have barely grown. The Skraelings who came outnumbered us and how many more wait on the mainland? Gytha is right, we need to find an accord with the people who live here. There may be a time when we are numerous enough to control these wild people but until then we have to find a peaceful way." My brother was not convinced. "Think how many of our people died because others tried to control us and then remember why we left Larswick. It was to find a home where we could live peacefully." I waved an arm around, "Is Bear Island not a paradise compared with the land of ice and fire?"

He nodded, "You are right but it does not sit well with the warrior in me." He put his arm around my shoulders and led me from the longhouse. "Before you go I would have us sail to Horse Deer Island. The horse deer…"

"Moos."

"Moos?"

"It is what the Skraelings call them."

He laughed, "The horse deer, for I am not a Skraeling, will have had their young and now would be a good time to hunt them. We will require the drekar for the snekke would need many journeys to take us. I hope to be there and back in one day. The days and nights are almost the same length, our seeds are in the ground and I am ready for meat."

I had planned on working on the snekke but I would have to delay that task. "It will take three days to ready the drekar."

"Good, I will use the time to choose the hunters and prepare the weapons."

The one thing we had not found, thus far, was iron to make arrowheads and spearheads. We had lost some arrowheads after the battle with the Skraelings. Despite searching the ground and the bodies we had not recovered every arrowhead. We would make shafts and we could fletch them but, without metal, we were as helpless as the Skraelings. We had used bone and stone, as the Skraelings did, to replace metal heads. We would use those for hunting.

I took Ebbe and Fótr with me when I went to check on the drekar, *'Njörðr'*. I would have taken Eidel and Sven to help me for they were skilled sailors but they now lived in the north part of the island and both had their own families. The three of us examined every rope and every sheet. That first day we replaced three of them. I knew we would have to make more rope. Perhaps we could use some of the hair we had seen on the bull moos. We ate our midday meal on the deck of the drekar.

"The sail, I fear, will need work for the voyage here caused much damage to it."

"Perhaps Gytha and the women could weave another one."

I shook my head, "You may not have noticed but we have few sheep for the wool and seal oil is lacking."

Fótr was more like me than Arne and my younger brother was a thinker. "Then, when we have hunted the Horse Deer, why not head north? Did not Padraig say that when he was lost in the fog, he saw seals in those waters? We could sail north and hunt them." He grinned, "Who knows, we might be able to explore some of the lands there. I know that you would like that, brother."

"Aye, I would but a voyage of that length, useful though it might be, would necessitate an examination of the hull and that would mean taking her out of the water, but I will give it some thought. The voyage to the island of the horse deer is so short that we might not need the sail but I would rather have it repaired than not."

The sail did need work but it was not as bad as I had first thought and the women were able to repair it. We had to use some of our precious oil to seal the repairs and I raised the problem of seal oil. Gytha suggested using some of the fat which would be rendered from the horse deer but Snorri had a better idea. "We use the sea. There are whales out there and we can hunt them, for a single whale is easier to hunt than seals and would give us all the oil and meat we might need."

The Savage Wilderness

That idea appealed to Arne, too, and would mean I did not need to haul the hull out of the water.

We took just half of the men from the island to go hunting. Older men like Snorri would stay to protect the women although as we were just going for one day there seemed little threat to our home. In truth, the women needed little protection for all of them could handle a sword and a spear quite adeptly. The deaths of Benni and most of his family had given them the encouragement to become more skilled. Loki decided that we would not use the sail for he sent winds which swirled in every direction. We did not bother to raise the mast; it rested on the mast fish. It would be just as easy to row and so, with each oar manned by a single oarsman, Arne had them sing to help us row the few miles to the island.

The Clan of the Fox has no king
We will not bow nor kiss a ring
We fled our home to start anew
We are strong in heart though we are few

Lars the jarl fears no foe
He sailed the ship from Finehair's woe
Drekar came to end our quest
Erik the Navigator proved the best
When Danes appeared to thwart our start
The Clan of the Fox showed their heart
While we healed the sad and the sick
We built our home, Larswick

The Clan of the Fox has no king
We will not bow nor kiss a ring
We fled our home to start anew
We are strong in heart though we are few

When Halfdan came with warriors armed
The Clan of the Fox was not alarmed
We had our jarl, a mighty man
But the Norns they spun they had a plan
When the jarl slew Halfdan the Dane

The Savage Wilderness

His last few blows caused great pain
With heart and arm, he raised his hand
'The Clan of the Fox is a mighty band!'

The Clan of the Fox has no king
We will not bow nor kiss a ring
We fled our home to start anew
We are strong in heart though we are few

 I was at the steering board with Fámr Haraldsson and it was I who saw the smoke drifting from the island. Arne and Sven Svenson were on the two leading oars I said, "There is smoke coming from the island. Fámr, up to the prow and climb onto the dragon's head. See what you can spy." This was the problem with not raising the mast; we could not see as far ahead.

 Arne said, "It must be Skraelings."

 "Perhaps we should have brought Bear Tooth."

 Arne remained unconvinced about the worth of the captive, "If it is the natives then he would have run back to them. We will deal with them if they are there." I did not point out that Bear Tooth had a lame leg and running was the last thing he would do. My brother was grinning for he saw the opportunity to go to war. It was a subtle change but since the last battle, my brother had begun to change. It was not just his estrangement from Gytha, he had distanced himself from Fótr and me. Ada put it down to his wife, Freja. When Arne had first married her, she had been a sweet young woman but she seemed to like the power of being the wife of the jarl.

 We were almost at the island when Fámr ran back down the drekar, "Captain, there are small boats drawn up on the beach."

 It was then I knew that the Skraelings had chosen to do what we were planning. While we could use our drekar to complete the task in one day they would have to take several days. The sounds of dogs barking confirmed that this was a hunt. As we neared the beach, I counted the boats which could be seen on the beach. We had examined them after the raid and discovered that they had a simple frame covered by birch bark. Each one could carry four or five men and I counted ten boats. In theory that meant fifty warriors but I knew there would be far less than that for they would not be fully laden and would have dogs as well. I guessed there would be half that number. I knew that what we should have done was to turn around and come back another day but I saw, in my brother's eyes, that he wished to fight and returning to Bear Island was not an option.

"Fámr, we will need an empty part of the beach on which to land for I will not risk the hull. Go back to the prow and signal me when you spy one."

As he ran Arne said, "Just crush their boats beneath our hull!"

"I am the captain and I will not risk our only drekar. We cannot make another drekar easily. We will find an empty part of the beach."

Arne shrugged, "You are the Navigator but I am the warrior!" He raised his voice to shout, "When we land, we arm ourselves for war and hunt Skraelings." He laughed, "Who knows, they may have done our work for us! Now let us pull for the sooner we land the sooner my blade can taste blood!"

Fámr's arm waved me slightly to steerboard and I could see, a little more easily, the bark boats on the beach. They would have had a guard and I could not see him. That meant they would be warned for he would have run to warn the hunters. The drekar was slicing through the water and we were approaching too quickly. I saw Fámr raise his arms and that told me that our course was perfect. One of the skills of a navigator is to know how to use a ship to do the work of men. Loki's wind was now coming from behind us and I shouted, "In oars! We have enough pace to reach the beach!"

My words pleased my brother and the oars were drawn in and the men stacked them on the mast fish. None of the men had come for war. We had neither shields nor helmets but a warrior does not leave his home without his sword. Even I had a weapon strapped to my belt. The spears and bows we had planned on using to hunt would now be used for war. The Norns had been spinning and they had made this happen. Had they conspired with Loki?

Fámr knew what he had to do and he had a rope already coiled. Ebbe and Sven, not to mention Fótr, had also sailed with me enough to take a rope and secure the drekar to the shore. Fámr shouted, "Thirty paces!"

The Savage Wilderness

There was an art to landing and I had to get this just right or risk damaging the irreplaceable drekar.

"Twenty paces!"

I put the steering board over so that almost all the way went from the drekar and she side-slipped towards the beach. The four warriors with ropes leapt into the water and I lost sight of them. Then I saw them rushing up the beach with their ropes. As soon as I felt the sand and shingle beneath the hull, I secured the steering board.

Arne turned to me; he had a spear as well as his sword. "You and Fámr will have to guard the drekar. Can you do that?"

I laughed, "Go, brother! We will manage."

The warriors quickly left us and waded ashore. I waved Fámr back to the drekar, "Fetch your bow for we may need it." I should have brought my yew bow for it was the best in the clan but the Norns had been spinning and it lay in my home.

As he strung his hunting bow, I walked the deck to check that all of the lines which held us to the shore were secure and that we were not close to any rocks. That done, I returned to the steering board. I had my sword and I had my dagger but if danger came, I could also use one of the spears which had been left aboard. I looked south to Bear Island and saw that it looked as though it was far out to sea yet the reality was, we were quite close to land. Perhaps that was why it had been uninhabited or it may have been the presence of the bear family. From what Bear Tooth had told me his tribe somewhat revered the bear. It would explain their aggressive behaviour for we would be seen to be a threat to the bear.

I could no longer hear the dogs nor could I hear the sound of fighting and I wondered who was hunting whom? Were the Skraelings using their knowledge of the island to lure our men into a trap or had my clever brother devised a way to hunt them? I soon had my answer for I caught sight of a movement in the woods which bordered the beach. It could have been an animal but it did not do to take chances and so I said, "Fámr, have your bow ready for there may be enemies out there. If there are do not panic. Better to slow your arrows as you release them and ensure that you hit what you intend."

The Savage Wilderness

There was a horn by the steering board, we used it to let those at home know that we were close, but I would not summon Arne and the others until I was certain that we were in danger. A second movement allowed me to fix the patch of wood with my eye and I saw the dark flesh of a Skraeling. I still did not sound the horn. If this was nothing more than a couple of scouts then I could handle it. I drew my sword and placed it between two of the planks on the deck. I could pick it up more easily that way. I hefted a spear. Perhaps my actions and those of Fámr alerted the natives for five of them burst from cover. Five could be handled by the two of us.

Fámr knew his limitations and he waited until the nearest Skraeling was forty paces away and then an iron tipped arrow slammed into the warrior's chest. As the man fell, with a surprised look on his face, I heard the sound of battle deep in the woods to the north of us. There was no point in sounding the horn for my brother and the others were already engaged. Fámr nocked a second arrow and hit another native in the chest. Then four others joined in the attack. There were now seven of them.

"Fámr, when they board get behind me and I will try to protect you."

The warriors who ran at us had spears and stone clubs in their hands. Had they had bows things might have turned out differently. Fámr's third arrow was sent as the first three warriors reached the water and his arrow drove deep into the warrior's collar bone between his head and his shoulder. Blood spurted and I rammed my spear into the face of a fourth Skraeling who was attempting to clamber up the side. He tried to grab the spearhead but we had well-sharpened spearheads and he merely succeeded in slashing his hand. I pushed, twisted and turned the spear, ensuring that he died. The second wave of attackers divided into two. The last of the original group jabbed his spear upwards. He could jab all he liked for while he jabbed, he could not climb.

"Fámr, aim at the ones nearer to the prow."

"Aye, Captain. I only have four arrows left."

"When they are gone use one of the hatchets or this spear."

Leaning over I took my spear in both hands and thrust it at the warrior who was trying to climb the side of the drekar. I caught his arm and he fell back into the water. Fámr then made his first mistake. He sent an arrow the length of the drekar and the warrior he aimed at was able to avoid it by ducking below the mast fish. The remaining warriors were now aboard and had seen that Fámr was unable to hit them if they used the mast fish as a barrier. They crawled along the deck.

"Fámr, take this spear and stay behind me."

The one in the water had been hurt and if he tried to climb the side then my sword could end his life quickly. The four who came towards us were the bigger threat. I took out my dagger and twirled my sword. I did it to catch the light from the sun. These natives had not seen metal weapons. Bear Tooth had told me that and I wanted them to think this was magic. It was then, as the four warriors rose and walked towards us that I had an idea. I put my dagger in my belt and holding the bear tooth necklace in my left hand, I shouted in the language of the Skraeling, "I am a shaman!" I was not sure if I said it right but the four men stopped and seemed to see the bear's teeth.

They stopped and stared; I am not sure what would have happened if the wounded warrior in the water had not begun to climb over the side. I seemed to sense him for I did not turn my head but some instinct took over and I took my dagger, King Raedwulf's dagger, and hurled it to the side without even looking. There was a scream and a splash as the body hit the water.

I shouted, "I am a shaman!" and began to move towards the four who had boarded. They turned and ran, barely pausing as they threw themselves into the sea. I ran to the side and saw that my hastily thrown dagger had caught the warrior in the chest. His body lay floating in the shallows. Fámr shook his head, "Captain! How did you do that?"

"I have no idea. Climb over and fetch the dagger back for me and then we had better collect the arrowheads."

I took his bow and nocked an arrow in case any of those we had hit were feigning death. I let the four we had chased run to the birch-bark boats. I watched them paddle away north as fast as they could. The shining sword, the necklace and my lucky throw must have convinced them that I had magical powers. I had been lucky and I knew it. Fámr was also lucky for he found all of his arrows and their heads. I now fretted about my brother and the hunters.

The distant sounds of battle had long ceased when I heard the sound of men running towards the beach and I took no chances. "Grab your bow! We may have to fight them off again!" I knew it was the natives and not our men for there was neither the sound of jingling metal nor the thud of sealskin boots. We heard the sound of bare feet pounding on the game trails. When the warriors burst forth, they did not come for the drekar but ran, instead, for their birch bark boats. Fámr pulled back on the bow but I said, "Let them go. They are done and the arrowhead is more valuable than the man you might just wound."

Most of the boats had but two or three men in them. There were four dogs with them too. Some of those who ran were supported by their fellows for they had been wounded. They had left the beach and were paddling out when my brother and the hunters arrived with bloody weapons. I did a quick headcount and saw that none had died although a couple had bloodied heads and arms. When Fótr and Arne saw the dead men around the drekar they hurried towards us.

"You were attacked too?"

"Aye brother. Four survived the attack and fled."

Fámr said, proudly, "Captain Erik waved his necklace at them and spoke their language! They ran!"

Arne laughed, "My brother constantly surprises me." He became serious and shook his head, "This was not just a deer hunt. They came and slaughtered every horse deer on the island. They must have been here for days."

"Why would they do that?"

"I know not except that if we had done this it would be to deny an enemy food. They have not done that; we can take the butchered animals back on the drekar but they have taken away a source of food. Now we will have to go to the mainland to hunt and they will, perhaps, gather their tribe to fight us."

I sensed that my brother was no longer as keen on war as he had been. I nodded, "Then it is lucky that we have a volva who can divine the future, for now my voyage south makes more sense, does it not, brother?"

"Aye, Erik, and, once more, our fate lies in your hands!"

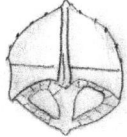

Chapter 2

The Skraeling had slaughtered every animal on the island including the young. It must have taken them more than a couple of days. We found the bodies of four or five dogs which had obviously died in the hunt. We would use the meat, the hides, the hooves, everything but it was a waste and I began to believe my brother, this had been an attempt to deny us food and these were not quite the barbarians we had first thought. When we reached home, I would have to speak with Gytha, Snorri and Bear Tooth. The row back was harder because we had been working all day loading the carcasses and that was after we had fought the Skraelings.

The work began the next day, to turn the horse deer into food and things which we could use. The mighty antlers were strong and along with the bones could be fashioned into serviceable tools. We did not have the metal we had used when we lived across the seas and we needed to improvise. The smaller bones would be carved too for we always needed needles and the like. Much of the meat was either dried or salted. I had the hair from the bulls gathered and the women began to weave ropes, for the hair proved to be as strong as that of the horse. Finally, the hides were cured for they were tough and could be used to make clothes which were hardy and could even stop a stone weapon from penetrating.

On the evening of the first night after our return, Arne, Fótr and I sat with Gytha, Snorri and Bear Tooth. It was the first time Arne had done so since he had been chastised and he only came because he wished to know what Bear Tooth knew. Snorri could now converse well with the captive and I could see a bond had developed between the two of them. The slave who had spent the first two months scowling or cowering at every word now smiled

The Savage Wilderness

and laughed for Snorri could be funny. I was also able to understand far more of the Mi'kmaq youth's words.

When Arne put forward his theory about the Skraeling and their slaughter, I saw Gytha nodding. "That makes sense but let us hear what the boy thinks."

Snorri rattled away some questions and Bear Tooth answered. Gytha and I could understand much of what was said while to Arne it was a series of grunts, but Snorri had the ear for it and we waited for his translation. I smiled at my brothers for they could not decipher a single word. When he had finished Snorri nodded, "You might be right, Arne, for Horse Deer Island has always been left by the Skraeling. Bear Tooth thinks that their chief, Wandering Moos, may be trying to starve us out. His people do not plant in the ground as we do and they move around their land searching for food they can forage, hunt, trap or fish. He does not understand how we plough and turn the soil; he thinks it is magic."

I nodded, "These must be a people who have very primitive beliefs for when my sword flashed in the sunlight, I saw them recoil, and by calling myself a shaman and pointing to the bear teeth I frightened them away." As I spoke, I saw Bear Tooth studying me. He was translating my words. Soon, we would have to be careful about what we spoke in front of him.

Arne waved an irritated hand, "That still does not help us. We have enough meat now to last six months but what about the future? What does Gytha the volva and mother of the clan think? Can she see the future?" He looked at her, "Your advice and my brother's skill have brought us here but is this the end of the voyage?"

Gytha smiled; she knew that Arne was flattering her but there was no harm in that. She nodded, "I have not dreamed, but I shall do so although the spirits may not inhabit this land. It may be a risk for the spirits I find might be Skraeling." I saw Arne's hand go to his hammer of Thor. Fighting a Skraeling was one thing but a Skraeling spirit was quite something else. She turned to me, "Erik the Navigator, there was talk of using the drekar to hunt the whale; is that possible?"

I had thought about this and I had an answer all ready, "I can see no reason why not but we have no metal to make the type of spearhead we used back in Orkneyjar and here we are closer to the ocean; we would need to have more than one whale spearhead for the whales here might be larger and would take more effort to capture."

"Then you need to hunt one sooner rather than later. Your visit to the mainland will have to wait." Disappointment must have shown on my face. The mainland and my search for the maid and the waterfall filled my dreams each night. She smiled, "Arne may be right. This Skraeling hunt might be an attempt to force us to land on the mainland where they might attempt to attack us. A delay of a few months will not hurt us and you need the oil for your sails, do you not?"

I nodded. Arne said, "The head of the whale spear is not a problem. We have the bones and antlers of the horse deer. I can throw well and there will be others who can do so. What you need to do, brother, is to find the whale. We cannot afford the time to have the drekar searching the seas for the beasts. You need to find where they feed and it will save us time."

Snorri had noticed Bear Tooth listening. I had also observed his eyes following the conversation. When Snorri spoke, I understood every word. "Bear Tooth, do you know where the whales can be found? Speak slowly so that Erik might understand."

"Do you mean, master, the fish which has a mouth large enough to fit a man whole and whose flesh has great layers of fat?"

Snorri nodded, "Aye, we call them whales. Do you know where they are to be found?"

He nodded, "I have only seen their bodies. To the north, they are sometimes washed up on the beaches and whole villages descend to take the harvest of the seas."

My uncle translated for the others and Gytha beamed, "This is *wyrd*! Erik, you must take the boy with you. I know you understood his words and this will help you when you go to the mainland."

Arne shook his head, "I am not certain. What if the boy escaped?"

I said, "Brother, it was I who captured Bear Tooth; I will watch him."

I could see my brother was reluctant but he agreed in principle. I turned to the Skraeling, "Bear Tooth, would you come with me on my boat and find the whale?"

He looked fearful, "The big ship with the fierce monster, the snake-headed beast at the front?" He shook his head.

"No, Bear Tooth, my snekke, the small ship which just holds four or five people. It is little larger than the birch bark boat you sailed."

He smiled, "I will, for the bear protects you and you have skill."

That settled I needed to choose a crew. Padraig and Aed were the best fishermen and both were keen to explore the waters further afield. They were happy to join me and I took Ebbe and Fótr too. This would be an opportunity to teach my brother skills he might need in the future and he was just a few years older than Bear Tooth. The five of us spent a day preparing the snekke and we took supplies for seven nights. I bade farewell to Ada, her daughter, Egilleif, and my son and, with my hourglass and compass, we set off north.

As we sailed, I recalled that these were the waters where we had lost Dreng and that sat heavily on my mind. I did not tell Ebbe that was where his brother had died but, as we passed the spit of land where he had died, I touched my hammer of Thor. Bear Tooth did not recognise the coast for he had never seen it from the sea and so I had to sail close to the land, hoping that he might recognise some feature. Smoke told us that some of the Skraeling had left the biting insects to come to the coast. We would have to be wary for their birch bark boats could surround us and take us. Much of that first day was spent in tacking north and teaching both Ebbe and Bear Tooth how to sail. I was the only one who could speak to the boy and, while Padraig and Aed handled the sails and Fótr made the map, I told first Ebbe and then Bear Tooth what we did and what they would do. Bear Tooth was a quick learner and he understood the new words far quicker than I might have hoped. Our mutual understanding increased dramatically on the hunt for the whale.

I had sailed along this coast in the snekke and the drekar and I knew there were large rocks and small islands where we could spend the night. They would be bare but we would be safe. We could even light a fire. As dusk approached, I found one which had a small beach where we could land and where we could camp in the lee of a low ridge of rock. We drew the boat up, and while I set about lighting a fire, the others collected shellfish. We had brought bread and some salted horse deer. We would eat well.

Darkness fell and we ate in the light of the fire. "Bear Tooth, do you recognise the coast?"

"This island and some of the others we passed look familiar. I thought they were further away than they are. The whales were washed up further along there." He pointed north.

I turned to the others and translated his words. Padraig nodded, "Then from tomorrow we look for the shiny backs as they come close to the surface. I do not know if they have the same beasts here as they do around the land we left, but some of them dive so deep that they cannot be easily hunted. We need smaller ones who stay close to the surface."

I had never hunted the whale and I had rarely seen one. Padraig and Aed would be invaluable in finding them. We rose early the next morning and, when we left our rocky perch, we sailed more slowly than we had the previous day. Now we did not mind tacking for we wanted to miss nothing. The sea is empty but when you sail slowly you see far more than when you are trying to get somewhere quickly. We saw huge shoals of fish coming to the surface and we spied flocks of seabirds trying to benefit from the bounty of the sea, but we saw no whales.

I took a decision, "I think we are too close to the land. We will sail further east." Padraig, Aed and Ebbe were unconcerned as we had already sailed out of sight of land to reach these waters. Bear Tooth, however, began to look fearfully to the west as the land disappeared and then the tiny rocks vanished. "Where are you taking us? Am I to be a sacrifice to your gods?"

Only I heard his words. I shook my head, "You are quite safe, Bear Tooth. My people come from a land over there towards the rising sun. We sailed for many days to reach this land. We will turn, eventually, and return to the land of the setting sun. Trust me."

He was not convinced and clutched the gunwale as though his life depended upon it. We sailed east until the sun began to move west and I had turned the hourglass before I turned the snekke to follow it. We had not seen any whales but Padraig was hopeful that this would be a good place to search. We sailed towards the coast of the mainland on our way back. The wind was with us and I was confident that we could make land before dark. Fótr had a piece of bark and he was using it to mark our position. I was teaching him to use the hourglass and compass. He would make a navigator and I was anxious for someone other than me to be able to sail the drekar. I knew I was not immortal and, one day, the clan might choose to return to Larswick.

It was Bear Tooth who spotted the whales. He was so excited when he did so that, despite the fact that we could see no land, he let go of the gunwale and stood and pointed north and east, "I see them!"

I turned the snekke to close with them. I saw that there were five whales, including two young. Their glossy, shiny backs rose to the surface and then disappeared again before rising once more. The size was hard to determine and so I asked Ebbe to shin up the mast. When he reached the crosspiece and sat with his legs around the mast I shouted, "How big are they?"

"There look to be two young with three adults. The young look to be five or six paces long while the adults are twelve paces or more."

That seemed a little large for us to take but Aed said, "These are slow-moving, Captain. We are catching up with them."

That was interesting for the wind was not with us and if we had the crew rowing then, with a good wind, we could catch them but we might need more than two whale spears to take them. We followed them north for an hour or so and I decided we had seen enough. "Fótr, mark where we spied them on the map and we will find a camp."

I saw Bear Tooth visibly relax when he saw the thin line that was land looming up on the horizon. I saw a number of islands and rocks. Finding one where we could land proved harder than the previous night and we were much closer to the coast when we found one. The smoke from the mainland told me that there were natives and we might have to be more careful. As we ate, I questioned Padraig and Aed about the hunting of the whale. Both had done it before in Hibernia but they had not done so in a drekar. The vessel which they had used had been rowed and sounded to be longer than a snekke and shorter than a drekar. "The snekke would be of little use to us. The whale is a powerful beast and if one dived it could take a little boat like this one to the bottom of the ocean. You would need to have at least two men with whale spears at the prow and another giving directions. If we had the sail it would be faster but you would find it harder to see. We would still need the men to row."

"And that means a larger crew," I nodded. "How many whale spears?"

"As many as can be made." Padraig used his arm as a guide, "The head should be long and narrow and as long as my arm. It needs to be barbed so that it sticks in the flesh. A perfect one would be made of metal but I am guessing it will be bone or antler." I nodded. "There is a thick layer of fat on the animals and you have to get through it to make them bleed. The more whale spears which are used the better and they all need a rope so that the whale is attached to the drekar. It is not as easy as simply fishing but the rewards…"

I could tell that Padraig was excited and his excitement communicated itself to me. "Fótr, how would you feel about being the guide for me? It will help you when you become a navigator."

"We have a navigator, brother, you!"

"And if the bear had killed me or the Skraelings overcome Fámr and myself?"

I saw Ebbe give me a sharp look; he had lost a father and a brother. He was terrified of losing a foster father.

"In that case, brother, I would be honoured and it sounds exciting. I would be able to watch our big brother when he hunts the monster of the deep!"

We reached Bear Island as the sun was setting. All the way south we had seen birch bark boats by the mainland and the fires of the Skraelings. The biting insects must have struck early or perhaps they feared that we would take their land if they did not come sooner. I spoke with Bear Tooth as we headed south. I could understand most of his words and his Norse had improved dramatically. The problem came when it was a word we did not have in our language and I still found difficulty getting my tongue around some of the sounds he made. As we spoke, I learned more about his people. It seemed there was no king but a loose confederation of tribes. The Skraeling sounded more like the Norse than the Saxons who liked their kings. Within tribes they also had clans. Occasionally a tribe would make war on another one and they were not averse to raiding another tribe for slaves. Like our people they had feuds and they had alliances but what did emerge was that they were far more numerous than the number of fires would suggest. He told me of rivers to the north and the south of our island which headed deep inland. He even told me about three huge waterfalls which lay well to the north between two pieces of water which were as big as a sea and yet were not salt water. He had never seen them but his people had heard about them. I wondered if one was the waterfall of my dream. Bear Tooth told me that they lay many days' travel to the north.

Arne and the men were on their farms when we returned but Gytha and Snorri joined Ada on the beach to greet us. I could see that they were all excited but for different reasons. Gytha and Snorri wanted our news while Ada was just grateful that her son and man had returned. After Padraig, Aed and Fótr had returned to their homes Ada, Ebbe and I joined my uncle and his family for food. Gytha was the cleverest person I knew and she was the one who saw and heard beyond my words. If we stayed on Bear Island, we would have to go to the mainland to hunt and that meant coming into conflict with the Skraeling. She was, however, delighted about the discovery of the whales. Oil from whales, not to mention the meat would guarantee that none of us starved and that our clothes would be protected from the wet. This new land was as wet as Orkneyjar and Larswick had been but there we had had plentiful seals and their skins.

The next day I told Arne what we would need. He had already planned when we would hunt. He was the jarl and he made such decisions. "We are still clearing ground and planting crops. Let us leave at Skerpla. That will give us the time to make six or seven whale spears. You have done well."

That gave me some time to work my own piece of land. I felt guilty for Ada and her children, Ebbe and Egilleif, did most of the work. They did not mind for I was the navigator but I still tried to do as much as I could. I tilled the land wearing just my breeks for this land was hot. Living so close to the few animals we had brought from our home across the sea meant I had access to their dung and I fetched some. The cow was in calf again and that was good. We had a second, young bull and, when he became fully grown, we could split the herd into two. We still did not have as much milk and cheese as we would like and more cattle would give us a better supply. We had tried to tame deer so that we could milk them but it had been a disastrous failure and all we had to show for it was venison we did not have to hunt. I spread more of the dung on the ground. Bear Tooth had shown us some of the growing things which we could eat and we were using the seeds of those plants to augment the barley, oats and beans on which we so heavily relied.

It was good to be with my foster family and laughter filled the air. My son, Lars, could walk but his crawling was so fast that we all needed lightning reactions to stop him from hurting himself. A Viking child grew quickly and Lars was no exception. We knew that it was unlikely that the Skraelings would risk attacking us on our island and so we relaxed more than we had, even in Orkneyjar and Larswick. Arne had set up a system of watchers who were young boys. The system worked and Ada and I chattered like magpies as we worked. I knew she had strong feelings for me and I hated not being able to reciprocate. The dream was a curse as much as anything. Had I not had the dream then I would have married Ada and both of us would be content. As it was, I was fated to wait until I had seen the maid and the waterfall. I was kind to her but Ada knew that one day, I would seek the fulfilment of my dream.

The fact that we could see more fires burning on the mainland was a little disconcerting for it told us that the Skraeling were there in greater numbers than the previous year. Bear Tooth had told us that, on the longest day of the year, all the clans of his tribe came together. It was a time to resolve any conflict between the clans and for their shamans to gather and speak to their gods. There would be much talking and celebration. That time was rapidly approaching and might explain why there were so many camps. However, Bear Tooth also told us that our arrival had caused the shamans and the chiefs great concern as there had been prophecies of men coming from the east who would take their land from them. When he told us that, I could understand their aggression for we would have done the same.

We left more than a fortnight before the longest day, leaving our families gathered close by Gytha and Snorri. The crops were in the ground and there was no need for any to be isolated. They would be safe. This time we had the repaired sail and the mast. We would easily be seen from the land and I wondered if they would fear an attack from us. Bear Tooth told us that they kept a watch for the beasts from the land of the rising sun. We headed north and east, needing no oars for the wind took us. With just men on board and the food we might need, *'Njörðr'* flew. Fótr and Ebbe were with me at the steering board and I was giving them both lessons. Ebbe was totally without skill and so my brother helped when I was busy. Fótr was a man now, with a wife and he had changed. We also had ship's boys as lookouts. They would be kept busier than usual for when we began to hunt, the sail would need almost constant trimming if we were to keep up with the whales.

Rather than landing on a rock or a small island which might threaten to rip the keel from beneath us, I headed out to sea, and with the sail furled and a sea anchor we slept aboard. The nights were so short that we were not in the dark for long and I shared the watch with Sven and Arne. We hoisted the sail and headed towards the rising sun. Stig Eidelsson spotted the whales not long before noon and signalled that the animals were directly ahead. It was a bright day and the sun reflected from their shiny backs. As soon as the shout came down, I gave my commands.

"To your oars! Arne, Siggi to your places."

We had decided to use just the two men although each would have another warrior close by to hand a second whale spear. Fótr ran down the centre of the drekar to stand between them. "Ebbe, remember that you need to say what Fótr is doing. It is important."

"Aye, Captain!"

I could hear the nervousness in his voice.

Arne and Siggi were standing with the whale spears in hand and the ropes coiled at their feet. Sven and Harald were each ready with a second whale spear.

The Savage Wilderness

Arne shouted when the whales were within a hundred paces and then raised his whale spear. That was his signal to me while his words were for the rowers, "Now we row and it is your speed that will catch this beast! Your power will light our homes at night and fill your children's bellies with food! Now row!" The men at the oars were looking at me and I sang the chorus of one of our chants. It was one which would enable us to travel really quickly but we could not keep it up for much above half an hour.

The Clan of the Fox has no king
We will not bow nor kiss a ring
We fled our home to start anew
We are strong in heart though we are few
The Clan of the Fox has no king
We will not bow nor kiss a ring
We fled our home to start anew
We are strong in heart though we are few

'Njörðr' had been flying before but now it was as though she sailed over the crests of the waves so swift was she.

"Steerboard, Captain."

I had seen Fótr's arm make the signal but Ebbe had been correct to speak to me. I adjusted the steering board ever so slightly. If it was not enough then Fótr would tell me. Exaggerated movements slowed a drekar down.

Stig Eidelsson shouted, "One is slower than the rest, Captain, and we are close!"

I confess that I was surprised although our ship, with the wind and the crew, had helped us to cover a great distance quickly. I saw Arne's arm come back and then he hurled the whale spear down. Fótr had both of his arms in the air and that meant we should sail straight ahead.

"Straight ahead, Captain!"

I deduced that the beast had shifted to the larboard side when Siggi hurled his whale spear and Arne took a second. Suddenly we lurched forward. The whale must have been hit again and dived down. As the coiled ropes reached their furthest extent the prow of the ship dipped alarming beneath a wave and water cascaded over the deck. The men at the oars were thrown from their chests. I wondered if any had fallen into the sea. Were we about to be taken to the bottom of the ocean by the wounded whale? I saw that Sven and Harald had axes ready to sever the two ropes if we began to sink.

Stig shouted, as the prow rose and a wall of water came down the drekar to wash around our feet, "I see the beast! He has two whale spears sticking in him."

"Steerboard, Captain!" I confess that I had not seen Fótr for I had been too concerned with the water flooding down the drekar. Fótr had had great presence of mind to concentrate upon his job when the whale threatened to drown us.

"Row! Row!"

The Clan of the Fox has no king
We will not bow nor kiss a ring
We fled our home to start anew
We are strong in heart though we are few
The Clan of the Fox has no king
We will not bow nor kiss a ring
We fled our home to start anew
We are strong in heart though we are few

I sang too for I could see the fear on the faces of the men. Even Padraig and Aed who had hunted whales before looked terrified.

"Sing!"

Arne was looking down the drekar and he waved his arm as though to exhort us to even greater efforts. Then he turned and raised his whale spear. This was a powerful beast for it had two of our best weapons embedded in it. Suddenly Arne hurled the whale spear and Siggi did so almost a heartbeat later. The whale must have been directly in front of the drekar. As soon as Siggi's spear struck we dipped again but less alarmingly and the men were able to continue rowing. I saw Arne speak to Fótr and then my young brother came running towards me. His face was flushed with excitement, "Arne says we have the beast and wishes you to slow the rowers until they stop."

I nodded, "Rowers, slow to this beat!" I began banging the spear we kept at the steering board. I gradually slowed it until I saw Arne raise his arm and then I shouted, "Stop! The Clan has done well and we have defeated the beast from the ocean!"

Padraig had told me that sometimes whales sank and so I began to turn the drekar to head west. The men at the bow began to walk back down the drekar holding the four ropes. They were pulling the dying animal to the stern. We would have to tow it to shore. The crew cheered and clapped them on the back as they passed. When they reached me, I handed the steering board to Fótr. "Keep us heading due west. We need an island." I took the ropes one by one and tied them off so that the two would be balanced. I saw that we had, indeed, caught a huge whale.

Padraig came to look and said, "That is an old bull and I see why we caught him." He pointed to his flank where his flesh had been attacked by some denizen of the deep. He looked astern, "We cannot keep towing him all the way back to Bear Island, look, already the sharks have arrived!"

He was right and I saw the fins of those terrifying creatures, "Ship's boys, use your slings and see if you can keep these sharks from feasting on our prize."

Arne looked as elated as Fótr. "By the Allfather but that was exciting; I would hunt one of these beasts again for we have taken on an animal the size of a drekar and won! This bodes well for the clan!"

With the animal, now dead, and our ship's boys hurling stones to smack into eager sharks, we headed west. Arne and the crew opened the barrel of beer they had brought. I did not begrudge them the pleasure. They had earned it. I had a ship to sail. Stig Eidelsson gave a mighty roar and the other ship's boys cheered. Fótr was still steering and I looked aft. One of the sharks had come too close to the whale and Stig's stone had hit so hard that it had drawn blood. The other sharks turned on him and soon the water astern of us was filled with the churning mob of animals now fighting each other. Our whale was safe.

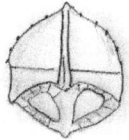

Chapter 3

We reached an island which had a beach and although I did not risk the keel, I turned the ship and our men jumped into the water to drag the whale to shore. We would butcher it and load it back on the drekar. It would be messy but it would be easier than towing and the stomach, heart and lungs could be left in the sea and our ship would be lighter.

As we headed south, the next morning, I looked ruefully at the bloody carcass of the butchered whale which almost filled the centre of the drekar. Ebbe and I would have to spend a long time cleaning it. That it had been necessary was never in doubt but a captain always wanted his ship to look its best. To me, *'Njörðr'* was a living thing and not just wood held together with nails and glue. I felt each movement beneath my feet as though it was a horse I was riding. I knew how to make the barest of touches to the steering board for *'Njörðr'* would almost anticipate my move. Arne would never understand although I hoped that Fótr, one day, would. As we headed south, I saw Arne at the prow already composing the song about our victory. He would not take all of the credit for that was not his way but he would not see that *'Njörðr'* helped us to take the beast which had, at one point, threatened to drag us beneath the waves. I had had the dream of the maid and the waterfall as we had slept except that the waterfall was now like the moment when the whale had begun to take us beneath the waves.

We could not row for the men were unable to sit at their oars and it was a long journey home into the prevailing wind so it was dark as we edged into the bay. There were lights lit, fires burning and folk watched for us. All were gathered together still and that was fortuitous as we had much work to do before we could go to sleep. When I saw the huge pots already hanging from the tripods above the fire, I knew that Gytha had used her powers to see across the seas. The blubber was put on to render down almost as soon as we manhandled it from the drekar. The women took over and gave commands to men to butcher the meat in certain ways so that they could begin to brine the whale flesh.

Only Ebbe and I were surplus to requirements and, once the mast and sail had been removed, we began to haul seawater up to wash the decks. It could have waited until morning but by then the sun would have started to dry the blood and the work would have taken longer. We worked methodically beginning at the prow and using pail after pail of water sluiced down the wood. We had hessian sacks filled with sand and we emptied those to help to cleanse the deck. I knew that Ebbe would soon tire and when we neared the mast fish, I was about to tell him to go ashore and I would finish when Gytha and Bear Tooth climbed aboard the drekar.

She said, "Bear Tooth, take over from the captain for I would speak with him. Copy Ebbe."

Bear Tooth seemed happy to join Ebbe as he squatted on the deck. I gave Bear Tooth the sack I had been using to rub the sand into the deck. Ebbe did not seem put out by the fact that he had to work and I did not and I saw him and Bear Tooth begin to talk to one another as they worked. *Wyrd*.

Gytha took me to the prow and she took my hands in hers and then she smiled as she stroked my cheek with her left hand, "It is strange but I feel closer to you than the sons I bore. I think that when your mother died the Norns attached your thread to mine." She pointed out to sea and swept her arm in a circle, "The sea is your domain and you have as much power there as I do here in the heart of the clan." When she turned back to me, I saw her eyes were wide and the black spot in the centre was as large as I had ever seen. Her cheeks were flushed and it was with excitement, I could clearly see that. "Since we left Orkneyjar and then Larswick I have felt as though I did not have the power I once had and I could not see beyond the horizon. I can see now that when you saved the life of Bear Tooth then you saved the life of the clan. Thanks to your uncle the boy now feels part of this clan. He expected to be mistreated and he was not. He also has a connection to you and when you sail to the mainland, he should be in your crew for he will not run, of that I am sure."

I nodded, "He would be a good addition and I can see that Ebbe and he get on." Ebbe and Bear Tooth were laughing at something one or the other had said; they were of an age and despite the cultural differences they had much in common, for they were both young men who enjoyed an adventure. I remembered when I had been the same age; that was when there had been blood on the blade and I had sworn an oath with Arne and Siggi.

She squeezed my hand, "I was in your mind when you were on the drekar and I saw the hunt through your eyes."

"How?"

She turned and pointed to Bear Tooth, "He found a plant for me. It seems that one reason Bear Tooth has an affinity for you is that his uncle was the shaman of the tribe. He was killed in the raid but Bear Tooth used to collect plants for him to use. He found one for me. It is a member of the sage family but this one, when pounded to a paste and added to other ingredients, makes a potion which increases my powers and fills me with such energy that I feel like a young girl once more. It has taken some months to make the potion work properly but I managed it and I saw your thoughts!"

I was not sure I liked the fact that this woman, who was as close to me as my mother had ever been and yet was still another person, could see my thoughts and dreams.

She smiled, "Do not fear this, Erik, for, as I said, our threads are bound and I could never hurt you nor would I judge you. This can only help and is just the beginning. There must be a way for me to speak to you in your head and imagine how that might help us. When you explore the mainland, I would be there with you."

I wondered why she was telling me this at this moment in time. What was the urgency?

Disconcertingly she had been staring at me and I think she read the thoughts in my head, "I tell you this now, Erik, for I do not want you to be afraid when you feel my presence inside your head. You will need to open your mind and let me in. Do not fight me."

"You know I will never do that."

The Savage Wilderness

She kissed me on the forehead and said, "Good, and now I must sleep for after I have felt the effects of the potion it drains me." She laughed, "But it is worth it and see, the boys have finished. You can go ashore and see Ada, she has need of you and she has words to speak to you!"

The crew had finished rubbing the deck and they had collected the sand in the sacks. Bear Tooth followed Gytha down the gangplank and I told Ebbe to go to his mother and I would follow. Despite Gytha's words and explanation I still felt strange. I touched my bear tooth necklace. I had been chosen as a navigator for the Norns had sent the piece of wood all those years ago to point me in this direction and I knew that my journey was not yet done. I realised that there was a connection between Gytha and the Norns and between Gytha and me. A man did not fight the Norns for therein lay disaster yet I still felt uneasy.

The men were all drinking ale when I stepped ashore. Half of the grain we grew went to make beer. Siggi clapped his arm around me, "Come, brother, drink with your blood brothers and your crew! We have much to celebrate for we fought a monster and won! The Saxons might have Beowulf but the Clan of the Fox have Arne, Siggi and Erik! What cannot we three do?"

I smiled, "I may join you later but first I need to see my son!"

Arne came over and put his arm around my other shoulder. I could smell his breath and knew that he had already consumed a great quantity of ale, "You know your trouble, brother, you think too much." He nodded towards the longhouse of Gytha and Snorri, "And our aunt has too much influence over you. Beware the volva!"

I began to fear for Arne as he did not know the power which Gytha had nor did he know that she could read my thoughts, "You may be right. I will see you later!"

I knew that Arne would soon fall asleep and the conversation would be forgotten. Ebbe was telling his mother of the voyage and I could hear the excitement in his voice. Ada smiled and said, "Get you to bed, Ebbe, and do not wake Lars! I will speak with your foster father and he will tell me of the voyage. You need to sleep!"

"Aye, mother! Thank you, Captain, for taking me with you. I learned much and I know I will learn more in the future."

"You did well and I will sail with you any time."

By the time Ada and I had eaten a little, I could hear his regular breathing as he fell asleep. Much later, after we had coupled, Ada said, as she snuggled next to me, "I have news for you."

It seemed to be a day for news. Had the killing of the whale set off events beyond my control? "News?"

"I am with child! You are to be a father again!"

I touched my bear teeth, "Did Gytha know this?"

Ada laughed, "Of course she did! She is the mother of the clan and we have no secrets from her." The light from the fire showed the concern in her eyes, "Why do you ask?"

I took a breath and told her what Gytha had told me.

Ada laughed, "Is that all? That is good for she is a volva."

"Aye, but it means she could know what we do when we are alone."

Ada giggled and suddenly seemed like a young girl again, "We all talk together about our men; there are no secrets between women. I do not mind and I am happy that she can watch over you when you are far out to sea."

It took some time for me to get to sleep and I reflected that I was happier at sea for I did not understand women at all. I was just glad that they seemed to understand me.

Our men all returned to their farms and I chose my crew for my next voyage. It was Gytha's choice of Bear Tooth that decided me. When I had found this land, I had had four youths and I would do so again rather than taking more experienced sailors such as Fótr or Aed. Besides, my brother's wife, Reginleif, was about to give birth and he was excited to be a father. I would take Ebbe along with Stig Eidelsson; both had proved themselves in the whale hunt. All were delighted to be going with me although Arne was less than happy that we would be taking the captive with us. Gytha, Snorri and I did not regard him as a slave. He had lost his family in the attack but appeared to bear no grudge against our people. It seemed his tribe had a philosophy similar to ours that a warrior killed in battle was guaranteed a place in their heaven. I did not tell Arne that I intended to arm my guide.

It took some weeks to be ready to sail. The snekke needed work. We took her from the water and sealed the strakes. I replaced all of the ropes on the steering board and had spares for the sheets and stays. We had a hide sail for we would not need speed on this voyage. I then had to teach my three crew how to sail. They would not have to do as Rek, Dreng and the others had done and stand a watch at night but I needed them to be able to steer and know how to set the sail perfectly to gain every piece of speed which we could. We loaded weapons. I had my sword and the dagger taken from Karl the Climber. I took my yew bow and I also took three spears as well as bows, arrows and slings for the crew. I only took four of the precious metal-tipped arrows. The rest were tipped with flint or bone. The Skraeling wore nothing even approaching mail. Most were bare-chested and a stone arrow could easily pierce their flesh. Ada spent two weeks attaching small pieces of bone to my leather jerkin. Had the natives had metal I would worry but their stone spears and arrows would not penetrate the whalebone. The compass, hourglass and old piece of white cloak which would serve as a map, along with the charcoal to make marks, were placed in my chest by the steering board.

Finally, we were ready to leave. As we would not need a great deal of food, we had more room than when I had left the land of ice and fire. Arne, Fótr and Siggi joined Gytha, Snorri and Ada to see me off.

"How long will you be away, brother? We need to know where we can hunt!"

"It will take but a day to reach the coast but as we might have to travel many miles inland, I do not think we will be back in less than seven nights."

Arne embraced me, "His voice was thick with emotion and that was unusual for him, "Come back safe, my blood brother, for you are a lucky charm. I know that I am the jarl but you are the clan's favourite and without you, there might be no Clan of the Fox."

After Ada had given me a hug too, Gytha came and, while embracing me, said quietly in my ear so that only I could hear her, "I have more potion and I would have you listen for my thoughts."

I nodded and climbed aboard the familiar snekke. The others were there already and I saw eagerness written all over their faces. Bear Tooth apart, they remembered Dreng, Rek and the others leaving and knew the risks and the rewards. I took out the hourglass and compass before I covered the chest with my bear fur and I sat close to the steering board. I left the putative map and charcoal in the chest. I turned the hourglass and then placed it in the holder I had made by the stern. I took a sun sight and marked the compass. We were ready.

"Ebbe, let fly the sail!"

Siggi and Fótr were holding us against the power of the wind and when they released us we flew south, *'Jötnar'* was a lively vessel and even though they had spent some days sailing her, I saw the shock on the faces of my crew as she leapt from the land to be in her true home, the sea. Once we cleared the bay and I had checked the wind I said, "Ebbe, Stig, go forrard and watch the hourglass. Tell me when it is ready to turn. Bear Tooth come here and sit by me."

I saw the look of apprehension on his face as he neared the bear fur; I had left the head on and the eyeless skull seemed to terrify him. He gave me a nervous smile, "I will sit here." He pointed to the gunwale.

I laughed, "Just so long as you do not fall in. Now tell me again, where is the boundary of your people's land?"

He pointed south and west, "There is a large river there although I have never seen it. Many other rivers flow into it and we call it the River of Peace. It runs north to south." I was pleased that Snorri had taught him the words for the points on a compass. It made life much easier for me. "Few people live on its banks for it is the boundary between our tribes and war is forbidden along it."

He had told Gytha and me that before and I had asked him to confirm in case he had changed his story. I was pleased that he had not. "And the people on the other side of the river, they are not your tribe?"

"No, they are the Penobscot; their language is like ours but they have different customs. We fight them sometimes for they raid us for slaves and we retaliate. Heads are taken as trophies and displayed outside our camps. The Penobscot do not travel as much as we do. Sometimes they just send hunting parties to gather animals or catch fish but their homes are similar to ours."

"So, do they live on the coast, in the summer, like your people?"

He shrugged, "I will be honest, Captain, I do not know for certain. What I do know is that when you find a wide river mouth that is the River of Peace and there will be few people, if any, living along its banks."

I had to trust this boy for the Norns had sent him to me and Gytha's faith rested upon the both of us. I reasoned that if there were none along the river then I could find its source and be able to view more land than if we explored on foot. I knew that we would, eventually, have to explore.

"And your people live on the side where the sun rises?" He nodded. If I found a tributary which looked promising then I would have to take one to the western side of the river for Bear Tooth's tribe knew and feared us. Of course, Bear Tooth had never seen this river and he had, certainly, never approached the coast from the sea. It would have to be up to me and my experienced eyes to find the likeliest place for a river mouth. I did not mind our sedate pace for I was looking to the west and the slow speed gave me time to evaluate what I saw. The land would be higher on the two sides of the estuary; they might not be much higher but they would be an indicator. Birds would be another. Where freshwater met the sea there was always a great deal of wildlife in the water and the birds would take advantage and the larger the river the greater the number of fish. We had been travelling for four hours when I saw the combination of birds in an area with higher ground on either side of a low-lying section. I headed to the south-west knowing that if I was wrong, we could still sail down the coast and look for the real river. To seaward we passed small islands but they were smaller than Bear Island and I dismissed them as places of interest. As we closed with the shore, I saw that there were many inlets but all appeared too close to be the mouth of the river we sought. Bear Tooth had no idea of distance, not at sea, at least.

The Savage Wilderness

I spied neither fires nor birch bark boats and that pleased me for I did not relish having to fight my way up a river. We passed one large river mouth but as it looked more like a bay and less like an estuary, I dismissed it. It was getting on for dusk and I had just taken a reading from the compass and turned the hourglass when I saw, just ahead, what looked like an estuary. Certainly, the entrance was narrow and so I headed along the coast. Bear Tooth had told me of an island, the natives called it Sebascodegan Island, and he said it was at the mouth of the bay which led to the river we sought. He said that the Penobscot tribe had made a natural cairn to mark their land. I had the crew looking for an impressive pile of stones and when I saw such a cairn on the south-eastern tip, I grew hopeful. I wondered if we would make the river before dark. If not, we would have to risk landing on an island which might be occupied.

In the distance I spied what I thought might be the mouth of the river; there were no large trees there but low lying and scrubby trees which were the sort which Bear Tooth had told me grew at the mouths of such large rivers. At home, it had not been so. I saw the churning waters which marked the meeting of river and sea.

I decided we had sailed far enough and we could halt. "This may well be it, Ebbe and Stig, nock an arrow, just in case but make them stone-tipped!"

"Aye, Captain."

"Bear Tooth, you will have to be ready to lower the mast if we hit trouble."

He nodded nervously for although we had practised all of these manoeuvres and actions, doing them quickly when there was danger, was a completely different matter.

"Do not worry, we should not need to do so for the wind is from the north and east, it will take us some way up the river." He nodded again. "Ebbe, you have the steerboard side; tell me when it is clear to turn."

"Aye, Captain!"

The motion of the ship became more violent as we approached the meeting of the sea and river water. That could not be helped. The three youths had all been told to hang on if the water became violent. I had the steering board to hold and I was less troubled and I had my feet braced against the thwarts. I saw that there were rocks which littered the estuary but there looked to be a clearer patch of water which suggested a channel. Ebbe would have to confirm that fact.

His voice was clear as he shouted, "Now, Captain!" And I put the steering board over to take us through the tidal race.

The bow rose and then fell, showering Ebbe and Stig as it did so. We slowed slightly. Had I had Ebbe or Stig on the sheets and stays, we might have been able to adjust the trim and make a more comfortable passage but Bear Tooth had the least experience of any aboard *'Jötnar'* and I said nothing, preferring to ride it out.

The river mouth was wide, perhaps three hundred paces and, to our right, I saw larger trees and forests. To the larboard side, the trees were smaller and they suggested another island. Bear Tooth had said there were many islands between the river and the open sea. So far, his description had been very accurate. The river narrowed dramatically and I saw streams entering the river from the west. It became just a hundred paces wide but the channel remained deep. Darkness would soon be upon us and we had not found a place to land. And then Stig shouted, "Captain, to larboard, I see a beach and what looks like a tiny stream."

I put the steering board over. "Ebbe, Stig, come and help Bear Tooth. When I give the command then lower the sail. We have enough way and the wind is pushing us west. I had learned to sail on this snekke and I knew just what it would do in almost any situation. "Now!" As the sail came down, I was already pushing hard to larboard and the bow grated along the sand of the tiny beach. The drekar would have ripped out her keel but *'Jötnar'* managed it with no problems at all.

"Bows!"

Ebbe and Stig jumped into the water with nocked bows looking for danger. The two of them leapt ashore and I gave the rope to Bear Tooth, "Tie us to the largest birch tree." I slipped over the side and stood in waist-deep water holding the stern of the snekke. Bear Tooth was a quick learner and he wound the rope around the tree and then pulled back towards the river to use the strength of the tree to pull the snekke out of the water. As soon as the snekke moved, I pushed it until it was half in and half out of the water. I held up my hand, "Tie it off."

Ebbe and Stig had taken the initiative and headed into the woods while Bear Tooth and I had beached the boat. The trees were relatively open on this side of the river but it was getting dark and I wanted to know that we were secure before I risked lighting a fire and making camp. I took out my sword. I saw Bear Tooth's eyes widen. Even in the gloom of dusk it still shone and I knew that the natives had nothing that was like it.

"Bear Tooth, find wood for a fire." While he did that, I stored my compass and hourglass in my chest.

Night fell within a few moments of the drawing of my sword and I began to worry about Ebbe and Stig. It was with some relief that I saw them both appear down the side of the small stream which fed the River of Peace. "There are no trails, Captain, either human or animals. If animals do come down to the water they do not do so in herds."

"Good, get a pot of water and our food. We will sleep aboard the snekke tonight but we will eat ashore. Hot food will help us on the morrow and the fire will keep away the biting insects."

Bear Tooth had shown us, on the island, a plant whose leaves could be burned and which seemed to lessen the number of insects. I knelt next to the kindling and used my steel and flint to spark and ignite the dried grass which lay beneath the pyramid of dried wood. Bear Tooth never tired of watching us make fire. His own people made fire but they had no metal and had used a piece of wood twisted and turned next to the kindling. He had told us our way was quicker. I saw him watching me closely and decide that I would allow him to do that the next time.

He picked some greens while I cut up a mixture of horse deer and whale meat into small chunks and Ebbe and Stig arranged some logs around the fire. Then they half-filled the pot and hung it from the tripod we had brought. When we had left Larswick, we had shown great foresight, as a clan, by buying many things, such as large pots and tripods which we could never have fashioned in this new world. The Norns had spun well and the threads were so complicated that I could not see how they could ever be undone. They waited until the fire had caught before they hung the pot and then I dropped the meat and fish into the water. Bear Tooth ripped the greens and then dropped them in too.

As we sat, watching the flames heat the pot and then the pot begin to bubble, I handed around the ale skin. We each took a drink. Bear Tooth did too. He knew what beer was and enjoyed it. As he passed it to Ebbe, I said, "Do your people have beer?"

He nodded, "Yes, Captain, but it is not as good as this. It is made from pines. My people would prefer this."

I wondered at that. Perhaps war was not the way we ought to approach these people. We had things we could offer them to make their life better. What if I could discover iron here, in this new world? We did not need gold for we had neither kings nor taxes, merchants nor markets. On Bear Island we bartered. Bear Tooth told us that was the way of his people for whatever was in short supply was expensive. I had much to think on. Before we retired for the night, I placed some logs and branches around the camp to trip anyone trying to sneak up on us and Bear Tooth put the pungent plant's leaves on the fire. I loosened the rope so that the snekke floated and any who tried to get at us would have to splash in the small stream. That done, I wrapped myself in my bear fur and slept.

I dreamed and I knew that Gytha was speaking to me. She was speaking in my head but I heard not a word and I was just aware that her mouth was moving. I saw Ada and I saw Lars but I know not how I saw them. What I did hear was music and I wondered what it was until I realised it was a lullaby my mother had sung to me when I was young. Then all went black and I dreamed no more.

I woke before dawn and I knew that some noise or movement had woken me. I was awake in an instant and I stared over the gunwale. My hand was on my sword but I moved only my head from beneath the bear fur. I saw a pair of white-tailed deer. They were drinking close to the rope which tied us to the tree and that must have woken me. As I lifted my head, they were startled and hurtled off back into the woods. Just to be safe I picked up Ebbe's bow and arrow and waded ashore. The deer had jumped over the timber and we were safe. The fire had died but the ashes were still warm. I made water and drank a mouthful of the ale. Going back to the snekke, I woke the others.

The Savage Wilderness

"Make water and then eat for we leave before dawn."

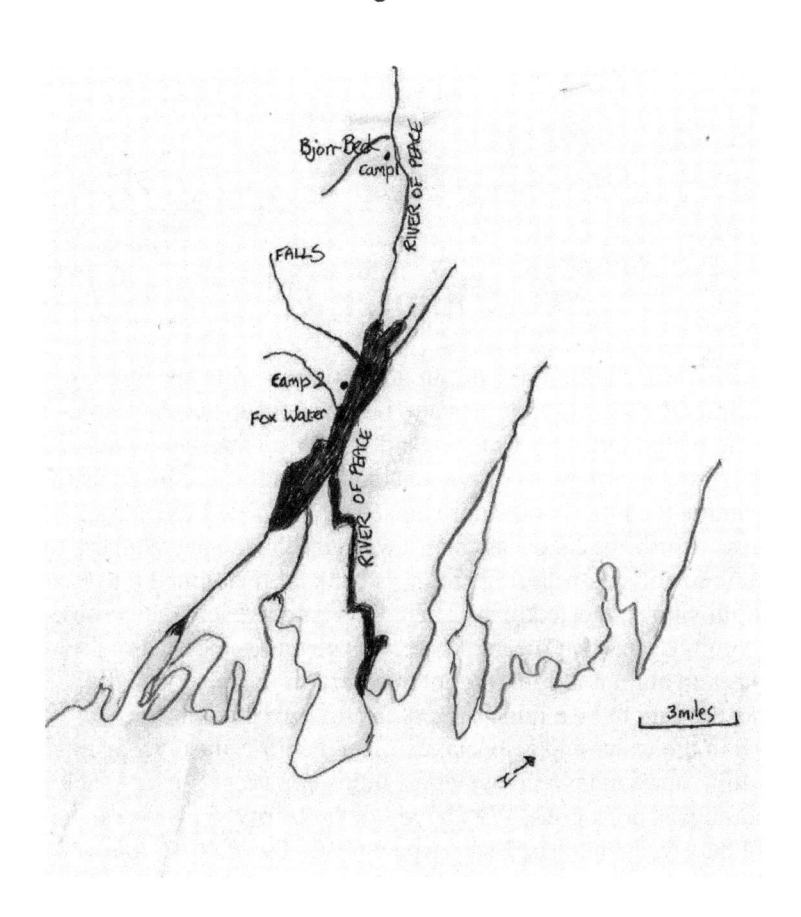

The Savage Wilderness

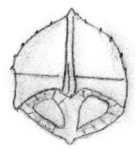

Chapter 4

This was the first day of our adventure in what appeared to be a wilderness or would it prove to be a bountiful garden? Time alone would tell. This time we had to tack up the river which took time and, in many ways, this helped us for it allowed us to examine the river banks more closely. As this was the border between tribes who occasionally warred, I had expected there to be more animals watering along its banks. I mentioned it to Bear Tooth who suggested that the small rivers were less dangerous. He pointed out that the banks were steep and somewhat rocky, and if an animal fell in, it would be hard to regain dry land. He was proving to be a mine of very useful information. We saw fish in the water and also snakes. Bear Tooth counselled against putting our hands in the water as, in his experience, every such reptile was poisonous. We obeyed with alacrity! The river did not narrow as much as I had expected and for the first mile or so remained about the same.

The river turned at one point to head due west and we gained speed as we did so. It only lasted for a hundred or so paces and then turned due north. A helmsman needed his wits about him on this river. The river appeared to be littered with islands and, as noon approached, I decided to stop at one of them and explore. We could make a good camp with plenty of time to examine what lay around us. That proved easier said than done and we passed three tiny islands, totally unsuitable for a camp, as well as four larger islands with no landing place. I could now see why animals shunned this river and I wondered if we should take a side river which might suit our people more. Finally, we found an island with just one tiny sliver of a beach. We almost missed it but Ebbe had sharp eyes and he spied the beach beneath the overhanging trees. It was a perfect place to land for we would be hidden from the Penobscot side of the river. We lowered the sail and the mast, and rowed in.

This time I put the snekke beam on to the shore and we pulled her securely up under the trees. After tethering her, we took ashore simply what we would need to cook and our sleeping furs.

"We will explore the island but we will do so together." I was aware of Rek's death. I did not want one of my young ship's boys to fall foul of some animal. I handed a bow and a handful of stone-tipped arrows to Bear Tooth. I had my spear and sword. I looked up and saw that the island had a high point. "We will head for that and we will watch all the way. If we can hunt then we will do so but it is not important for I wish to know what is here."

The three nodded but I saw the excitement in their eyes. They knew that they would be the envy of every boy in the clan. Even Bear Tooth felt part of the clan, as his actions and words so ably demonstrated. I headed up what looked like a game trail but, to be truthful, I was not hopeful. From the hoof prints I spied, there appeared to be no horse deer on this island. As I wound my way up through the trees, I saw what looked like squirrels with long ears but they scurried away along the ground so quickly I had no idea what they were, except that if they had been squirrels, they would have raced up into the trees. At one point I found animal dung that looked like a wolf, dog, fox or a large cat. I sniffed it and deduced it was a cat but a larger cat than I had ever encountered. We also found plants that were unpleasant. We avoided nettles as every sensible person did but we brushed against other plants and felt pain and our flesh burned. Bear Tooth apologised when Ebbe was thus burned for he had assumed we knew what they were.

I shook my head, "Bear Tooth, we come from a land which is not like yours. You must tell us of all the dangers in this land!"

"I will, Captain, and I am sorry."

I smiled for I could see he was making an effort. "I am not angry but we are one clan and we watch out for one another."

He smiled, "I am of your clan?"

I smiled back, "You are now!"

The Savage Wilderness

A change came over Bear Tooth then for it was as though he made a conscious decision to cease being a Mi'kmaq and become a Fox! We also found briars and brambles which impeded our route. The game did not use this path and we were breaking trail. It was not easy. When we reached the high point, I could see nothing. I would have sent Bear Tooth up the nearest tree but he would see with Skraeling eyes. "Ebbe, climb the tree and tell me what you can see." He nodded and went to climb. "Do not shout your answer down. Wait until you descend."

"Aye, Captain!"

It seemed to take an age and I began to fret but, eventually, he slid down and shook his head, "To the east, west and north there is forest stretching as far as the eye can see. To the north is a piece of water which looks larger than a river."

"A tarn?"

"It could be but the water moves."

I nodded, "We will descend but we will go that way and walk around the island." I pointed to the south-west. "We look for game. I need to know what animals we can hunt." I was disappointed for there was less here than on Bear Island. As we walked down, I worked out that, if we wished to find the horse deer, we would have to find the mainland and head inland. I did not want to risk the land of Bear Tooth's people and that meant heading to the west and the land of the Penobscot. What we did discover were the bones of animals which had been hunted but, from the condition of the bones, it was an animal which had hunted them.

As we cooked our food, I asked Bear Tooth about such predators. "There are wolves and large wild dogs which both hunt in packs. The dogs can be captured and trained and we use them to hunt the moos. There are foxes," he smiled, "you are the Clan of the Fox and I do not think you hunt them."

"We have hunted them but we are the Clan of the Fox for, like the fox, we are clever and can adapt wherever we live."

"Then there are the large," he used a word I had never heard and could not pronounce. I asked him to describe the animal. "It has sharp teeth and two are like fangs. Its claws are deadlier than the wolf and it does not bark."

The Savage Wilderness

I nodded, it sounded like a large cat. There were such animals back on the mainland in the land of the Picts; they were wildcats and they had been known to take small children and babies. There were no such creatures on Bear Island; perhaps the bears had killed them. It was a danger I had not anticipated. Such cats could ambush and, if they were like the wildcats of the land of the Picts then, unlike the wolf and the dog, they could climb and that made them dangerous.

"There are none on the islands for they do not like to swim." Bear Tooth's words were reassuring.

We prepared our food and I stored all of the information. I had the map I was making and I refined it a little with the information we had discovered on this voyage so far. I marked on the map the game we had seen. So far it was just white-tailed deer, squirrels and the long-eared creatures which lived under the ground. We had not been able to hunt anything and so we ate river shellfish and the meat we had brought.

I asked Bear Tooth what his people hunted. "We use traps more than we hunt, Captain." He described a whole series of traps which were used and, from his words, I deduced that there had to be a natural vine they used for ropes as they did not appear to be ropemakers. I had not looked for them when we had been walking as I was more concerned with that which we could hunt. He also told us of a creature which built its home in the water and dammed rivers. From his words, I ascertained that it was trapped, not for food but for its fur. That made sense for if it lived underwater then, like the seal, its fur would repel water. It sounded to me like the animal they had in Norway and the land of the Picts, the bjorr. He told us that they were found on the smaller rivers and that decided me that we would take a tributary as soon as one presented itself.

Of my crew, I knew Stig the least well. I knew that his father was the last of his family and Stig the eldest of the children but, other than that, I knew little about him. His father, Eidel, had been keen for me to take his son with me and I wondered why.

"So, Stig, you wish to be a navigator?"

He shook his head, "In all truth, Captain, no, but my father was keen that I should know how to sail for he said that we may not stay in this new world forever."

The Savage Wilderness

"He wishes to return to the land of ice and fire?"

He shook his head, "After Benni died, he and some of the others spoke of returning to Larswick. They said that the King of Norway might not rule that land and there would be treasure for them to raid. Here, there is food and the weather is clement but the Skraelings appear to be poor people. They have no metal and we have seen neither gold nor silver. There are others like my father who wish to have the opportunity to raid for such treasures."

As we ate, I reflected on his words. That he had been honest was a good thing but his father and some of the others had been less than honest with us. I understood that there was little treasure and metal and that was a problem, but I knew that the Allfather would have put such metals in this land and we had yet to begin to search for them. The problem was that we knew where to look for such metals in the east. When the Clan of the Wolf had had their stronghold in the Land of the Wolf, the mountainsides of Úlfarrberg and mountain of Old Olaf had yielded iron, copper and lead. South of Wyddfa there were mines with gold and jewels buried in them. Both places were now barred to us but I knew, in my heart, that there would be such places here in this new world. We just had to find them.

The next morning, we set sail north and after just a mile, or so I estimated, we found ourselves in a huge piece of open water. I scooped a handful and tasted it; it was freshwater. I looked south and deduced that this must be a river and rock had narrowed it to form this natural stretch of water. To the north, I saw the water narrow and become the River of Peace once more. This was a perfect place for the drekar. We could easily sail up the River of Peace as there had been nowhere which was too shallow or too narrow. I decided to spend the day exploring the river and seek somewhere to make a camp.

First, I sailed due west and discovered that the water was more than two miles wide. I found a navigable river which headed north and west. I also spied many places to land. This was where we had been meant to come. Further south there were too few safe places to land. Then I sailed south and west to see how long the piece of water I had already named in my mind, Fox Water, was. It narrowed where two rocky pieces of land forced it and it became a single river, and so I turned us around and tacked back up Fox Water past the place we had joined it, and we headed north until I saw another island. Once more the water narrowed and flowed around the island. It was getting on for dark, and as I spied a beach on the island we could see as we headed north, I landed us there. As we had sailed, I had estimated the distance we had travelled; Fox Water was over nine miles long. There had been fish in it all the way along and some were large ones, the type of which I had never seen before. When we sailed south, on our way home, I would have the boys trail fishing lines to see what we could catch.

We had seen no sign of Skraeling and Bear Tooth's words appeared to be true. This was a border and was kept free of people. After ascertaining that the beach was safe, we landed. Bear Tooth had told us of the traps his people made for the long-eared animals and he went with Stig and Ebbe to show them how to set them. He told me that the creatures came out at night. I lit the fire and threw long fishing lines into the water which flowed from the north. Then, once the fire had caught and began to throw off light, I worked on my map.

The three youths came back and began to toss food into the pot as they no longer needed instruction from me. Suddenly Ebbe said, "Captain, the fishing lines, we have a bite!"

He ran with the other two and they hauled from the water two fish, which were both as long as a child's arm. Bear Tooth said their name. They looked similar to fish I had seen in the river close to Larswick but they were not the same. Bear Tooth gutted them using my dagger. He loved using the sharp metal and even when he cut himself, he never minded, regarding it as something which was spiritual. *Wyrd* for this was the blade which Siggi, Arne and I had used to make ourselves blood brothers. King Raedwulf's knife had been sent to us for a purpose. I saw that the flesh was pink and I knew that it would be good to eat. We threw the two pink-fleshed fish into the pot. They would not take long to cook and would be flavoured with the meat and the greens we had used whilst also imparting a fish taste to the deer meat stew. I saw then that this place would be a better home for the clan if we could find the horse deer for there were more fish which were easier to catch and game, although so far small, was in

The Savage Wilderness

abundance. The smell of the cooking food made me hasten my map making and I put the precious map back in my chest. I placed the two fish on the wooden platter we used and divided them into four. As captain, I took one of the delicious heads for me. I saw that when I divided the fish the flesh came easily away from the bones. It tasted as delicious as it looked and we did not need to eat all of the meat. We left it to cook while we went to sleep. We would have a stew when we woke.

Once more I dreamed and it was Gytha who came to me. She was smiling and I struggled to hear her words. I heard one phrase before she disappeared, '*You have done well, Navigator.*' Or perhaps they were the words I wished her to say, I truly know not.

We rose and finished off the stew. While I prepared the snekke for our voyage, the boys checked the traps and brought back three of the long-eared creatures. Bear Tooth showed us how to gut them. They stank and I wondered what the flesh would taste like. Bear Tooth grinned, "They taste good, Captain, like the birds who lay eggs for the clan on Bear Island but they should be cooked now!"

"Add wood to the fire. There is still water in the pot. We will cook them and then head north. Save the guts for bait and we will trail lines as we sail. Then come back to me and I will tell you what I plan for I think we have found a place to live."

While they obeyed my commands, I walked to the western side of the island. I only had to walk two hundred paces. I looked at the river bank. The trees were much larger than they had been downstream and I could see no game but they would probably use smaller rivers to frequent. We had seen many rivers when we had sailed along Fox Water and looking at the river bank decided me. I returned to the boys who had finished their tasks.

"Today we sail north until we find a river to the west. I will sail until we find a beach and then we will land, make a camp and then explore. Bear Tooth has told us that there are Skraelings who live here and they may be belligerent. You will listen for my words and when I tell you to run then you head back to the snekke. If anything happens to me and you have to leave me then do so and return to Bear Island."

Ebbe looked appalled, "We cannot leave you!"

The Savage Wilderness

One by one, I looked at each of them in the eyes as I spoke, "I will leave any of you if I have to. What we do is for the clan. We serve the families on Bear Island who rely on us, do you understand?"

They nodded.

"We seek the horse deer and when we find where it lives then we return home."

We waited until the animals had cooked and then packed them in leaves and placed them back in the snekke. We left the island and sailed up the western channel seeking a side river. It was not as easy as I had thought. While we had passed many before Fox Water, we sailed all day without spying one and, when we did, in the late afternoon, it came from the south-west. I had made my plan and I stuck to it. We turned and headed upstream along the smaller river and sought a beach or a landing place. Within a hundred paces it became obvious that the drekar could not navigate what I had taken to be a river but was little more than a wide and shallow beck, but in many ways that suited us for the trees which grew along the banks arched and met giving cover to the river. We would not need a beach for the banks were not high and we could tie up to a tree. As it was coming on to dark, we landed.

I saw a small clearing and pulled the snekke over to the larboard bank. I estimated that the River of Peace lay less than four hundred paces to the east of us and while we set up camp, I sent Ebbe to confirm this. While he was away, I scouted out the land around us and discovered no signs of Skraeling but many animal trails and dung. When both Ebbe and I returned, I knew that we would travel no further inland using the snekke. We would scout out the land around this stream and see if it was suitable. Certainly, the campsite showed more promise because the land was flatter. Thus far the banks of the river had been steep and clearing them for farming would have proved too difficult. Here the land was flat and looked fertile. Ebbe reported that the river bank close to the River of Peace was rocky and too high for us to land. That was good for it meant this land would not flood. As we ate, I put the finishing touches to the map and the outline was done. There were empty areas and I would need to mark them with the animals I had found. Heading upstream with gut baited lines had yielded half a dozen fish. While none were as large as the two we had caught off the large island, they were more than enough for us and we did not need to use the pot. We put fishing lines out and set traps for the long-eared animals. We had each made water on the pelts of the animals we had skinned and I thought to make two of them into a hat which would be useful in winter.

As we ate, I saw that the clearing was man-made. I spied stumps of saplings in the ground and wild plants, bushes and shrubs had begun to colonise it. The fact that they had done so reassured me for it meant whoever had cleared it had not returned for some time.

As we were now in the land of the Penobscot, I took the precaution of using some of the vines we found and cut them down to make trips and traps. I did not wish to be visited in the night although as we had had to pick our way into the centre of the clearing it was unlikely that we would be disturbed. We drank the last of the ale; we would now have to drink river water and that was always fraught with danger. I decided that we would boil it before we drank. I knew not what lay in the waters of this new world. That night, when I slept, Gytha came to me, but this time Ada was with her and it was Ada's voice I heard in my head and not Gytha's but Gytha's mouth moved. '*You have found a good land. Find the horse deer and return. Find the horse deer.*' And then they were gone but I still dreamed and I saw the maid again. This time there was no waterfall and she was not alone but, in my dream, I only had eyes for her and this time she looked at me and she smiled. Then I woke and it was still dark and I needed to make water.

I tried to return to the dream but failed and so I set about making food. I took some of the kindling we had gathered and rekindled the fire. I took some of the water from the stream and put it on to boil. I checked the fish lines and pulled out half a dozen fish. I quickly gutted them and threw the guts into the stream. As I sat on a fallen log and watched the flames grow, I listened to the noises around us in the dark for there were many animals. When I heard the growl, even though it seemed to be far off, I clutched the hilt of my sword. Was this one of those sharp-toothed cats Bear Tooth had told me about? Bear Island might lack horse deer but it was safe for the people. I took off the pot with the boiled water and put on the pot we had used to cook the stew the previous night. There were still the remains of food in it. I added more water and I put some dried meat in the stew pot, and then I used twigs to skewer some of the fish I had taken from the lines and gutted. I would put those next to the fire to cook later. Before dawn truly broke, I woke the boys. They collected the animals from the traps. We skinned and we gutted them. After I had filled the water and ale skins with the boiled water, I added more water to the stew and put in the long-eared animals to cook with some greens. The fish were small and they did not take long to cook; we ate well.

Stig wiped his greasy fingers on his breeks, "The fish here, Captain, are amongst the finest I have tasted and the meat from the long ear is good too. Could we live here?"

I shook my head, "I heard wild animals in the night and we have yet to meet the Penobscot. Until we do that and find the horse deer, I will be unable to make a decision."

Ebbe said, "The clan will heed your words?"

"I am honoured that they trust me but it is a great responsibility for I was one who persuaded them to leave Larswick and then the land of ice and fire. The land of ice and fire was a mistake; will this prove to be a similar one?"

Arne was the jarl but I was the one who thought of the needs of the clan and I was not yet convinced that this new world was the world we had hoped. Arne was a warrior and while I saw the dangers, he saw it as a land filled with potential for we had defeated the Skraeling at every turn. I thought we had been lucky. As we prepared to leave to explore, I knew that this adventure would become more dangerous before it reached its end. We headed south and east as I wished to stay as close to the River of Peace and the invisible border as I could. It would make it much less likely that we would meet Penobscot.

There were animal trails for us to follow and I used them for we sought the herds of horse deer. We found the spoor of a smaller deer which Bear Tooth told us were the white-tailed deer. They appeared to abound and would provide the food we might need but I had been sent to find the horse deer which the Skraeling hunted. We found bushes with berries and fruit upon them. Bear Tooth told us which were poisonous and which were not. He told us which ones could be fermented to brew an ale. I collected some and put them in my satchel. I would dry them and take them back for Gytha. Then we found evidence of Skraeling. We would not have known that what we saw was evidence but Bear Tooth knew. My decision not to kill him and make him one of us was proving a good one. We found a tall birch and the bark had been taken off in one piece. When Bear Tooth saw it, he nodded and said, "Penobscot have done this for they are skilled in the making of birch bark boats as they can take off the bark in one piece and they do not harm the tree."

While I admired the skill involved, I became warier. They might not occupy this borderland but they did harvest it. I moved more slowly. It was just after noon when, not only did we spy the spoor of the horse deer, we found a small herd of them grazing. We did not attack them for there were not enough of us and I had only been sent to find them. As we were upwind of them and kept still, they did not move but continued to graze. We watched them for a while until they moved off. We sat, when they had gone, and ate some salted meat and drank some of the cold boiled water. Ebbe and Stig wrinkled their noses, "Foster father, we should have brought more ale! This has no taste!"

I laughed, "The hardships of exploration. Your brother Dreng would have swapped this water for the foul-tasting dregs we had when we sailed the mighty ocean."

We were about to move when a small herd of the white-tailed deer nervously came to graze in the same place that the horse deer had been. I knew not the name of the leaves upon which they grazed but I decided to take a sample back to the clan. They would help us hunt a little easier for both species appeared to like them. As the deer began to graze, I had a thought. I said, quietly, "String your bows and let us see if we can hunt a deer." I had never seen the three hunt and I knew not their skill level. In addition, we were not using metal-tipped arrows but bone arrows. It was worth the risk for the meat would be useful. "I pointed to an older female who favoured a hind leg. She would be easier to hunt and would be just as good to eat. "We take her."

They strung their bows and I hefted my spear. It had a metal spearhead but it would be a long throw and I knew not if I had

The Savage Wilderness

the skill to kill, but I would try. Ebbe and Stig flanked me while Bear Tooth moved to the right of Ebbe. The boys might be untried but they knew what to do. Each watched their feet before placing them on the ground. We moved to within twenty paces and I saw the male raise his antlered head; they were going to bolt. I raised my spear and as I hurled it, I said, "Now!" The movement of the spear, the sound of my voice and their sense of smell made the herd move, but the old female was slow and the Allfather must have guided my hand for my spear hit her in the shoulder. Two of the boys' arrows also hit her and one must have struck an artery for blood flowed and she stumbled a dozen paces before collapsing.

We reached the animal and I took out my spear. While the boys recovered their arrows, I found a birch sapling and, using my sword like an axe, cut it down to help carry the animal. As we headed back to our camp, the boys were in high spirits. This had been their first real hunt and they had succeeded. Only the one whose arrow had missed knew that he had failed and none spoke of it. That was good for it showed that the three were a crew and I knew the value of that.

We spent the afternoon skinning and gutting the animal. We would have to burn the guts for if we left them it would invite carrion. We would also have to cook the beast and so I began to butcher it while Ebbe and Stig put water on to boil. Bear Tooth went to set more traps. It was almost dark by the time I had finished. We pegged out the hide and made water on it. Half of the deer was in the pot and while it was cooking, we would salt the rest and dry it on the snekke when we returned to Bear Island. We hung the half we had not yet cooked from the branch of a tree.

As we waited for it to cook, Ebbe said, "We leave for home tomorrow?"

I shook my head, "Bear Tooth said that the little river we used is the sort which is the home of the animals with the highly prized fur and who make dams. We managed to hunt a deer today, let us see if we can hunt one of these animals which make dams. I think they are a bjorr, a water bear, but I will need to see one, first."

Bear Tooth was sceptical, "We trap them for they are hard to hunt as they have thick fur."

I smiled, "I have the spear so let us see, eh?"

I took some of the meat out of the stew to test. It was a little tough but tasty and I put in the bones for that would make them easier to use and extract all the meat from them. The longer we cooked the deer, the tenderer it would become.

That night I dreamed once more but it was not Gytha who came to me nor Ada. Perhaps the hunt and the richness of the food had affected me, I knew not, but the dream was of the maid. She was running and men were hunting her. I ran after them with my spear and sword but my feet seemed incapable of moving, and it was as though I was in quicksand. She was taken and vanished before me then the men, I saw they were Skraelings with bones in their hair and paint on their faces, came towards me. They had stone clubs and stone-tipped spears. I prepared to sell my life dearly when suddenly I was awake.

The dream had been a warning of danger and I grabbed my sword. I saw eyes in the dark and I leapt to my feet, "Alarm! Alarm.!"

Something leapt at me and I swung my sword blindly at the golden eyes. I connected with something and I heard a scream which sounded fox-like and then, whatever animal it was, raced off through the woods.

The three boys were awake and armed in an instant. They ran to me, "What was it, foster father?"

"An animal of some kind." I went to the meat we had hung from a tree and saw that the animal had climbed the tree and ripped down the meat. There were teeth marks on one of the haunches and scratch marks on the branch. "I would guess the creature was one of those large cats which Bear Tooth mentioned. Whatever it was, I hurt it." I showed them the blood on my blade. You boys go back to sleep and I will keep watch."

I doubted that they would sleep well but they would rest and I was The Navigator. We could go for days without sleep and we would be home within a few days. I rehung the meat and built up the fire. I made water and then took the fish from the lines and put them in the water. I sat and watched the flames dancing red, yellow and blue and saw, again, the face of the maid in the fire.

Had she warned me? If so, was this the work of the Norns? How could that be for she was a Skraeling and I was Norse? The threads were, indeed, long and complicated.

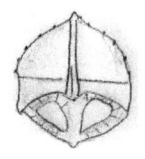

Chapter 5

I was anxious to leave but, first, I had to find the bjorr, if that was what the animal which Bear Tooth had described, was. We loaded the snekke and, after facing it downstream, headed up the small stream which I had hopefully named Bjorr Beck. My dream and the incident with the cat had made me wary and we moved up the river bank far more slowly than I would have otherwise wished. We soon found where the bjorr were to be found. I saw a jumble of logs across the river and spied one of the creatures sitting like a sentry on the top of the jumbly structure. I had never seen a live one but when we had been in Orkneyjar I had met a Saxon who had hunted them and wore one as a hat. This had the same fur, however, before I could even think about hurling my spear, the sentry, for that was what he was, had given the alarm and he had disappeared beneath the waters.

Bear Tooth seemed to find it amusing, "I told you, Captain!"

I nodded, "Let us get closer then and I can see their home. Then we return to our snekke and begin our voyage home."

I saw that it was a considerable structure and behind it was a large patch of flat water; I would not have liked to drink from it for it looked to be filled with wildlife and one did not drink water which did not move! I was about to turn when I heard, from ahead in the woods, a scream. It was human. Our hands went to our weapons and the three boys prepared to flee for that was the right thing to do, but something kept my feet rooted to the spot. I knew that it was my dream.

"Let us investigate. Bear Tooth, with me, Ebbe and Stig, guard our backs!"

We headed into the woods to our left and I followed an animal trail. It had been made by the horse deer for I saw where their antlers had scraped and scratched the bark. I stored the knowledge in my head. The sound had ceased but I knew the direction we should take and we moved silently along the trail. When I stood on a stone and it hurt, I realised that the soles of my sealskin boots were getting too thin and I would need to repair them. Our minds work in strange ways for I immediately slowed. It was fortunate that I did for ahead of me I saw two Skraeling. They were women. One had her back to me and was kneeling over another who lay on the ground. I knew they were both females for the Skraeling warriors we had seen thus far wore just breeches or a loincloth. These women wore a hide shift of some kind.

It was Stig who made the mistake and stepped on the twig which broke. The woman turned and I saw it was the maid of my dreams. I said, quickly to Bear Tooth, "Tell her we mean her no harm. We can help!"

The other Skraeling was an older woman; I saw that when she turned her face. She did not scream but looked in terror at us. Bear Tooth rattled off some words so quickly that I barely understood them but I heard enough to know that he had spoken the truth, although he said more than I had told him to. When the maid replied, I understood less but there was the hint of a smile and the smile was in her eyes.

"She says her mother is hurt. She has cut her leg and there is much blood. I have told her that you are the shaman of the Clan of the Fox and have the sign of the bear about your neck. You can approach but not Ebbe and Stig."

"You two stay here." I handed my spear to Ebbe, and Bear Tooth and I approached. I saw that the older woman had stepped onto a hidden, sharpened stump. Some animal had broken it off and the grass had grown around it. I knelt. I could see the woman shaking with fear and I smiled. Bear Tooth spoke and the maid replied but I was concentrating so much upon the wound that I heard nothing. I took my waterskin and washed the blood away. Then I tied a piece of thong tightly around her ankle. The woman was brave for she made not a sound. I washed the blood again and then wiped the wound with the sweat cloth I wore around my neck.

"Tell her this may hurt."

The Savage Wilderness

This time Bear Tooth spoke to the older woman and he said, "The young one is Laughing Deer and this is her mother Long Standing. Long Standing is afraid that you are some creature from another world who will hurt her."

"Tell her that this will hurt but it will heal her."

I took my vinegar skin which I always carried and poured some on to the wound. The woman screamed and Laughing Deer turned and looked west. As I began to smear honey on the wound, the maid spoke again and Bear Tooth said, "We must leave, Captain. She said that there are warriors close by. I am with you and they will see you as an enemy. She says thank you but you must run! She will watch her mother!"

I heard a shout in the distance and knew this was not the time to try diplomacy. I nodded and said, in Skraeling, "I know you from my sleep!" I did not know the word for dreams and it was the best that I could do.

I saw her smile and she said something. Bear Tooth grabbed my arm and pulled me, "She said, '*Me too*', but we must go, Captain, for if I am caught, they will do terrible things to me."

I nodded and rose, "Ebbe, Stig, let us run and run fast. We go straight to the snekke and head downstream!"

My dream had come true and been shattered in the same instance. The Norns were toying with me. I had so much I wished to say and now I could not. I heard shouts behind us and it spurred me on. Ebbe led and I shouted, "Do not look back. I will watch the back but run!"

We kept a steady pace along the river trail and when I saw the mast in the distance, I felt relief. It was then I risked turning. I saw the Skraelings. They were not painted as Bear Tooth had said they were when they went to war but they were fierce looking for they had the sides of their heads shaved. Worse, they were less than three hundred paces behind us and catching us.

Ebbe was almost at the snekke for he could run swiftly; I shouted to him, "Get aboard and cast off. Stig be ready to send an arrow at the Skraelings, and Bear Tooth, raise the sail!"

I risked another look and saw that one warrior was less than forty paces behind me but he was forty ahead of his companions. He would reach us before we had left the river bank. I heard his feet pounding. I had seen, in that glance, that he had a short fire-hardened spear and a stone club in his breeches. I watched Ebbe fumble as he tried to untie the rope, and then Stig was on board and he turned to aim the bow. The feet were even closer and I knew that I would not reach the snekke before I was struck from behind. As Bear Tooth leapt aboard and Ebbe finally untied the first of the ropes, I drew my sword and turned. It was not before time for the fire-hardened spear was rammed at my chest. Even as my sword bit into his side, scraping off his ribs, the spearhead hit one of my bone scales. Stig sent an arrow at the Skraeling's companions who slowed and then the Skraeling warrior fell at my feet looking in horror at the sword.

"Captain!"

I turned and saw the snekke moving away from the shore. I ran and jumped as high in the air as I could manage. My ship's boys had moved and I landed awkwardly on my chest. I had hurt my ankle but I was alive. Stig sent another arrow at the Skraelings as Ebbe helped Bear Tooth to raise the sail, and I grabbed the steering board to put us in the centre of Bjorr Beck. The dam of the bjorr saved us for it made the beck move faster than the Skraeling could run.

Stig said, "They have stopped, Captain, and returned to the warrior you wounded."

I nodded but my ankle was hurting. "Ebbe, fetch a pail and fill it with water. I have hurt my ankle. When it is filled then put my right foot, after you have removed my boot, into it."

"Aye, Captain! They are fierce-looking warriors!"

I nodded, "I can see why Bear Tooth and his clan fear them." I almost screamed when the boot was removed, but when Ebbe plunged my foot into the icy water, I felt relief. "Be ready with your bows for we know how close the River of Peace is to Bjorr Beck." Just then we hit the River of Peace and the stronger current caught us. This was a wider river and I hoped we could outrun the Skraeling.

Bear Tooth was at the prow and it was he saw the Skraeling some way down the river. They had known the land and raced across from Bjorr Beck to where the River of Peace narrowed to less than fifty paces and, to make matter worse, there were rocks and rapids on the shore opposite. They knew their land well and would be well within range of us. I guessed that others would already be carrying their birch bark boats to catch us. The ones on the shore would use bows. Bear Tooth turned, horror written all over his face, "They are waiting, Captain! They will kill us and I will lose my manhood! I will spend eternity alone!"

Ebbe said much more calmly than Bear Tooth, "Should we get our bows, foster father?"

I shook my head, "There is too much risk to you!" Taking my injured ankle from the leather pail, I stood and pain coursed up my leg. "Take the bear fur and go to the mast. Lie as flat as you can. The pelt is thick and, with your leather vests, you should be safe."

"But what about you, foster father?"

"I will trust to the bear teeth and this." I opened the chest and took out my helmet. "Now go!" I sat on the chest and sank my ankle into the leather pail once more. The relief was exquisite.

We were less than one hundred paces from the Skraeling but the snekke was picking up speed. Even so, there were fifteen Skraeling with bows and I knew that some would hit me. It was then I prayed to the Allfather to help me. I had to sail within thirty paces of the Skraeling to avoid the rocks and rapids. At that range, even a stone or bone tipped arrow might penetrate flesh. I saw them draw back their bows and arch their backs. They must have seen my crew take cover and they would use plunging arrows. The other half were aiming for me. I tried to keep my head down to look at the prow for my helmet had a face mask. The danger would be if an arrow came between my helmet and leather jerkin.

The arrows, when they came, did not come as a volley and I stored that information. It looked now as though we might have to fight the Penobscot, and if we did then our disciplined archers might well carry the day. Then the arrows struck. I heard some hit the sail and the mast. A grunt told me that one had hit the bear fur but not penetrated. Then I was hit. My helmet was well made and the arrows pinged and banged off it but did not penetrate. Some hit the gunwale and one hit the steering board but the Allfather watched over us and we were not hurt. I calculated that, at this speed, we would have to endure two more flights before we had passed them. The second flight sent two-thirds of their arrows at me. This time they hit my bone covered leather jerkin. One scored a hit on my right arm and I felt the blood drip. It had missed the bone but I dared not move the arrow in case it increased the blood flow. I would have to endure the wound. I risked looking up and saw that we were now downstream of them. We had one more flight to endure and then we would be safe. This time the arrows thudded into the steering board, my back and my helmet, but one found the gap between helmet and jerkin. I felt it hit my neck and yet there was neither pain nor blood. Then I realised what had happened. The stone arrow had hit one of the bear's teeth. The Allfather had saved me!

I risked turning my head and saw that their arrows were falling short. "You can come out now. Are you hurt?"

Stig shouted as he emerged from the fur, "One hit me on the back but I will just have a bruise to show!"

Ebbe was grinning until he saw my arm, "Foster father, you are wounded!"

"Aye, and now we will have to see if you can heal me. Take off my helmet and then get the honey, water and vinegar. Stig, come and fashion a leather thong around my arm to prevent the blood from flowing."

"Why do we not pull over to the bank, Captain, and take the arrow out when the snekke is motionless?"

"Because, Stig, those Skraeling had birch bark boats and they can move quickly down the river. We have a head start but they will eat into it soon enough. It will not be long before the three of you will have to take it in turns to row."

He tied the thong around my arm as Ebbe appeared next to me with the healing kit. "I have never done this."

"Do not worry, I will guide you through it. First, pull out the arrow. There will be blood at first, but if Stig has tied the thong well it will soon stop." I did not tell him that it would hurt me for I did not want to put such thoughts in his head. He pulled and blood poured out. I was pleased, despite the agony I felt, for any fragments of stone should be washed out with the blood. "Good. Now wash the blood away and examine it. If there are any fragments of stone then use the tip of your dagger to remove them." He looked shocked, "If you do not then I might die!"

He nodded and used the water skin to clear the blood. I watched him look at the bloody wound and he nodded, "I can see but flesh and blood."

"Good, then pour vinegar on and then seal the wound with honey. There are some strips of cloth in the healing kit, bind the wound with them and then, when that is done, I want the three of you to drink something and then eat some of the dried meat. We will not be stopping now until we reach the open sea."

Stig shook his head, "That will take a day and a night, at the very least! You cannot do it alone!"

"I must, but if I do fall asleep then one of you must steer. It is easy enough to steer but you must follow the course we took to reach here. The map is in the chest and you can use that." I smiled at the terror on their faces. "With luck and the Allfather's help then you will not need to do so!"

I knew that I needed to rest and that my two wounds would lessen our chances of survival but I also knew that the Skraeling would be chasing after us in their birch bark boats and that they would be faster than we were. We had an advantage for they had to travel north on the Bjorr Beck before they could join the River of Peace, and that was why I was so anxious for my crew to eat. With three of them, I could have two rowing and a spare to refresh them. I did not want them steering for that was a skill they had yet to master. I watched them eat and drink. Ebbe brought me some food and some water.

"Ebbe, fetch me my healing kit and put some honey on the end of your spoon."

"Honey, Captain?"

"Gytha has told me that it helps a man if he eats some when he is wounded. Let us give the remedy a test, eh, foster son?"

He grinned, "Aye, for I would not wish to face my mother if I brought home a corpse!"

The honey did help for I felt much more alert and, I know not how, the pain and the ache diminished. The bee was truly a wondrous creature. I turned and looked astern; the fact that I could not see the Skraeling did not fill me with hope for this was their river and they knew it better than I did. My hope lay in the fact that I hoped they would think we would stop for the night. I would not do so and I would push on through the dark and hope to lose them.

When they had finished eating, Ebbe said, "Would you like me to take the steering board?"

I was going to say no when I felt the need to make water. This would be a good chance for me to see how Ebbe handled the steering board. I nodded, "Aye, for I need to do so."

He slid next to me and I relinquished the steering board to him. I stood but kept my foot in the pail. Soon I would refresh the water for it was not as cold as when the pail had been filled. I made water over the side and stared astern. It was becoming late but I saw the first birch bark boat some five hundred paces behind us. With five Skraeling in the boat, they were powering through the water.

I took the steering board from Ebbe. "Refresh the water in the pail and then fetch the oars. Soon you may have to row."

He nodded and looked to Bear Tooth whose face was a picture of terror, "Bear Tooth thinks that they will do terrible things to us."

I would not lie to my foster son. "If they catch us, they will, but we are Vikings and we will not go peacefully. If they come for us there is no thought of surrender. We fight until we see Valhalla and Odin greets us. If you heed my words then they will not catch us. Trust to me and to the Allfather!" He looked reassured and I felt guilty for I did not believe my own words.

When night fell, the leading birch bark boat was less than one hundred paces from us and I gambled that they would soon tire. "Ebbe and Stig, take an oar but wait until I give the command before you put the blade in the river!"

They both chorused, "Aye, Captain!"

I saw that Bear Tooth was fingering the beads he wore around his neck, I smiled, "You will row soon enough Bear Tooth and then we shall leave your enemies far behind, for now, you are Clan of the Fox and we have great power!"

We had yet to learn the new song of the whale and so I began to sing our clan chant. Ebbe and Stig took their oars and I nodded as I sang. They joined in. Bear Tooth did not know it but he soon picked it up almost as though he knew it might be his salvation.

The Savage Wilderness

The Clan of the Fox has no king
We will not bow nor kiss a ring
We fled our home to start anew
We are strong in heart though we are few

Lars the jarl fears no foe
He sailed the ship from Finehair's woe
Drekar came to end our quest
Erik the Navigator proved the best
When Danes appeared to thwart our start
The Clan of the Fox showed their heart
While we healed the sad and the sick
We built our home, Larswick

The Clan of the Fox has no king
We will not bow nor kiss a ring
We fled our home to start anew
We are strong in heart though we are few

When Halfdan came with warriors armed
The Clan of the Fox was not alarmed
We had our jarl, a mighty man
But the Norns they spun they had a plan
When the jarl slew Halfdan the Dane
His last few blows caused great pain
With heart and arm, he raised his hand
'The Clan of the Fox is a mighty band!'

The Clan of the Fox has no king
We will not bow nor kiss a ring
We fled our home to start anew
We are strong in heart though we are few

    I glanced astern once we reached the end of the chant. We were losing them. Perhaps the song took the heart from them or it may have been that they were tiring, but whatever the reason I saw the white foam at the prow of their boat begin to fade.

"Sing!" My crew sang even louder and I watched their faces. They were tiring. "Bear Tooth take both oars. Let us see what a new member of the Clan of the Fox can do!" I relied on his terror of the consequences of being caught. There was a slight hiatus as they swapped over but then I felt the power in his arms. It made all the difference and when I next looked astern I saw no white foam beneath the birch bark boat. I let him row a while longer and then said, when the boat following had disappeared into the dark, "Rest! We will let the river and the wind help us. Thank you, Allfather!" I smiled, "Now eat some food and drink water, then rest. I will wake you when I tire!"

They had done well but rowing had exhausted them as they were not yet men grown. A warrior could row for many hours before his back ached and his thighs and arms burned. A warrior had a crew to row with him and there is something about rowing in unison with others which increases a warrior's capacity to go beyond what is physically possible. It is as though the crew is greater than the individual warriors. I do not understand it but I know that it works. The three of them slept and I concentrated on the river and tried to take my mind off my ankle and my arm. The ache was going from my foot but my arm throbbed. Bear Tooth had told me that some tribes poisoned their arrowheads and I hoped that the arrow which had struck me was not one of those.

When we passed the large island where we had camped on our way north then I knew that Fox Water was not far away and that would be a good opportunity for me to turn and see if we were still pursued. I knew that we could not stop until we reached the open sea but if I knew they were far behind I could cease worrying that they would close with us. It was the wind and the current which shifted *'Jötnar'*, the Skraelings had to use their arms. The moon came out as I reached the middle of the Water and bathed it in white light. Turning, I saw no birch bark boats and I shifted the steering board to take us a little further east. I had an easy sail for a mile or two before I took the twisting and turning river to the sea. I had a dilemma. I had been sent to find out if the land was suitable for the clan. I had been asked to find a place with less belligerent warriors. The land of the Penobscot was not such a place and yet I had seen the maid

The Savage Wilderness

and she had seen me. I wanted to return and yet, if I did, then I am sure it would result in my death. As I turned the steering board to head down the river, I decided I would not twist the reality to suit my purpose, I would tell them the truth and leave the decision to the others: Gytha, Snorri, Siggi and, of course, the jarl, Arne. My mind was a maelstrom and that is never a good thing when you sail strange waters in the night.

It was then that I heard Gytha in my head. It was night time and she would be dreaming in the spirit world. I was not but I heard her speaking to me. She was asking me to be safe. I could not see her but her voice was soft and soothing and seemed to ease the ache in my arm and my foot. More than that she calmed my mind and the troubled waters seemed to flatten to become like the bjorr water above their dam. I was content and I looked ahead to the twists and turns of this river.

Ebbe woke as I turned the steering board to take us on a sharp turn and the snekke heeled a little. He came to the stern, "Foster father, your arm must ache. I know that you will not sleep but can you not let me steer the snekke while you watch?"

He was right and I nodded. I was becoming stiff and, as he had rested, he would be able to react quicker, "Very well. Take the board with your left arm while I shift out of the way and then sit on my chest and use your sword arm to steer." Every captain and helmsman that I knew always steered with their right arm, their sword arm. I knew not why that was but we all did it and Ebbe might as well learn the right way. I sat with my back against the steerboard side with my foot still in the leather pail. I could look both up and downstream.

"The Skraeling women that we saw, one seemed to know you, foster father. How could that be? For this was all new land to us."

"I had dreamed of her and knew her face. She told Bear Tooth she had dreamed of me."

"But we are not the same people!"

"Perhaps they have the Allfather as their god, and the spirits, the Norns, they are everywhere. It was they who tie and spin our threads." He nodded. "A little to larboard." He made small movements and I said, "Good. That is perfect. You are learning well."

He concentrated for a while and was obviously still digesting the words I had said, "And my mother?"

I sighed, "Your mother knows I dreamed of the Skraeling. She knew it before we lay together and made Lars. No matter what happens, I will still be your foster father and I will still watch out for your mother and our family."

"But how?"

I shrugged, "The Norns spin and they weave; their threads are long and complicated; I do not know, but first, we get home to Bear Island, and then we tell the clan what we found. We have done our part and it is up to the others to make the decision."

Bear Tooth woke too and he said, "Captain, there is something I need to tell you." I nodded. "Those women we saw were not Penobscot. When the young one spoke, I understood her easily. She is Mi'kmaq but not of our clan and it was her clan markings which confused me. In the heat of the moment that thought did not connect with me but I have been sleeping and, in my sleep, I remembered and it woke me for I knew I had to tell you. It may explain why they were with a hunting party. They are slaves."

I clutched my hammer of Thor. The Norns had spun and I now saw the thread from Bear Tooth to Laughing Deer. "Thank you, now the two of you sleep a little while longer and I will sail. The pain in my arm and foot stops me from sleeping anyway." Was the answer to my dream closer to home than the land of the Penobscot?

We sailed south and I saw a lightening of the sky to the east. Dawn was not far away and I woke the boys. Ebbe was more confident now and he busied himself with the tasks which needed to be done. He had grown on this voyage while he had faced death, he had learned much about himself. A long voyage will do that to any be they man or boy. He had begun to use his mind. "If it was not for the Penobscot, this would be a perfect land for the clan. The drekar could get almost as far as Bjorr Beck and there are islands we could fortify but…" he had grown but he was still not a man and could not follow such thoughts to their logical conclusion.

"But the Penobscot live there and the only land we saw which we could farm lay in their territory, aye, I know. As I said, the

Norns spin complicated webs. Gytha and the volvas of the clan will have to unravel them, and my brother will decide if it is worth the risk."

I watched the sky to the east become even lighter as Ebbe said, very quietly, "But you wish to return here, foster father."

"I wish to return for I have seen part of my dream but not the other."

"The other?"

"The waterfall. The Spirits planted that dream in my head and I cannot shift it." I laughed, "Pray that they do not do so to you, Ebbe, for the worm they plant grows and grows with each passing night until it consumes you."

"Know, Erik the Navigator, that if you wish to return to this land then I will come with you."

From my right I heard Stig, "And I, Captain."

"And even though it might mean my death, shaman of the bear, I would come too." Bear Tooth was truly one of the clan now.

They had been listening to what I had thought were quiet words between my foster son and me. The Norns had not finished spinning.

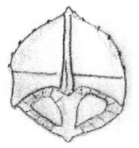

Chapter 6

We reached the open sea and there was no sign of pursuit. I sailed towards one of two small islands we had passed when heading towards the River of Peace. I needed sleep and to examine the wound from the arrow. We landed on a flat, shelving rock. The three ship's boys were quite skilful now and the snekke was hauled to safety with no damage to her keel. I used the spear as a stick to help me walk. The ankle was sore but not swollen and the first thing I did, after I had made water and emptied my bowels, was to put on the sealskin boot. It hurt but I knew that it would restrict any further swelling for we still had far to go. Although I was not hungry, the boys were and so, after I had taken off the dressing and sniffed the wound and applied more honey, they cooked some shellfish they had collected augmented with deer meat.

As we ate the food, I said, "Bear Tooth, you said that the river was a border and that none lived there. We saw women and there were many warriors."

He nodded, "They do not live there permanently but the bjorr are a source of income for them. They come and they trap them before returning west into their heartland."

"Do your people do the same?"

"Aye, Captain, but we do not do so close to the River of Peace. It is only since my grandfather's time that we hunted the land to the east of the River of Peace. There are some of our tribe who wish to be more aggressive and take over the land beyond the River of Peace, for our tribe, the Mi'kmaq, has more warriors than the Penobscot. The men of peace say that this is not the time. The chief's son, Eyes of Fire, wishes to make war on the Penobscot. It was he who counselled that we should drive you into the sea."

"Perhaps he was slain in one of the battles."

Bear Tooth shrugged, "I only saw my family fall."

Bear Tooth's observations explained much and I ate my food while thinking about the implications. If we returned to hunt the horse deer then we would have to do so when the Penobscot were not trapping the bjorr. We would have to choose our time well. I wondered if there was an alternative and I could not see it. I wrapped myself in my bear fur and slept a dreamless sleep.

I woke at noon and I was hungry by then. I ate some of the deer meat and saw that they had cooked up the rest of it. Our plan to dry it on the way home had come to nought and cooked, it would last a little longer. The clear skies and the full moon of the previous night encouraged me and, as we loaded the snekke, I said, "We will sail directly for Bear Island." I held up the map, "Once we clear this headland we can sail north and east and, by my reckoning, with this wind, it will take us between eight and ten hours. We will arrive home in the dark but I am anxious to return to the clan. What say you?"

Stig nodded, "We escaped the Penobscot in the dark and sailed down a dangerous river. You are Erik the Navigator; what cannot we do?"

Their confidence was inspiring and we set sail. *'Jötnar'* seemed anxious too and she fairly flew across the empty seas. The only two large vessels in this vast ocean were our snekke and drekar. It was as though the Allfather had sent us here to make this land Norse. It was as I sailed, with the sun to larboard, that I realised that, with the new children and animals, the clan, even if the clan wished to, we could not go to the land of the Penobscot. There were too many of us. We would have to build a knarr or a second drekar. Unlike the land of ice and fire, we had the wood to do so but it would take time. Each question seemed to pose more and I yearned to give the responsibility to another. I was not clever enough!

The Allfather had smiled upon us with his moon and, as we approached our bay, I saw our drekar illuminated in its light. Since the attack by the Skraeling, we had kept a watch at night. Each of the men and youths of the stad took it in turns to stand atop the wooden tower we had built. Bear Tooth had told us that his people did not like to attack at night but the loss of one night of sleep each month was no hardship. It was Halsten Haakensson who greeted us.

"Welcome, Erik the Navigator." He spied my wound, "I can see that you have a tale to tell here."

"Aye, Halsten, and it can wait for the morning. First, we will unload the snekke and then Ebbe and I will go to my wife and son. Bear Tooth, do not disturb Gytha and Snorri, come to my home and sleep there."

I was weary and I ached but, when we opened the door to my longhouse and Ada greeted me, then all thoughts of sleep went from me. She hugged the two of us, "You are home and I will now enjoy a good sleep." She saw Bear Tooth, "Welcome, Bear Tooth. There is a sleeping fur there." She pointed to a corner we kept for guests.

Ebbe said, "I will show you, for now we are brothers of the snekke and you can sleep in our home any time you choose."

As Ada and I lay down on the fur she said, "My son has grown and is becoming a man. You are good for him."

"It is good for us both. My foster son gives me the opportunity to practise being a father for Lars and this unborn one."

"Your son has missed you. He is now old enough to know when you are gone and he cried himself to sleep for two nights. It is good that you are back." Her eyes showed her concern when she said, "You will not be sailing soon, will you?"

"That is up to the clan but I hope not. My ankle and arm will need time to heal."

She jumped up, "I was so pleased to see you both that I did not notice. What happened?"

"An arrow but it is clean and can wait for the morning. Come and lie with me for I have missed the smell of your hair!"

Despite myself, I rose late the next day for it was comfortable to lie in my wife's arms and Lars also slept beyond his normal time. By the time I had eaten and we had left the hall, the stad was busy. I took with me the skin of the long-eared animal in my satchel. As I expected, I was greeted with a multitude of questions. My voyage had been for the clan and they wished to know all. I did not wish to repeat myself and so I said, "I will first speak with my brother for it may well be that we wish to hold a Thing and let all of the clan hear my words."

Gytha and Snorri had emerged from their home and she gave her seal of approval, "The Navigator is right. This is for the clan, and those on the farms which lie some way away will need to come here too!"

Young boys were dispatched to fetch them and I went to my brother's hall. He and his wife were within. He was pleased to see me, "You have returned! All is well?"

I nodded and Freja said, smiling, although the smile was not in her eyes, "I will leave you alone."

I told Arne what I had discovered and that Gytha had asked for a Thing. "That is good but your news is mixed."

"There is more that I learned and it was about our clan and not this new world."

"More?" I told him what Stig had said about some of the men wishing to return to Larswick. He nodded, "I have heard the whisperings too, as has my wife. It annoys me for a man should speak his mind and not hide behind his hand. This news may decide more of the clan to leave." I said nothing and he smiled, "But you would not leave?"

I shook my head and told him of the maid. He touched his hammer of Thor, "This is truly *wyrd*. When you had the dream, I took it to be a fancy and nothing more but this... Did you see the waterfall?"

I shook my head, "And that is why I cannot leave for it might anger the Norns and we would not be able to return across the ocean. My feet are on a path which is not of my making."

He nodded, "We are ever their playthings. Well, let us go and meet the clan and then we will have your arm seen to. We would not have the Navigator lose an arm!"

I looked at the jug of ale, "But first I will have a beaker of Freja's ale. We have drunk boiled water for three days!"

He laughed as he poured the foaming ale, "Then you have truly suffered."

By the time we had finished the ale and left the hall, the meeting place was filled with families. I saw Fótr and Reginleif with their new babe, I knew neither its sex nor its name. While

Arne went to the centre, I joined my little brother, "You have a babe!"

"Aye, brother, and we have named him after you. He will be Erik Fótrsson."

"I am honoured and are you well, Reginleif?" I was her foster father too.

She looked radiant, "I am and I pray that the Allfather will smile upon my son as he smiles upon you."

I saw that Bear Tooth had brought out seats for Gytha and Snorri. It was only then that I saw the grey hairs on them both and that Gytha looked thin. I had grown used to Snorri's lameness but Gytha had always looked a picture of health. Then I remembered I had only seen her in the dim light of the hall. Here it was daylight, and every line, hollow and grey hair could be seen. Gytha was the only woman allowed in the inner circle. The rest were men, warriors. Every Viking had their own version of the Thing but the rules were the same for us all. When you were in the centre then you could speak until you signified you had finished and stepped back. Until then no one could speak. It allowed for order and prevented violence.

Arne shouted, "Silence so that we may hold a Thing. My brother Erik the Navigator has returned and he will tell all what he has found. When he is done then I would urge all who have words to say to speak them and not to whisper them in secret." His eyes flashed and glared at the ones he suspected of disloyalty. Most could not meet his gaze.

I stepped forward. "What I say is the truth and I will not add my opinion. It is for the clan to make a decision based upon my words." I saw Gytha smile and nod. She was the only one whose approval I sought. "We found the river which Bear Tooth called the River of Peace. The drekar can sail up it for many days. We found the horse deer as well as a smaller, white-tailed deer. They are plentiful. We trapped these," I took out the skin I had brought with me. "They, too, are plentiful and are easy to trap and skin. They make good eating. We found the bjorr too and they fill the smaller rivers. What we did not find was land for cultivation. However, we found Skraelings, the Penobscot. They are as belligerent as the Mi'kmaq. If we made a home on the River of Peace then we would have to fight." I saw the looks of disappointment on the faces of many of the men. "There is something else. I am the Navigator and I sail the drekar. I have to tell you the clan has now grown in numbers because this is a land of bounty. We have lost but one family since we came here and there are many more babies. Our children are growing. If we were to move either to the River of Peace or, as I have heard whispered, back to Larswick, then we would need another vessel. We have the timber but that would take time. That is all I have to say." I stepped back to stand beside Fótr, Arne and Siggi.

I saw warriors just looking at each other and none would speak. Gytha broke the silence, "I am a woman and I have no right to speak at a Thing but I ask the clan for their indulgence." The men all nodded. "I am the oldest woman in the clan and I will never return to Larswick nor leave this island for I am ill and there is a worm which eats me from within!" I was shocked and I saw that most of the men were too. Tostig dropped to one knee next to his mother and took her hand. She smiled at him. Ada and the other women were not surprised and I knew then that the women were as close as any shield wall of warriors. "I tell you this, not to evoke sympathy, that is not my way, but so that you know the words I will say are what I truly feel and not because Erik and Arne are my nephews. I have heard the words which are spoken in secret. Even now there are men who stand on their lips so that they do not speak what they truly feel, and that is a shame. I know there is no treasure in this new world. That is because we have not yet found it. There are no markets and towns and there is no one to raid. What we do have is control over our lives for there is no king to command us. We are more powerful than any Skraeling and we could not say that when we lived in Orkneyjar. That is all I have to say but my grave will be in this land and I will not see another summer so no matter what this Thing decides it will not affect me."

She had read my thoughts for I had had that in my head when I had sailed down the River of Peace.

Harold of Dyroy stepped forward and said, "I am a loyal member of this clan and will abide by whatever is said here but I am a weaponsmith and I work in iron. There is none here and I cannot do that which the Allfather gave me the skills to do. I would return to a land where there is iron but if the clan wishes to stay here then so be it but, unlike some, I will not hide behind the words of others. That is all I have to say." He stepped back.

Eidel Eidelsson was the one with courage and he spoke as I knew he would. "I am one, Gytha, jarl, who has kept silent. I lost my father and that has weighed heavily upon me. I have a son, Stig, and I think about his future. I would return to Larswick." There were murmurings but Arne held up his hand. There were rules and no other could speak until Eidel relinquished the centre. "But Erik is my friend and he speaks not only the truth but he is wise. We could not take this clan back to Larswick with just *'Njörðr'*. Even with the snekke, we could not." He smiled, "And I am guessing, from what my son has told me, that Erik the Navigator and his snekke will stay in this new world come what may. I suggest that we do as Erik suggests and build a second drekar. I know that it will take time to build one for we have no shipyard here. That will give us at least a year, maybe longer, before we have to make a decision about the future of the clan. Those who wished to stay could and those who wished to return would have the means. That is all I have to say."

He stepped back. Sven, who had been one of my companions when we had found this land, stepped into the circle. "Let us build this drekar but let us not forget that we are warriors. The Skraelings wish to fight us so I say let us take war to them. Their treasure is the horse deer. I say that we sail up this River of Peace as warriors and hunters. We take as many of the horse deer and bjorr as we can. If this tribe, the Penobscot, wish to fight us, I am not afraid, are you?" He waved a hand around the circle of men. That is all I have to say."

Halsten Haakensson stepped forward, "We came here because we were told it was better than the land of ice and fire. Erik was right, it is better than that icy rock but is it better than Larswick? I left Larswick because I did not want to be ruled by a King. I have had many nights to think about this. We could have gone to the Land of the Wolf for they have no king and Sámr, the Dragonheart's heir, is a good man. He came to our aid when we fled Larswick. That is all I have to say." He stepped back.

Halsten was an honest man and he had spoken in a reasonable tone; I saw nods and murmurs of agreement.

Kalman Martinsson stepped into the circle, "What of Bear Tooth's people? I know that he is of this clan now but his people have horse deer and they have killed our people. It would be a shorter journey would it not? That is all I have to say."

Snorri used his stick to push himself to his feet. He was the clan elder now and none had more respect than he. He smiled and tapped his leg with his stick, "I have lost to the Skraeling and yet I know that the Mi'kmaq are not a threat to us now. If they were then they would have come again after we defeated them on Horse Deer Island. Sven is right and a raid on the land of the Penobscot will blood young warriors who have yet to have their swords taste blood. When the horse deer rut at Gormánuður would be a good time. That will give the clan the time to begin work on the drekar and that, too, is good for it will unite the clan. The Mi'kmaq will have returned to their winter camps and we will be safe on the island. The ship could be finished over winter and we could hold another Thing in Spring. That is all I have to say."

No one else spoke and Arne stepped back into the circle. "We have had many ideas put forward but the last one, spoken by Snorri Long Fingers, has not been questioned. Do we agree with Snorri or is there more to be said?"

I took out my sword and held it in the air, signifying my approval. Every warrior followed suit and there were no dissenters.

Arne nodded, "Then it is decided. Erik, you are the Navigator, we will need your advice when we begin to build this drekar."

I nodded, "Then tomorrow we will seek the tallest tree on this island. If there are none suitable to be found then we must sail to the mainland. That will mean war."

Arne nodded, "And the clan knows that. This is good but I urge any man who harbours thoughts to spill them for if they are kept within a man's head, they will poison him."

Thus warned, the clan dispersed. Arne, Fótr and I went directly to Gytha. She smiled, "Your father would be proud of you! You have kept the clan together."

Arne said, "Why did you not tell us of this worm?" He seemed almost angry.

"I have told you now and what difference would it have made? Are you a healer?" Arne shook his head, "But I am and I need to hear Erik the Navigator for he still has much to tell me!"

She leaned on her younger son, Tostig, as we walked to her hall. Arne and Fótr stayed to speak with Sven and Siggi. That there was bad blood was now obvious. Despite the words spoken by Eidel and Kalman, the two warriors and, no doubt, others were clearly unhappy. Once in the hall, Gytha said, "Now leave us, Tostig. Go and speak with your cousins. They will need your support. There were others who did not have the courage of Kalman and Eidel and they are the ones to be feared." He left us and Gytha said, "Now, while I tend to this wound, tell me all and leave nothing out! I know much for I read your dreams but you did not sleep on the river when you came home."

"You can read my mind from across the sea?"

"That is my gift but the Allfather has given me the worm as a curse. I can see into your mind and heart but the cost is a shortened life." She smiled, "It is worth it!"

I told her everything. Even she was surprised that the maid had had the same dream. When I had finished and she had bound my arm, she nodded, "I can see that the Norns have chosen you. They sent that piece of driftwood to you for a reason and it is they who have spun this web which is so vast that I cannot see how it would be unpicked. You and this maid are meant to be with each other and you are right to pursue the dream but you know that there may come a time when you have to choose between the maid and the clan; a new life and a life without Ada, Lars and your unborn daughter."

"Daughter?"

She smiled, "As I said, it is a gift and I use it wisely."

I looked at Snorri, "Uncle, what are your thoughts?"

"Like my wife, I will never leave this island and I am content. I have buried too many friends not to mention my brother whom I loved! Gytha has seen a little into the future. The volva, Ylva, still lives and Sámr, Dragonheart's heir, who saved us once might offer a home to our people. Gytha has dreamed and Tostig will not end his days here in this new world. That is good for not all are meant to live here but one thing I know, you are!"

I looked at him as he spoke for he had not mentioned his eldest, Siggi. Did that mean Siggi would stay with me in this new world? Would the brothers of the blade be the ones who remained?

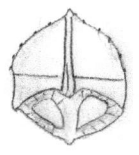

Chapter 7

Finding a tree big enough to make the keel of a ship sounds like a simple task but it is more complicated than that. It has to be straight and strong enough to take the weight of half a clan! It took three days to search our island until we found such a tree. I did not know what was the wood but those who farmed nearby said that the wood was a hardwood and that was what we needed. There were others more skilled with axes than I and I let them hack down the mighty timber. I identified another six trees that would be hewn to make the strakes. It would take them days to trim all of the branches from them and while they did that, I returned to the bay to begin the next part; we had to build a shipyard! My words at the Thing had stirred the clan and we had every man not involved in trimming the trees we had felled to manhandle stones to make supports for the ribs of the ship and the keel. It took many days of hard work to do so but we had freshly brewed ale to help us. That done, we needed every man in the clan to fetch the timbers. There would be much work in shaping the timbers to fit. We had brought the tools we needed from Larswick: breast auger, side axe, moulding irons, hafted wedge, tongs, hammer and bits. Now we would get to use them. We also had improvised tools made from whale and horse deer bone. Every man helped to carry the timber because that would bond us to the vessel when it was made. Carrying it also showed me what the size of the unborn drekar would be. I had chosen the largest piece of timber we had and that gave us a vessel that would be sixteen paces long. It would be slightly bigger than **'Njörðr'**.

When all the wood was gathered, most of the men returned to their farms leaving just eight of us who would work on the drekar. Not all of us would work all the time but I would be there for every part of the process. Padraig and Aed would also

The Savage Wilderness

contribute much of their time too. They were fishermen and knew ships. It would be slow going for it would take us a month to fashion the keel and ribs to size and to prepare to fit them. We did not have the luxury of metal nails and so would have to make wooden ones. It was time-consuming. The bulk of the work would have to wait until we had hunted the horse deer for we would need both pine tar and the hooves of the horse deer to make the glue. We also needed, instead of sheep's' wool, the fur of animals. Snorri had said that he would carve the prow for it was something he could contribute. I had told no one except Arne and Snorri but I planned in naming this drekar, Gytha, in honour of the clan's matriarch. Having Snorri carve it would imbue the prow with more magic than if another did so.

It took a long month and more to finish the ribs and the keel and have them ready to be assembled. The assembly would have to wait until the trenails and glue were ready. I went with Arne, Fótr, Siggi, Sven and Padraig to cut the pine we would need for the mast and the yard and crosspiece. We would have to go to the mainland for that was where the pine was to be found. My wounded arm and ankle had healed and I was able to move freely and help with the hewing of the timber. We could not take more, for men were needed to tend their land while others were working on the nails for the ship. We could not take the drekar and so we took the next best thing: the snekke and the best warriors we had. There were still Mi'kmaq close to the coast and while they had not bothered us for a while, an incursion into their land might make them keen to fight us. For that reason, we went mailed, with shields and spears.

We had seen the pines when I had first explored the coast and I knew there was a good stand less than half a mile from the coast, up an animal trail which climbed up the cliff. It was not close to any of the summer Mi'kmaq villages and gave us the best opportunity to get ashore, fell the trees and return before they discovered us. I took Ebbe with us and he would wait, off the beach, in case the Skraeling came. We left before dawn and I took the steering board. We had experienced eyes looking for signs of danger but we saw none. In addition to our weapons, we also had wood axes. All we needed was to find two pine trees of suitable height, hew them and then tow them back to Bear Island. It sounded easy enough but the Norns were spinning.

Arne and Siggi led us up the path. I confess that I found it hard to wear the mail byrnie. I had rarely worn it but, if we were attacked, then until Ebbe and Fótr had been trained as navigators then I was the most valuable thing the clan owned for I was the only one who could sail them back to Larswick! When we reached the top, I looked down. The cliff was not high and we could lower the two trees down the side when we found them. I could not help smiling as I thought back all those years to when I had gone with my father, uncle and brother to the land of the Picts to do this self-same thing. Then we had had to fear wild Picts and now it was savage Skraelings.

Arne and Siggi led us through the woods seeking a tall straight pair of pines we could fell. Although I was at the back, I was still able to examine the trail and I saw evidence of Skraeling; the signs were not recent but I still felt uneasy. We had chosen a stand of pines which were not near one of their beach camps but they had been here and that made me loosen my sword in my scabbard. Bear Tooth's tribe might have primitive weapons but they could still hurt us and the best of our warriors had put their necks out. When Arne stopped, just five hundred paces from the clifftop, I knew that he had found a good tree. The others parted to let me forward.

My elder brother patted the tree and said, "Well?"

I looked up and saw that it was longer than we needed and that was no bad thing. More importantly, it was of the correct girth. "This is a good one." I turned and saw its twin just three trees away. "And that one for the yard."

While the other four would hew the trees, Fótr and I would stand a watch. We made certain we knew which way that the trees would fall and then moved in the opposite direction. I hung my helmet from my sword scabbard so that I could hear better and peered into the forest. Arne and Siggi were chopping the first tree while Padraig and Sven hewed the other. The sound of their blades striking the trees was regular and in the silence between each stroke, we listened for sounds ahead. The four men would work competitively; that was our way. When we heard Arne shout, we knew which pair had won, Siggi and Arne. The pine crashed through the forest. If there were any Skraeling close by then they would hear it. Then Arne and Siggi would be attaching the vines we had gathered to the trees to allow us to pull them back, and then trimming all the branches which might hinder our progress. Fótr and I waited until we heard Padraig shout and then we knew that the other was down. The second tree crashed and fell. Our duty was almost done.

As we waited for the vines to be attached and the branches trimmed, Fótr said, "I think I would like to return to Larswick, brother."

I nodded for I was not surprised. "Reginleif has bad memories."

"Aye, and her dreams are haunted; she often wakes with the terrors of the night and they are not easily dismissed."

Arne shouted, "Ready, Erik."

As we turned to go, I said, "Then you will need to become as skilled a navigator as I. Move your family close to the shipyard and help me make this drekar. If your hands and blood are in the hull then you will hear the ship when she sails."

"You will stay?"

"Until I have seen the waterfall then, aye."

When we reached the trees, I saw that they had brought down lesser trees in their path. Had we so wished we could have taken five trees back to Bear Island. Arne was grinning, "You have had an easy time, my little brothers, now you will sweat!"

The vines we used were tougher than I had first thought. They were not suitable to be used as ropes on a drekar but they were strong enough to haul trees and so plentiful that we each had our own vine, and when Arne said, "Pull!" we all moved together. We could have moved it quicker if we had chanted but we did not wish to let the Skraeling know where we were. The time we had spent on the drekar helped us and we moved with the same rhythm and we made good time. We reached the cliff and the other four laid down their axes. We began to lower the tree.

Ebbe waved from the beach and I could see the relief on his face. We lowered the tree down the slope away from the snekke. I cupped my hands, "Tie the tree to the thwarts!" He waved his hand in acknowledgement. We returned for the second. Arne said, "We might as well come back when we have taken this one and fetch some of the other trees which the mast tree felled. They are the Allfather's bounty."

I was not certain that this was a wise decision but we appeared to be alone and I agreed with Arne, the fallen trees were an unexpected bounty, for pine decking was the best.

The second tree was easier to move as the first had cleared a path. I saw that Ebbe had done as I suggested. This time I said, "Use the vines to bind the two trees together." He waved and we returned to the fallen trees. They were all much smaller than the ones we had taken but some had a wider girth and would yield more planks. We attached the vines and this time we lifted. It made progress much quicker although my back and arms burned. It encouraged us to return for a fourth tree. We were halfway back when the Skraeling found us.

Bear Tooth's people were brave, of that there was no doubt, but they fought as individuals and not as we did, together. Although we had no shields, when Arne shouted, "Wall!" we acted as though we did. I turned and put my helmet on my head as I drew my sword and then my dagger. Fótr was between Arne and me for he was the least experienced of us. The warriors who ran at us had stone spears and clubs. They hurled the spears at us as they came. One hit my mail byrnie. It hurt but did not penetrate. I saw the look of horror on the warrior's face when he saw that I had not been hurt. He had a stone club and a bone knife and he ran at me. I swung my sword in an arc, aware that to my left the others were also sweeping their weapons at the individuals who ran at us. Their stone weapons could break limbs but they could not penetrate mail. We had to face them and discourage them. If we turned our backs then we were at risk. My sword tore through the bare flesh of the Skraeling. It ripped through to his guts which poured from him. I doubted that any of them had ever seen such a wound for while a stone knife could cut, it could not cut deeply.

Fótr showed his inexperience by using the tip of his sword. It caught on the ribs of the man who attacked him but did not kill. As the warrior raised his stone club to smash Fótr's head, I flicked up my dagger and ripped across his throat. A spear came at my side and hurt me. I swept my sword in an arc and hit not only the warrior whose spear had hit me but the one behind who sought to stab me in the back. Neither was dead and so I turned and ended both of their lives with my dagger.

Arne shouted, "Let us move back towards the snekke but face them as we do so! We have broken their first attack."

There were more Skraeling hurtling through the trees to get at us but we stepped backwards away from them. One, who had a painted face, used the bodies of the dead to leap into the air. Arne was the strongest warrior we had and he used his two hands to sweep his sword and dagger across the warrior's body. He hacked through to the spine and the body was almost cut in two halves. It had a sobering effect on the others for the man must have been a chief. Bear Tooth had told us that within his clan they had a number of chiefs. We used the hiatus to move back more quickly. I could hear the sea behind me and then I heard a cry from the Skraeling. Another chief must have arrived.

Arne said, "Quickly, we run back to the snekke!" Turning, we hurtled towards the cliff path. As I had known he would be, Arne was at the rear. He was the jarl. Siggi was with him. I was the captain and I had to be first to the snekke. I shouted as I approached the edge of the slope, "Ebbe, get aboard and untie the snekke!"

Although I ran down the trail, I did so carefully for I did not want to risk falling. I saw that Ebbe had done well and the three tree trunks were tied together like a raft. When I reached the beach, I took off my helmet and sheathed my sword. I did not turn for I had to have the snekke ready for sea. I said, for I knew he would be behind me, "Fótr, you and Ebbe raise the sail." I knew that it would take the wind time to push us away from the shore as we had three logs as a deadweight behind us. Once we got going then we would move quickly but it would take time to gather speed. I reached the snekke and threw my helmet to the bottom of the boat. Turning, I saw that the other four had turned to face the next onslaught. They were just twenty paces from the snekke but the Skraeling had closed with them. There were fifteen Skraeling who were closing with them but many more were standing on the clifftop already descending. It was a slaughter for none of the weapons the Skraeling had could kill our men but, as Ebbe and Fótr lifted the sail and the snekke tried to move away from the beach, I saw that Padraig had been hit in the arm with a stone club. It hung down. I saw that Ebbe's bow and arrows were at the bottom of the boat. I picked it up and nocked an arrow. I was less than thirty paces from the Skraeling who raised his club to finish off Padraig and my arrow knocked him from his feet as it slammed into his chest.

I shouted, "Back! Use the logs as a raft!" Already the snekke was drifting away from the beach and with mail byrnies, they would find it hard to board. The raft would be easier. When I saw them help Padraig back, I turned the steering board. Ebbe and Fótr had the sail fully in place and Ebbe grabbed the bow I had dropped and sent two more arrows at the Skraeling while Arne and the others waded through the surf to the raft of timber. It was waist-deep where they tried to board. I adjusted the steering board to keep us close to the beach while they struggled aboard. Spears and arrows hit the mail of our warriors and the raft but Ebbe and his bow deterred the Mi'kmaq from closing with us.

Fótr shouted, "They are aboard!" and I pushed the steering board over so that the wind caught us and the snekke headed east. Some of the Skraeling had jumped into the sea to try to catch us. The ones who reached the raft were stabbed by Arne and Siggi while Sven tended to Padraig's arm.

I touched my bear tooth necklace. We had been lucky. Perhaps Fótr was right and this wilderness was too savage for us to tame. The Skraeling seemed to be fearless and were as plentiful as the sand on the beach. Were we doomed?

It took longer to tow the logs across to Bear Island than I had expected and I was worried about Padraig's arm. It was obviously broken. Our slow approach meant that there were many hands ready to help us land the timber; Helga took her husband to her mother, Gytha, to be tended to. Arne was in an ebullient mood as I knew he would be for he enjoyed combat and liked being a warrior. At times I feared that he might be a berserker.

"These Skraeling are nothing! We need not have run for we could have slaughtered them all."

Siggi grinned and nodded, "Aye, cousin, for they have no weapon which can compare with our swords!"

"And yet," I counselled, "Padraig has a broken arm and if they had surrounded us then their stone axes and clubs could have broken our bones."

"Brother, you are a navigator and not a warrior yet you killed many of them. If we took all of the clan's warriors then we could destroy the whole tribe!"

"Have you not spoken to Bear Tooth? He has told us that his tribe is allied to many others; would they countenance such a slaughter? I think not. They would gather together and come in such numbers as to overwhelm even a shield wall"

Arne shrugged, "We have your wood, now you need to let it season and I need to prepare the warriors for the raid on the Penobscot. You are right, their weapons can break limbs. We will need better padding beneath our byrnies."

Sven and Fótr remained with me and Fótr said, "I agree with you, brother, we need to speak with the Skraeling. Perhaps we could send Bear Tooth to begin talks."

Sven shook his head, "Until we went for the wood that might have been possible but not now. The fight on the Island of the Horse Deer was an accident. We both visited the same place but today was different. We took from their land and we slaughtered their warriors, and besides, Bear Tooth has been here too long. They would be suspicious and might harm him."

I believed that Sven was right and Bear Tooth was no longer seen as a Skraeling. He spoke our language and worked as hard as any. However, I also wondered if there was a way to begin peace talks with our neighbours. "My brother has set the course for the clan, Fótr, and we must follow it. There are already those who do not wish to follow him. We must support him or the clan might fall apart." Gytha's ailment and Snorri's sat heavily on my mind. They were, quite literally, the heart of the clan and if they were not around then Arne would have no-one to rein him in. I feared for the future.

Arne was right, the wood needed to be seasoned. First, we removed the bark from the logs and put them where they could dry. I had the timber to grade and to sort. I looked for natural curves which might help the ribs and I examined the trunks to see how they might be split. There was a great temptation to begin straight away but this drekar might have to sail across the ocean; it was not a forgiving sea. The keel and the ribs were not attached; they were just cut to size. The men who would help me began to use the smaller pieces of wood to make pegs and trenails. We had some metal nails left from the land of ice and fire but they were precious and would be used to secure the most vital parts of the hull.

As the sun began to set, I went to visit with Gytha before returning to my home. "How is Padraig?"

"It was a clean break and he is lucky. I heard what you said to Arne and you are right, the Skraeling are too numerous for us to defeat, despite what your brother says. Your uncle and I could live here on Bear Island quite happily for it has all we need but I can see why others are looking at the land to the west with greedy eyes."

I took her hands in mine, "You may be wrong about your illness!"

She shook her head, "I am a healer and a volva. I know that I am doomed and I have seen my end but know this, Erik, when I go to the spirit world, I will still watch over you. You have heard my voice and I shall use that when I am no longer here."

"But it is not right! Why should the worm choose you?"

"Did you not heed my words? I was given greater powers for the time which is left to me. The worm is the price I pay. I have been training Ada to take over when I am gone and Helga also has powers that I will develop. Both will be powerful volvas. They will not have my power but the price they would have to pay for such powers is too high. I have yet to approach her but Siggi's wife, Gefn, also has some skill. If I could have three to follow me then I would die a happy woman, for three is a magic number." She lifted my head, "Do not be sad, Erik. Before I leave this life, I will put as much magic into the drekar you are building as I can and Bear Tooth can help you to build. There is a bond between the two of you for you saved his life and one day he may save yours."

I went to my hall a sadder man. Ada sensed my unhappiness and said, "We will both have much to occupy us over the next months and that is good but you must spend as much time with Lars as you can. He missed you when you were away and you will be voyaging again after the harvest is in."

"You are right and now that he can walk and I am able to understand some of his words it will be easier. Besides, Bear Tooth can watch him. Perhaps the Skraeling will understand more of his words than I." She busied herself with the food. Like all Viking women, she was a good cook and knew the kind of food a hungry warrior enjoyed. Whatever the shortcomings of Bear Island, we had better and more plentiful food than when we had been in Larswick. The difference was in the kind of food. "And you are happy to be trained as a volva, along with Helga and Gefn?"

"I am honoured although I know that it is a great responsibility. I know I can never be as great as Gytha but if I can serve the clan then I am happy. You have given me a new purpose. Since Ebbe's father and Dreng died, I was lost and knew not where to go. You have given me a better life than the one I had for you are held in high esteem by the clan and I am your woman. I thank you for that."

Ada was too good for me; I could see that. Any other woman would have demanded I marry her and forget the maid and the waterfall but Ada truly understood my heart and the wandering spirit which lay hidden in my body.

The next day I took Lars with me when I went to the shipyard to resume work on the trenails, cleats and pegs. I found a job he could do. He filled hessian sacks with sand and then placed the pegs, cleats and trenails within. He shook the bag of sand until the wood was much smoother. It was a necessary job but one which few would take on. To Lars, it was a game and with Bear Tooth to watch him he could ensure that he came to no harm in a work area filled with sharp-edged weapons. Each day I would turn the timbers so that the seasoning was even and I resisted the temptation to begin work too early. We knew that the winters here were benign, at least compared with Orkneyjar, and we could continue to build the drekar in the short days of winter. I estimated that it would take at least a year to build her.

I also had to give some time to *'Njörðr'*. She had not been to sea since the whale hunt and we had treated her harshly on that hunt. I went over every part of her, including the masthead and I checked every rope, sheer and stay not to mention, joint, strake, gunwale, block and withy. By the time we reached the beginning of Heyannir, we had enough pegs, cleats and trenails and the ribs and keel were ready for us to begin work on them. This was the most crucial part of the building, for while the rest of the ship could be repaired if damage occurred, the keel and ribs had to be perfect and the four of us who worked on her, Sven, Padraig, Harald and Fótr, worked slowly with much consultation between tasks. Lars and Bear Tooth were still helping and Ebbe wished to but he had to help tend our fields and animals. We shaped, first the keel, and then the ribs. Once they were all attached, we would be able to invert her and then, after the winter solstice, we could begin to fir her strakes. That was in the future.

Bear Tooth had shown great skill in carving. Despite Arne's misgivings, I trusted him and I had given him a seax which had lain hidden in the bottom of my chest. He was so skilled that I gave him the task of carving the weather vane which could go on the top of the mast. It was a vital piece of equipment. I showed him the one on the snekke and that on *'Njörðr'* and he had the framework in his head. He knew what we would name the ship and so he incorporated a carving of Gytha. We had learned to use pine to stick sand to a piece of wood and Lars happily used the tool to rub the wood smooth for Bear Tooth. Of course, Ada was less than happy at the mess it made of Lars' clothes and hands.

So it was that late summer passed peacefully and smoothly with each member of the clan engaged in work for the whole clan. None was idle. Even though Ada grew with our new child, her work continued as well as her training with Gytha. Each night we would be so exhausted that we would fall into each other's arms, have one kiss and then fall asleep. Life was good.

We worked hard on the drekar and it was infuriatingly slow work. Shaping wood to exact specifications was not quick work and often, by the end of the day, we appeared to have little to show for all the work we had done. Amazingly, what made us all feel good was the work done by Bear Tooth and Lars. Bear Tooth carved beautifully and Lars enjoyed the simple task of rubbing the sand-covered wood against the weather vane. Lars was growing into a boy before my very eyes. Bear Tooth had carved a bear which stood against the triangular section of wood which would catch the wind. I was not surprised that he had done such a good job for he was a follower of the bear but I was surprised at the incredible detail and the way he made the bear so lifelike. The detail was actually unnecessary as it would not be seen from the deck but he had done a good job and it made all of the boat builders happy. I realised that Bear Tooth no longer belonged to Gytha and Snorri. He was a member of our family. We had put Snorri and Bear Tooth together because of their mutual lameness but one hardly noticed that now in either of them. Neither could run but they did not need to. When we had had to flee the Penobscot, I had, deliberately, moved slower than the Skraeling and Bear Tooth had been in no danger. I now saw him as a protector for Lars. I would be away soon and Ada would be ready to give birth. Bear Tooth could help.

The harvest came and it was a good one. We would not really need the meat of the horse deer but we would need the hooves and we would need the hide. In addition, the fur from the bjorr was valuable and we planned on trapping. As much as Arne wished to hunt the whale again, he knew that would have to wait until after the winter. The second drekar would not even have been placed in the water by then. The clan had said they wished a second drekar and they wished another Thing. Everyone would abide by those decisions for to do other was to make a mockery of giving every man in the clan a say. The fact that their women had also contributed meant that the will of the Thing was the will of the clan!

By the time the harvest had all been stored and salt collected for the meat we would hunt, we had the keel and the ribs attached. We had even begun to split the pine for the decks. The mast and the yard had been stripped of all bark, shaped and cut. A couple more months of seasoning would only improve them. However, it was time to leave the skeleton of the new drekar for Arne wished to hunt. *'Njörðr'* was ready for sea and so Arne summoned all of the outlying farmers to come to our stad. It would be easier to defend. We were ready to set sail but I feared for Gytha. In the last months, she had shrunk in a quite frightening way. I was reluctant to leave for I would not go if I thought she would go to the Otherworld. I went to see her and told her my fears.

She smiled, "You are the son I never bore and I feel closer to you than any other than Snorri. I will not die while you are away, for I have dreamed and I see you returning from this raid."

"It is successful then?"

She shook her head, "Do not put words in the mouth of a volva for it is dangerous. I said that I saw you return and the drekar too. You are concerned you will be able to say goodbye and I am here to tell you that you shall. I may be a shell of the woman you remember but my mind will work and I shall breathe. We can say all that we need to say then. Now Bear Tooth will watch your son and Snorri and I will ensure that the clan is well. You do what you do best and sail the drekar. Arne thinks he leads the clan but it is not true. Without you, your brother is nothing."

I left but I did not believe the last statement she had made. My brother was a rock and he kept the clan together. I sailed the drekar and I had found this new land but if we faced enemies then it would be Arne and Siggi who would be the strength of the clan. I had told the clan of Bear Tooth's words about the trapping camp and we had decided that just before winter was the time that they would be in their heartland. Bear Tooth had been closely questioned by Arne and he had revealed more about the Penobscot tribe and where they lived. Some lived within a day's march of the River of Peace and it was a warning to us. We would have to be armed and prepared to fight.

We would be taking a full crew and some of the ship's boys, like Fámr Haraldsson, now took an oar and had a shield. Ebbe would be the senior ship's boy. Along with Stig, they knew the river and would be able to help the six other boys who came with us. The raid would allow them to become familiar with the drekar and to help us should it come to a fight. They could all use a sling and I knew that the Penobscot would outnumber us if they chose to resist our raid. I hoped that they, like the Mi'kmaq, would be inland once more in their winter quarters. I did not wish a full-blown war.

Ada was so large with our child that I felt sure that she would have given birth before we had reached the mainland but I dared not delay. This was the time of the rut and the perfect time to hunt the horse deer.

Fótr was being trained to be a navigator and I put him in charge of the compass, hourglass and map. I took out my map and handed it to him. "When you have the chance then copy this and add your own details to it. A good navigator uses his own maps. If you return to Larswick then you will be the only one, except for Sven, who can sail the drekar for I will not be returning."

He knew this but he still shook his head, "And this is the fault of the maid and the waterfall?"

I nodded and I laughed, "And the Norns!" It was a mistake to utter such thoughts for they were listening and they were spinning.

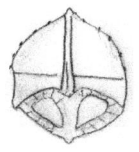

Chapter 8

I was as relaxed at the steering board as I had ever been when sailing but poor Fótr was a mass of nerves. It was easy for me as we just had to sail to the coast and then follow it down the River of Peace. The last time I had completed the voyage I had had boys as a crew. Now I had the whole of the clan and we were mailed and armed. Arne was right, the Penobscot could not hurt us this time, but if they chose to bring every Skraeling to fight us then we might be in trouble but, as we sailed along the coast, I felt as comfortable and easy as a man could. Fótr now knew that he would have to be a navigator and commanding the mighty drekar was a daunting prospect

That first day of sailing was easy but I knew that the ones which followed would be harder. It was one thing to tack a handy snekke up the river but we would have to use oars for much of the journey. The Allfather thought to send us a good wind for the first part of the voyage and we made such good progress that I wanted to keep sailing, however, it was getting on to dark and we needed to stop. The drekar was too valuable to risk sailing at night time. When we had sailed the snekke, we had avoided any islands and beaches on the east bank. We did not need to do so with the drekar and I found a large island where the river Bear Tooth had called Black Biting Insect River joined the River of Peace. The name of that river was enough of a deterrent that we would not sail it. Despite Gytha's potions, lotions and salves, the insects in this new world were still as much of an enemy as any Skraeling!

We used a couple of trees to moor the drekar and we waded through knee-deep water to reach the land. We were numerous enough not to fear Skraeling and we lit a fire and put on food to cook. We had two barrels of freshly brewed beer and it washed down the food and the bread we had brought. When the beer was

The Savage Wilderness

finished then we would use them for the meat we would hunt. Barrels were valuable!

Arne had more need of my advice and as we ate, he and Siggi spoke to me of what we would find. "We have seen no Skraeling fires, little brother, will it be like this all the way north?"

"We saw none but, of course, my snekke will have alerted them that there are strangers in their land. Bear Tooth told us that the Penobscot are not as numerous as the Mi'kmaq, but they are protective of their land. We may not have as far to go, brother, for there is a huge stretch of water just a day or so north of here. I did not explore it but it is so large that there must be horse deer close by."

"And bjorr?"

I shook my head, "I did not look for them."

Siggi threw the horse deer bone into the river, "Then I say we stick to the original plan. From the map you showed me, we can find white-tailed deer, horse deer and bjorr all within a short walk from the river. We are ready to fight if we have to, but better to have an easy hunt and return to finish the other drekar." He lowered his voice. "Those who wish to leave need the ability to sail home. The Thing did not silence all their fears and some talk of forcing the clan to go home."

Arne's eyes flashed as he scanned the other fires around which men were seated. Before he could become angry and say something or do something we would all regret, I said, "Brother, even if they thought that, they could not for I am the only navigator and I would not agree. Even the most critical warrior knows that a drekar needs a navigator."

Arne jabbed a finger at Fótr, "And our little brother, here, is becoming a navigator and he wishes to sail home!"

Some of the warriors around the other fires looked over at the raised voice. Siggi said, "Peace, Arne! Peace!"

I saw Fótr's face colour in the firelight, "Do you think so little of me, brother, that I would go behind your back and sail with the others? I have made no secret of the fact that I wish to return to Larswick but I will only do so when we have built *'Gytha'* and held another Thing. If that is your worry then put it from your mind but I, for one, am disappointed in the lack of trust. I will sleep aboard the drekar tonight!"

The Savage Wilderness

Siggi shook his head and gave a sad laugh, "Arne, you are one of the closest friends I have. Along with Erik here, the three of us are blood brothers but lately you seem to open your mouth and let words pour forth without giving them thought."

Arne did not raise his head but stared into the fire, "When we left the land of ice and fire, all the clan wished to come to this new world and when we reached it, I thought it was all that Erik had promised and more. What has changed? Am I a bad jarl?"

I shook my head, "It is the others who have changed. What they thought they wanted they have discovered they did not. The threat of the King of Norway has faded and men think back to the first days at Larswick before we fought the Dane and the Norse. They think of the weapons and the treasure we took from the dead, and not the cost to get it. I do not think that the return of one drekar of Vikings to Larswick will hurt those of us who choose to stay in this new world. When they reach our old home, they will tell others of what we have found and there will be other Vikings who wish to come. We are the start of a colony and, who knows, when your son is jarl, we may have a land here which is ruled by us, think on that!"

Arne put his arm around me and said, "We three are the brothers of the blade and it is good that we are together. I will go and speak with Fótr for you are both right. I will not let him go to sleep angry."

He left us. Siggi put another piece of kindling on the fire. "It is Freja makes him the way he is. She is not like Ada or Gefn. She is the wife of the jarl and she thinks they should have more respect for she wishes them to bow and curtsy as though she is, in some way, better. She tells your brother that and also the other women. It is another reason why some families are unhappy and wish to return home, across the seas. Do not worry, he will come to his senses and put his wife in her place. She is not my mother; she is nothing like Gytha."

"I had not seen that side of her."

"And whom did Gytha, the matriarch of our clan, choose to train as volvas? Was Freja one?" He shook his head, "Gytha can see into all of our hearts and she knows Freja's. When Gytha passes over then the three of them, Ada, Helga and Gefn, will have to deal with Freja."

As I wrapped myself in my bear fur, I realised that all of my voyages had set me apart from the clan. I did not see the day to day interactions which shaped the clan. They knew more of me than I did of them. The Norns were spinning.

Fótr and Arne had settled their differences but, from that moment on, I saw that there was a growing rift between Fótr and Arne. Fótr had always been closer to me as I had had more time for him. Now he threw himself into the sailing of the drekar. He was constantly at my side and his questions showed that he was serious about becoming a navigator.

The next day the wind veered to come from the north and we stepped the mast. I had known it would be inevitable. Now our speed would slow as we were forced to row north. We only needed the chant to begin the voyage up the river for we would keep up a regular rhythm. I had the drekar manned with a single man on each oar and we would replace them when they tired. That way we could row all day. We made for the island we had found when I had sailed in the snekke. It lay a short way away from Fox Water. This was the island we had explored and I knew that there were the long-eared animals on the island. We reached the island before dark for the men were tired. We had not had to row for as long since we had left the land of ice and fire. Ebbe and Stig showed the other ship's boys how to make traps to catch small animals and I told the others what we would find the next day.

"There is a large piece of water, I named it Fox Water and it is like a small sea. From there we have two short days of rowing before we reach Bjorr Beck. That is where we will camp and hunt. When we catch these animals, we can use their guts to fish as we sail up Fox Water for there are some mighty fish there."

I saw that my words brought smiles and looks of eager anticipation to the faces of the warriors. They would row happily but only if they knew there was a reward at the end; a raid or a hunt.

Arne, of course, saw the opportunity to establish his authority. "My brother and his crew found a place which might well prove to be a place we could live. When we hunt, we go armed and with shields for there are Skraeling who might dispute our right to be here. Clan of the Fox, we may have a battle in a few days' time!"

The other warriors showed that they hoped this was true but I, for one, hoped not. If I was to find my maid and speak with her then I needed peace with the Penobscot.

Morning found that we had been successful with our traps. The animals had not been hunted before we had come, for we saw no evidence of the Skraeling living on the island. We had time and so we cooked them before we left. The crew found the meat was sweet and I saw some of the ones who wished to return to Larswick speaking with their oar brothers. The bounty of the land was making some reconsider their decision.

As we sailed up the river, the ship's boys hauled fish after fish from the river. Some were as long as a boy's arm while others were as long as a leg. The sheer size and richness of Fox Water filled the drekar with the murmur of approval as they saw the forests which surrounded it, the fish which rose to the surface and the birds which soared and then swooped. As we headed north, we saw horse deer and white-tailed deer which came down to the water to drink.

Arne had the lead oar and he grinned at me, "Brother, you have a nose for navigation! This is a good land and we have seen no Skraeling!"

I shook my head, "This is the River of Peace and they do not live along it but," I pointed to the west, "they are over there and they are as the fish in this water, plentiful!"

I was allowing Fótr to have the steering board more and more. He was becoming used to *'Njörðr'* and she to him. He was also learning to gauge the effect of the rowers so that he knew the most opportune moment to make a course correction. It was easier here than on the great ocean, which was where I had learned, but that was no bad thing. We came to the island where we had eaten many of the long-eared creatures and we stopped for the night. It would be a short day of sailing ahead of us and we needed daylight to build a defensive camp at Bjorr Beck.

We had fish to cook and animals to trap; this was a land full of bounty and we knew how to harvest it. That evening there was an air of anticipation in the camp for I had promised them much and all were eager to see if I had, once more, delivered. Ebbe and

The Savage Wilderness

Stig had already told them of the bjorr and the dam they had made. We had heard of the bjorr but there had been none on Orkneyjar and Larswick. The name, small bear, suggested something grander than it was and I hoped that they would not be disappointed.

I took the steering board as we headed up the narrow channel next to the island. I kept a wary eye to the shore to the west for that had been where the Penobscot had attacked us and I had been wounded. I thought we could turn the drekar at the Bjorr Beck but I was not certain and that row up the River of Peace was a tense one for me. When I saw where the two rivers met, I breathed a sigh of relief for it was as I had remembered it; indeed, the river was slightly wider than I had remembered. Perhaps being chased by Skraelings had narrowed it in my mind. I turned the drekar around and moored it next to the western bank of the River of Peace.

As Arne organised the warriors and while the ship's boys fastened us securely to the shore, I spoke with Fótr. "I would have you and the ship's boys stay aboard. You will need to fit the mast, yard and sail. If we are successful then there will not be enough room for the rowers. We might have to use the current and the wind."

He nodded, "That suits me for, despite Arne's attempt at an apology, I am still unhappy to be close to him. Since he became jarl of the clan he has changed."

"He is blood and he is family; you cannot have a feud."

He shook his head, "He is jarl and you are the only family, save Reginleif, that I have. Do not worry, Erik, I will smile and I will play the dutiful brother but it cannot change that which is in my heart."

He was right.

The rest of the warriors took their mail byrnies, helmets and shields ashore. I did not. I would trust to my bone covered leather. Arne was waiting for me as I descended. He frowned when he saw that I had no shield, "Are you not a warrior?"

I said, "Aye, but today you need me as a scout and to find where we were ambushed and where the bjorr are to be found. If there are large numbers of Penobscot here then the Allfather does not wish us to be here. Anyway, there are enough warriors to do the fighting. I will fight when it is necessary."

Siggi nodded, "He is right, Arne. We cannot hunt in mail can we and shields will be of little use when we set traps? Let us scout the land, choose our camp and make it defensible. If the Allfather smiles upon us then we will be here for some time."

Siggi's words persuaded Arne and I led them down the river path to the bjorr. Some were disappointed at the diminutive size of the creatures, but when they saw the fact that they could swim and that their fur kept them dry, they changed their minds.

"There are the bjorr, now where are the horse deer?"

I headed away from the river and followed the trail we had discovered. I soon spotted the spoor of the horse deer and we also startled some white-tailed deer. Men with mail and shields make a noise. I stopped when I found the clearing where we had seen the horse deer grazing. I waved a hand, "We saw them here but we are making so much noise that we cannot expect to surprise them."

Æimundr Loud Voice, who was the best hunter we had, nodded and said, "I have seen their spoor and the marks of their antlers on the trees. This is where we will find them." He patted me on the back, "You have good eyes, Erik the Navigator."

Arne was mollified, "Then let us head back closer to the drekar and make a camp. If the Skraeling come then I want to be able to defend what we have!"

There was a clearing which was close to the confluence of the two rivers. I suspected that in the spring when there was a thaw, it would flood. We cut down the saplings which grew there but did not discard them. We cut them into shorter lengths and sharpened them. They would make a palisade when we had dug our ditch. We hacked down the brambles and briars which grew and we would use them to disguise the ditch whilst clearing ground in the centre of our camp. We needed a large camp as we would not just be sleeping there, we would be butchering animals, salting and drying them. Fótr and the boys would be kept busy. I had already decided that I would explore more of this land. I would find the maid.

By the time darkness came, we had the camp built with a ditch and mound topped with the saplings. We wound briars and brambles between and covering the ditch; we left just two entrances. One led to the drekar and the other was the one we would use to leave the camp to hunt and to trap. I had organised the food and used a mixture of the long-eared animals, fish and some preserved whale we had left. It was a hearty stew and, if all went well, we would eat horse deer the next night.

As we lay down to sleep with two men on duty, I heard the sounds of the night. I heard a wolf and I heard a wild cat. We were no longer in a safe place like Bear Island; we were in the heart of the wilderness and, from the sounds we heard, it was a savage one with predators in abundance.

The next day Arne and Æimundr Loud Voice led two groups of hunters and trappers out. Arne would lay bjorr traps while Æimundr Loud Voice would find the horse deer and the white-tailed deer. Arne would join him when he had set the traps. Arne also hoped to hunt some of the bjorr, and he and Siggi had their bows with them. I stayed in the camp to help Fótr to organize it and to ensure that the mast and sail were secure. We might have to leave in a hurry. Fótr had done a good job and, as the ship's boys lit fires to cook the meat we would hunt, Fótr showed me his copy of the maps. "I have not wasted my time, brother. I have copied all of your maps and added detail to them both. I am not yet ready to sail across the wide ocean but I am closer. If you would allow me, I would sail the drekar back to Bear Island."

I smiled, "Of course, Fótr. I am honoured that you follow in my footsteps."

By the time the hunters returned, it was early afternoon but we had the camp organised and ready. One of the beer barrels had been emptied and we had the other ones we would use to store the meat. Æimundr Loud Voice was pleased for they had found a small herd and managed to kill five of the beasts. Arne had laid traps and managed to hunt four of the bjorr who were too slow to move away from danger. It confirmed what Bear Tooth had told us, they trapped the bjorr and did not hunt it. The men began their work; they would strip the hides and then butcher the meat. This was not like when we had hurriedly butchered the whale. We had time to make the cuts the way we wished to have them and nothing would be wasted. The guts

The Savage Wilderness

would be used to bait fishing lines in the River of Peace while the hearts and liver would be eaten fresh.

I went to my brother, "Arne, I will scout."

My brother and Siggi both stared at me. "Why?"

I had thought it all through. "When we came here, we were surprised by a large number of warriors. I believe that they have a summer camp close by."

Siggi shook his head, "And if it was still there then we would be battling Skraeling instead of butchering horse deer."

"Perhaps, but it will put my mind at rest if I find it empty."

Arne nodded, "That makes sense. Ebbe, come here."

"Yes, Jarl?"

"You will go with my brother to scout."

I shook my head, "I can go alone, Arne."

"You could but if you were caught then we would have no navigator. Two of you doubles the chances that at least one of you will return. It is not open for debate; that is my command!"

I nodded but knew that the next time I went scouting I would wait until the hunters had left and I did not have to seek permission! "Ebbe, fetch your bow. We might find something to hunt."

Ebbe was happy to be with me and I did not mind the company; I just disliked the imperative from my brother. Perhaps Fótr was right. Arne had changed since he became jarl. I picked up my yew bow and we headed towards the place I had seen the maid. The warriors had come down the path and it was a good place to begin our search. I was not a fool and I did not wish to stumble upon Skraeling; for one thing, I had Ebbe with me and I could not risk him. "Ebbe, stay five paces behind me. Arne is right and if we come across the Penobscot, you can take word back to the jarl."

"I could not leave you alone, foster father."

I stopped and faced him, "You will leave me if I am in danger for the clan and the drekar are more important than my life." He nodded, albeit reluctantly.

We found the place where I had tended to the maid's mother and I nocked an arrow before heading down the trail. There had been rain in the past week but there appeared to be no human prints. The Skraeling wore a kind of hide shoe which Bear Tooth

The Savage Wilderness

had called a mockasin; I saw no recent sign of them but I did see where birds had been down and walked and another small creature which appeared to have feet like the long-eared animal but smaller. The lack of mockasin prints emboldened me and I moved more confidently. When I found a track which headed away from the river trail, I became warier. I moved more slowly and saw that there was a clearing ahead.

"Ebbe, stay in the trees and nock an arrow."

"Aye, foster father."

I stood behind a birch tree and I noticed that it had had the bark removed. I peered into the clearing and saw the blackened remains of some fires. There were also patches of grass which were a different colour from those around them. This had been their summer camp. I could see no one and, taking a chance, I stepped out and entered what I soon confirmed to be the Penobscot camp. The circles were clearly where their homes had been. Bear Tooth told me that they were portable and easy to repair. He had also told me how many warriors and their families could be accommodated in each one. I went around and counted them. There had to be at least two hundred Penobscot who had lived in the village. They had moved inland but would they send scouts back? I waved Ebbe forward and I continued to explore. I saw broken wood which suggested racks for drying fish or meat. There were chips and flakes showing where they had made new bone weapons and there was a section of freshly turned earth. I guessed that was where they buried their dead and I also knew, I know not how, that we had killed some of them when we had been pursued.

"Come, we can return to the camp. The Penobscot have left for their winter camps and I am relieved. We will not have to fight."

By the time we reached the camp, it was getting on towards night but we could have found the camp with our eyes closed for the smell of cooking meat and the laughter told us where it was. Arne had placed men on watch and I heard Ǫlmóðr Ragnarsson shout, "Someone approaches!"

I shouted back, "It is Erik the Navigator and Ebbe!"

Ǫlmóðr's voice sounded relieved, "That is what I hoped. Advance."

The Savage Wilderness

The entire camp of warriors stopped what they were doing when we entered through the narrow gap in the palisade and Arne said, "Well?"

"I have found the Penobscot village and it is deserted. They have returned to their winter homes."

"Good, then the Allfather smiles upon us! This is a good place to hunt. Æimundr Loud Voice, here, is convinced that we can take another twenty animals before we leave and I am keen to see how many bjorr we can trap." He added, more quietly, "Perhaps this might make those who wish to return to Larswick change their minds."

I was not convinced. The desire to return east was not about hunting and food it was about raiding and taking women and treasure. There was no treasure and I did not think that the warriors wished anything to do with the women. Then it struck me; I was the only one who had seen a woman. When they did so, they might change their minds.

The next day we found eight bjorr that we had successfully trapped. We also trapped ten of the long-eared creatures. When Æimundr Loud Voice and his hunters brought back another ten of the horse deer and four white-tailed deer carcasses, I feared that we would run out of salt! We had two days of butchery in the camp and then we began to load the drekar with the barrels of meat. We had brought plenty of barrels from the land of ice and fire but we could not make new ones as we did not have the metal. We were, therefore, very careful about how we looked after them. When the barrels were full, we would have to leave for there was little point in hunting just to have the meat go rotten. There were fewer bjorr in the traps and I deduced that we had almost wiped out the colony.

Before the warriors left the next day to check the traps again, I slipped out of the camp for I wished to see if I could discover another river with a colony of bjorr. I had to leave early or I risked Arne spotting me and I did not want another argument. I used the bjorr dam to cross the river and headed due west for I could see a piece of higher ground which suggested a natural divide or valley. There were no roads whatsoever in this land and, as far as I could see, there were only trails made by animals and used by the Skraeling. As they moved their homes too, it was hard to see what kind of mark these people left on the ground.

Moving alone, I did not disturb as many animals and I saw birds and animals I had neither seen nor imagined. This was truly a magical place. Being animal trails, they followed the line of least resistance and twisted and turned. I suddenly came upon a piece of flat water. It had to be a bjorr dam. I followed the water and saw the bjorr dam at the end. Below it, the stream headed north and east. I guessed it would join on to the River of Peace. I had brought my map and I roughly marked the position of the dam. I estimated that I had travelled, perhaps five miles. Noon was still some hours away and so I estimated the time. I drank some of the ale I had brought and ate some of the dried meat. I was tempted to eat the bright berries I saw but Bear Tooth was not with me and I did not want to risk poison. I put my map and ale-skin back in my satchel which I slung over my shoulder and I headed back.

As I headed over the trail, I saw a high point to my right. The animal tracks did not go towards it and there was no reason why they should, for to silhouette themselves against the skyline would invite a predator. There were only thin trees there and I deduced from the size of the trees that the rock was close to the surface and inhibited growth. It suited me for I knew I would have a good view in every direction. By the time I broke into the sun, I was hot and sweaty. My leather jerkin was not as heavy as my mail burnie but I could see why the Skraeling went bare-chested.

I looked north and saw the River of Peace, twinkling in the distance; it was a long river. Looking to the east, I saw the smoke from our fires. I frowned for it was the only smoke to be seen and if the Penobscot were close by, they would see it. It was fortunate that we had almost finished. Then I looked south and, as I did so, my heart fell for I saw the painted bodies and heads of a Penobscot warband and they were heading for our camp! I ran!

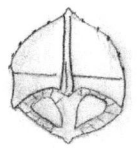

Chapter 9

By my estimate I had two miles to go; fortunately, I had no more ridges to climb but I would have to swim the Bjorr Beck. By the time I was there, I would be able to shout a warning. I cursed the fact that I had not brought my bow. If I had then I could have attacked these Skraeling. As it was, I would have to close to within a sword's length if I was to do anything about them. They had also been about two miles from the camp and this was a foot race, except that they knew the land and the trails and I was a stranger! I hoped, as I ran, that my ankle would hold up. I had not had any trouble for some time but I knew that it would be a weakness, as would my right arm. Working on the new drekar had strengthened it but combat was something different.

The trail I had followed when I had searched out the new river headed towards the dam at Bjorr Beck and I did not want that for I would run into the warband. I needed the most direct route as that would be shorter and, I hoped, quicker. I ran down the gentle slope through the saplings and scrubby trees. The closer to the beck that I came, the thicker were the trees. As I neared the beck, I risked shouting. If it drew the Skraelings to me then so be it but Ebbe and the ship's boys were in the camp. I was not certain that Arne and his half of the warriors had returned from the dam yet.

"Clan of the Fox! Alarm! Clan of the Fox! Alarm!"

I saw the beck just forty paces from me and I realised it looked wider than I had remembered. The snekke had been able to turn around and that should have warned me. I did not slow but threw myself in and found that the current was stronger than I might have hoped. The seal skin boots began to drag me down as did my sword and I contemplated discarding them both, but something made me retain them and I kicked and used my arms to drag myself closer to the other bank. I found myself going under but I kicked off the bottom and, as my head broke the surface a rope snaked out and Gandálfr shouted, "Grab this, Erik the Navigator, lest you sink a second time and do not rise."

I grabbed the rope and he and Uddi Sharp Tooth, hauled me out of the water. As I landed spluttering on the bank, I said, "Sound the horn! Skraelings are about to attack!" Gandálfr ran off leaving Uddi to lift me to my feet. I pointed upstream. "They are coming down the river trail!"

I heard Gandálfr shouting, "Arm yourselves! Skraelings!" I heard the horn sound three times; it was the call to return to camp urgently for we were under attack. I wondered who was in camp. With luck, it would be all of our warriors and we would meet the Skraeling from behind our ramparts!

Uddi Sharp Tooth and I rushed towards the camp and ran through the single opening from the beck side. Our precautions looked as though they had been justified. I saw that Æimundr Loud Voice and the rest of his hunters were donning their byrnies for they were already in the camp. The ship's boys and Fótr were on the drekar just standing with gaping mouths.

"Fótr, you and the boys will use your bows! Stand behind Æimundr Loud Voice and his warriors. Loose over the top of them when you see the Skraelings."

"Our brother?"

"Will be able to handle himself."

I grabbed my shield and helmet. I did not have time to go aboard and fetch my mail. I would stand in the second rank. I picked up a spear. Æimundr Loud Voice was the senior warrior and he said, "Present two lines. If they reach us, we let Arne and the others through but if they do not come, we slaughter everyone else. We are the Clan of the Fox!"

I began to sing, as I stood between Uddi Sharp Tooth and Sigismund Shape Shifter. I sang the song of the whale hunt. If Arne and the trappers heard it then they would take heart and know that they were not alone.

Lars and Snorri had five fine heirs
They hunted enemies in all their lairs
Wolf or fish, dragon or bears

The Savage Wilderness

They could not be taken unawares
From Bear Island the five set sail
Hunting the monstrous big black whale
The whale that came from Ran's deep home
Rose like a monster through sea and foam.
The clan feared no black-skinned beast
On its flesh, the clan would feast
Njörðr flew like a hunting bird
Waiting for Ebbe to give the word
Lars and Snorri had five fine heirs
They hunted enemies in all their lairs
Wolf or fish, dragon or bears
They could not be taken unawares
Longer than a drekar and foiled with teeth
The whale was like a black-skinned reef
None was dismayed as the creatures rose
Arne and Siggi were the hunters chose
And two spears hung in mid-air
Waiting to strike at flesh laid bare
Arne hurt first and struck down fast
While Siggi's spear made a hole so vast
The beast it dived down to Ran's sea bed
Erik Navigator kept his head
As Njörðr fought her own hard battle
The whale rose and gave a deadly rattle
The clan had fought and the clan had won
Their great sea battle was over and won.
Lars and Snorri had five fine heirs
They hunted enemies in all their lairs
Wolf or fish, dragon or bears
They could not be taken unawares

I heard the sound of the song taken up in the distance. Arne had heard our song and he was rallying our men with its call. We had shields presented with spears sticking over the tops. Æimundr Loud Voice, Faramir and Folkman would have to move apart to allow Arne and the others through. Once they opened their ranks then Uddi Sharp Tooth, Sigismund Shape

Shifter and I might have to bear the blows of the Skraeling until the gap could be closed again.

As the last line was sung, I shouted, "Fótr, are you ready?"

"Aye, Erik the Navigator!"

As we waited for either the Skraelings or our men, whichever came first, I had time to work out that it was our fires which had drawn our enemy to us. I had no doubt that they had sent scouts when they had first seen the fires and, having ascertained our numbers, gathered a large enough warband. It was in that moment that I knew they might have their birch bark boats close to hand too. They had almost caught me the first time and I knew they had learned from that encounter.

Arne's voice came down the trail, "Let us through! We have wounded!"

Æimundr Loud Voice, Faramir and Folkman stepped back as did Uddi and Sigismund. I stood as our men ran through the gap they had left. I saw that Palni and Mikel had both been hurt. They were bleeding but had managed to run without assistance. Tostig was still alive and he ran through with more of our men. I saw Arne and Siggi. They were walking backwards down the narrow trail and jabbing at the Penobscot with their spears. Arne and his band had taken shields each time they had left the camp and I now saw the wisdom of that.

I shouted, "The men are safe! Turn and run! Fótr! Arrows!"

Once Arne heard my command, he would know that we had him covered. He and Siggi ran. They had forty paces to cover but the Penobscot were close behind. My brother and cousin held their shields above their heads as eight arrows plunged down. One hit Siggi's shield but three of ours hit Skraeling and those three arrows bought the time for Arne and Siggi to join us. As soon as they burst through then Æimundr Loud Voice, Faramir and Folkman resumed their places. Behind me, I heard Arne shout, "Don your mail!"

I had been watching Arne's hunting group when they had returned and I knew that one was missing: Danr Danrsson was one of the older warriors and also one of Arne's faithful followers. He would be missed. I had little time to ponder the future for a hail of spears, arrows and stone axes were hurled at us. This time we all had shields and wore helmets. The weapons rattled and cracked off our shields. They did little harm but they enabled the Penobscot to close with us for Fótr and the boys dared not risk the arrows close to us. The warriors ran into a wall of spears held by ten of our men in the front rank.

I heard Arne shout, "Siggi, take the left side, the rest of my men to the right!" The Skraeling were trying to use their superior numbers to outflank us and he moved the trappers to plug the gaps.

Æimundr was called Loud Voice for a good reason, he could be heard in the noisiest of places. He bellowed, "Second rank, on my command, push!" I placed my shield in his back and put my right foot behind me. "Push!"

As I pushed into his back, I jabbed my spear forward at head height. It was a blindly struck blow but I connected with something. Æimundr moved forward as did Faramir and Folkman. I pulled back my spear and jabbed again. I caught something a glancing blow and there was a scream. As I pulled it back for a third strike, I saw an eyeball hanging from the end of my spear. Our warriors in the front rank were pulling back and punching with the regularity of a weaponsmith making a sword. I heard screams and shouts. I recognised some of the Skraeling words and they were cursing us and demanding that their gods punish us. Then there were splashes as warriors were knocked, some dead, some wounded, into the beck.

Arne shouted, "Break ranks!"

Every one of our warriors obeyed instantly and we hurried to find a Skraeling to kill. There could be no mercy. It would be a case of kill or be killed and I did not want to die. I faced a Skraeling with a spear and a small hide shield. He was smaller than I was and his spear just had a stone tip. I moved my shield away to invite him to strike and he did so. I brought my shield over to smash into the head of his spear and then stabbed at the warrior's leg. I struck his knee and, as I twisted the blade in the wound, he fell. He lay helpless beneath me and I picked my spear out of his knee and rammed it into his chest. He died quickly but my spear was caught on his ribs and a second warrior leapt at me with a stone axe. I barely had time to bring up my shield and block the blow. I pulled out my sword and swept it around; the edge caught his left arm and grated off bone as I slid it back. I punched with my shield and, catching him in the face, he reeled. I brought my sword from behind me and struck down. I split his skull in two. We were now racing up the trail to the bjorr dam. I was no longer at the fore and I saw bodies hacked and broken on the trail, in the woods to the side and hanging over the beck. This was not a battle, it was a slaughter. I saw Siggi and Arne hurrying ahead, slicing and chopping with their swords. They were like men possessed and I wondered why until we reached the dam and I saw the naked body of Danr Danrsson. It was lying next to his head which had his manhood stuffed in his mouth. He had been gutted and his entrails were spread across the path. We showed no mercy.

We sounded the horn an hour or so before dark for the Penobscot had fled and we were too tired to pursue. I was one of the first back and I went to the two wounded men. Both had been hit by stone weapons and Mikel would have a terrible scar until the day he died. As I tended to his wound, he told me how the Penobscot had appeared from nowhere. Danr had been the sentry and he had been overwhelmed by sheer weight of numbers. In the time it had taken to grab weapons, Mikel and Palni had been wounded and then they had heard the horn sound and Arne had ordered a retreat.

The last in were the men of Siggi and Arne. They carried the body of Danr with them. I saw anger in Arne's eyes but there was something else. His arrogance had gone. He had lost only one man but that had been a close companion. More, he had had two men hurt. I knew that it was a good thing that we had almost finished our hunting.

"Before we do anything, let us bury Danr Danrsson here where the clan fought a battle which will be told whenever the clan remembers great deeds."

We all banged our shields with our spears for blood still boiled in our heads. Had the Penobscot returned they would have suffered far worse than in their first attack. We had counted over eighty bodies. In terms of numbers, we had won but they could afford to lose more than we!

We had food prepared and I drew Fótr to one side, "Tonight, you and the boys sleep aboard the drekar. I will join you."

"You are worried?"

I rubbed the back of my neck, "It is just a feeling. Bear Tooth said his tribe do not like to fight at night. That may be true of the Penobscot but if we sleep aboard the drekar then I will be happier. Tell the boys to go aboard when they have eaten and to sleep with a knife close to hand." He nodded. "Let them know that they did well and showed much courage in the battle."

Fótr nodded, almost absentmindedly, "I have never seen berserkers but these Skraeling seem to fight like that; as though they do not care if they will live or die. They threw themselves upon your blades."

I nodded, "Those were my thoughts too. They must guarantee themselves a place in their Valhalla by such deaths!"

I went to join Siggi and Arne who were deep in conversation. They stopped as I approached, "How were you able to raise the alarm, brother?"

"I went to scout out another river and I found bjorr."

Arne became angry and his tone was that of a father reprimanding a naughty child, "You should not have gone alone; you might have been killed and then where would we be?"

"Fótr could have sailed you back to Bear Island."

Arne's voice became quiet, "Do you not hear me, brother? Without you, none can sail back to Larswick."

"But everyone knows I do not wish to return there."

Siggi leaned in to me, "There is talk of making you sail them home. Since the Thing, those dissenters who wish to leave have begun to meet. Your brother has heard whispers."

I laughed, "How can they make me? I am my own man and I make my own decisions."

"There is Ada and your son!"

"Arne, Ada knows that I will stay and she can choose to go back to Larswick. We have spoken and Gytha knows all."

Siggi could see that we were getting nowhere, "Now we have to decide what we do here."

Arne stretched, "That is simple. We finish what we were doing. The difference will be that we will keep a better watch and we begin to load the drekar tomorrow. Before we leave, we will destroy the bjorr dam."

I said, "But that will flood this place!"

"I know and it will destroy the place the Penobscot trap the bjorr. I wish them to remember the price they pay for attacking the Clan of the Fox." It would be a vindictive act but I saw the wisdom in it for we would not be returning here.

While we waited for the food, men sharpened weapons and checked byrnies for damage. I would need two bone plates replacing on my vest but that could wait. I then added the information I had found to my map. There was another bjorr colony. And, while we might never trap them again, the navigator in me wanted to complete the job I had begun. In anticipation of loading the drekar, I had the deck removed from the centre. The stones that were our ballast were exposed. We would have to remove some before we loaded. That task could wait and there were enough stones on Bear Island to refill the hull.

That night I slept by the steering board with my sword and dagger close to hand. Fótr slept at the prow. The other boys spread themselves around the drekar with Ebbe sleeping next to the gangplank from the camp. Gytha had not come to me on this voyage and I wondered if the illness was preventing her from doing so. Perhaps the worm was affecting her. That night she came to me. She looked different from normal and was a sort of thin grey fog-like form with hollowed eyes and wild white hair. I might have thought that she was a spirit come to harm me had I not heard her words. 'Erik, awake! There is danger! Erik, awake!"

My eyes popped wide and I listened. I heard nothing except for the sound of warriors snoring in the main camp. I was about to return to sleep when I heard the slightest of bumps. Had I not been awake I would not have heard it. The sound could have been a piece of driftwood coming down the river but Gytha had warned me and I jumped to my feet, sword and dagger in hand. I went to the stern and saw two Skraeling climbing up.

"Clan of the Fox! Attack!"

I swung my sword and the sharpened blade hacked through the skull of one Skraeling and across the neck of the other. They fell and I heard the splash as they hit the river. Looking over, I saw a mass of birch bark boats; they were attacking at night! My boys were awake and Arne was leading men from the camp to come to our aid.

I laid down my sword and grabbed one of the ballast stones. It was heavy and I dropped it into the boat which lay by the stern. Two of the warriors from the boat were about to climb but the stone plunged into the bottom of the birch bark boat smashing a hole in the bottom and it began to sink. Grabbing my weapons again I shouted, "Sink the boats with the ballast!" I ran down the decking which remained along the side of the drekar and hacked into the neck of the Penobscot who had climbed the side and was about to attack Stig Eidelsson. Ebbe had gone to the prow to help Fótr, for although that was the highest part of the drekar, the figurehead would help them to climb aboard. Arne and our men were now on board, although with the centre decking removed, our fighting platform was narrower than it ought to have been but our warriors fought with a ferocity which terrified me for I had never seen it before. The Penobscot warriors were not simply killed, they were butchered. Perhaps the sight of Danr's body had affected them.

I hurried back to the stern. I saw three boats which had been approaching now sail along the side of the drekar, downstream. At that moment I knew that this was not over. They could wait for us where the river narrowed and attack us with spears and arrows. I dropped stones into the boats which were lining our sides. Any who managed to clamber aboard were hacked to pieces. By the time the first hint of dawn could be seen, it was over. The dead were hurled over the side and our wounded tended to. All of the ship's boys had wounds. The Skraeling might only have stone, flint and bone weapons but their knives were sharp and they had cut the boys. None of the wounds was serious and I think that the boys all regarded them as a badge of honour.

Arne wiped the blood from his blade, "You may be right about these people, Erik. They do not know when they are beaten. We will load the drekar and leave. The meat is almost all prepared. Yesterday's hunt can be salted as we sail and when we reach the sea, the salt air will help preserve it. While it is loaded, Siggi and I will take men and destroy the dam."

I shook my head, "Leave that until the last moment and use all of the warriors."

Arne was going to dismiss the idea when Siggi held up his hand, "Why, Erik the Navigator?"

"When last we came, they tried to attack us at the narrows. They can use arrows, spears and stones but they can also block the river. If you first weaken the dam and then pull the wood from the base, it will still burst the dam but give you and the men the chance to reboard the drekar. The river will rush down and join this River of Peace. The river will be higher and take us down the river quicker. It might stop them from blocking our escape."

Arne smiled and put his arm around my shoulder, "I sometimes forget how clever you are. We will do this."

Some of the ballast had already been removed but more was needed to be shifted. Then we loaded first the hides and the furs followed by the bones and antlers. The smaller barrels were placed under the deck close to the mast. Then we replaced the deck. That was time-consuming. The larger barrels had been readied and they were all loaded and stored around the mast fish. I wanted the drekar balanced. We would have to keep the sides of the drekar free in case we had to fight. Finally, we loaded the freshly salted meat and that was placed in the centre of the drekar. I gave a rueful shake of the head. The deck would be bloody when we reached Bear Island and, before I could start work on the new drekar, I would have to clean this one first.

The men placed their shields along the side of the drekar and then returned ashore. Our two wounded warriors came aboard while the rest went with Arne to destroy the dam. I had the sail ready to be hoisted and I allocated ship's boys to the ropes which tied us to the shore. "When the jarl returns with the warriors, you must begin to loosen the ropes as soon as they begin to board. Ebbe and Stig, you will unfasten your ropes as soon as the last warrior is aboard and then ensure that you are able to board too. When I raise the sail, there will be no stopping us. The river will come with a rush and *'Njörðr'* will fly as though a whale pulls us!"

They both grinned. The fact that they had survived an attack by the Penobscot and killed their first enemies had made them more confident. *Wyrd.* We waited and we watched. Suddenly Tostig led the warriors back, they were running, and they began to pour aboard. The lines were untied leaving just Ebbe and Stig ashore.

"Let fly the sail!" As the sail was hoisted, the wind and the current began to tug us against the two ropes which held us. I heard them creak. Our men were not slow and their feet pounded on the gangplank. When I saw Arne and Siggi race through the camp, I stood by the steering board. I had said that Fótr could sail the drekar and he could, but not down a river which would be like a maelstrom! The two warriors and two ship's boys hurled themselves over the gunwale as *'Njörðr'* was struck by the wall of water from the burst dam. The gangplank was lost but that was a small price to pay for our escape.

The waters flooded over the banks to fill our camp. Danr's grave disappeared under the wood-filled water. I clung on to the steering board. It was like riding a wild horse. The drekar was fighting the river and I was fighting the ship. "Fótr! I need your help!"

Fótr joined me and the two of us clung to the steering board as we hurtled down the river. One advantage I had not anticipated was that the extra water made the river wider. I still kept to the centre for I knew that close to the banks were rocks and branches which threatened to tear into the hull, but as we approached the narrows, I saw that they were not as narrow and Skraeling, waiting to attack us on the sides, were floundering in the river. Heads were cracked open like eggs and limbs were shattered as the half-naked warriors were smashed into the rock walls.

Eidel was at the prow and he shouted down to us, his voice barely audible above the roar of water and the sound of trees crashing. "They had a barrier of boats! They are destroyed!" I saw some of the wrecked and ruined birch bark boats as we raced towards Fox Water.

By the time we reached that vast expanse of the river, the force of the broken dam had been expended and we sailed into a sea of calm. The warriors cheered and banged the deck with their feet. They called my name and Arne and Siggi joined me. Siggi put his arm around me, "None other could have done that, Erik the Navigator."

I shook my head and put my arm around Fótr, "Our brother had his rite of passage this day. Had he not been with me then things might have gone awry. This was meant to be. The Norns have been spinning. Fótr has taken some serious steps to become a navigator!"

The rest of the voyage back was slow and uneventful and that pleased me for I had had enough danger to last a lifetime. Arne and Siggi stood with me at the prow while Fótr sailed us across the sea to our home. Arne stared at the west bank of the river, "We cannot go back to Bjorr Beck, that is certain."

I looked at Arne, "You would return to the land of the Penobscot?"

He sighed, "Erik, I am no fool. I know the dangers but I also know the rewards. The bjorr has good fur and it is easy to trap. When we sailed across Fox Water, I spied rivers which joined it. We just follow those rivers up and we will find the bjorr. I do not say this season but, after next summer, we come again."

"But why? Why do we need the fur?"

He smiled, "I know that you are the thinker but I am not stupid and I can make plans too. We are not just warriors, we are traders. When those of the clan who wish to, return home, we will send furs to trade. Siggi here will return to Bear Island with metal and new settlers who wish to join our clan. The ones who wish to sail home can do so but they will not keep the drekar. The drekar is ours! I have spent some time thinking about this. There will be others who do not wish to bend their knee to the King of Norway nor the Saxon kings. We offer them sanctuary here."

"You forget one important matter, who would sail the drekar across the seas? Fótr wishes to stay in the east."

Siggi and Arne looked at each other and Arne shrugged, "The plan is not totally thought out but these small details are not beyond our wit to solve. For now, we have had a great victory and none will starve this winter! It is good."

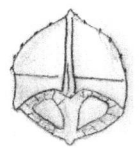

Chapter 10

Fótr showed his increasing skills by guiding us into our bay without recourse to me and that pleased me but I was still concerned and worried about Arne's plan. He was my brother and he was the jarl; I would do anything for the clan but until I had seen my dream become a reality, I could not return to Larswick. I would not return across the seas.

When Gytha was not there to greet us, I was concerned, although the sight of Ada, heavy with child, made me happy. I had not missed the birth of my daughter. The rest of the clan who lived close by the bay were also present for their men had been aboard. Some were tending their fields but the sound of the horn announcing our arrival would soon recall them. We had food for the winter and there was little time for reunions and embraces. A human chain carried the salted meat to be preserved as well as the full barrels and, after the shields and the chests had been removed, I lifted the decking. Although it had only been a day or so, the smell from the hold told me we had taken out our cargo none too soon. I would leave the deck off for a week or so to allow fresher air into the hull and I would examine it for leaks. I would also have to set Ebbe and the others to seek out more stones for ballast as well as for the new drekar.

Once the drekar was secured and the mast stepped, I hurried to greet Ada, "The baby?"

Ada shook her head, "This one is wild and headstrong. Lars was little trouble but this one kicks and wriggles like a bag full of cats."

"But you are well?"

She kissed me, "I am well."

"And Gytha?"

"She was fine until two nights ago and she has not risen since."

The Savage Wilderness

Two nights ago, she had come to me. "I must go to her. Ebbe, take your mother to our home and then you and Bear Tooth can gather all the hooves from every animal we hunted and begin to boil them to make glue. The sooner we start the better." I saw Lars looking at me, "And take Lars with you. He can be useful." He looked delighted although the smell would be quite horrible. "Make the fire downwind of the stad and close to the shipyard. I will speak with Gytha."

It should have been Arne who visited Gytha but since Freja had been overlooked as a future volva there had been an ever-widening rift between them. It was all on Arne's part, I knew that, but it was something I could do without.

Snorri was next to the bed and holding his wife's hand. My immediate thought was that she was dying. Her voice was stronger than I had expected from her appearance when she spoke, "I am not yet ready to die, Erik, but I am weary. Warning you took much out of me. I will recover but it is rest which I need."

I was relieved, "Thank you for the warning."

"And the rest?"

"Went well and we have all that we need for food and to finish the second drekar."

"But you did not see the maid?" I shook my head. "When the time is right you will, of that I am certain."

I then told her of Arne's plan to trade with our homeland. I was not being disloyal to Arne but it felt that way.

"That will not work for the voyage is a hard one and without the skill of Erik the Navigator it will only be attempted once." She smiled, "I will not be here and I shall have to watch that voyage from the Otherworld. Some things cannot be changed." She smiled, "Your daughter will be born soon."

I knew that it was not a question, Gytha actually knew. "Ada says she is eager to be out."

"Aye, Ýrr will be a restless spirit."

"Ýrr?"

"That will be her name. It means wild and restless and she will be that for she will grow up without her father and she will seek him." I had not thought that far ahead. Ada and my children, what would happen to them when my dream was fulfilled? "Do not try to anticipate the future, not all the threads are spun and the Norns are not yet finished."

"But you know that Lars and my daughter will not see me and I will not see them."

"In your heart, Erik, you know that too."

She was right.

When I spoke with Ada, at the end of a very long day, I told her of Gytha's words concerning the naming of our child. Ada said the name as though tasting it. "I like that and it is like the greatest volva, Ylva. I should like to have met her."

"When we fled Larswick, it was her powers and the drekar of her kin, Sámr, Dragonheart's heir, that saved us. Our threads are joined."

"And now you will be home." I nodded. "That is good for Lars has missed you and he needs to get to know his father while he can."

I saw understanding in her eyes. "I will be spending all of my days at the shipyard."

"And I can be there until Ýrr is born for the crops are all in and I can spin and weave there just as easily as in the hall. I, too, need to see you as often as I can." She was becoming more like Gytha and seemed able to read my thoughts.

Everyone in the clan was busy. We had used all of the salt and we needed to make more. Already salt pans were being prepared. One advantage of living by the sea was that salt was easy to produce. The bones of the animals had to be cleaned and sorted before they were used as tools. After we had taken the longer hair from them then the hides would be tanned before use. The meat was sorted, and while some was cooked for a feast, most was stored in our storehouses. At the same time, men fished and we still collected late berries and greens. I had asked for one of the white-tailed deer hides for myself as I wished a new pair of boots. My sealskin ones had seen better days, and until we could travel north to hunt them again, I needed something to wear on my feet. Ada would make them for me.

We now had the glue. There was some pine tar we had made from the last of the small pines we had found and cleared when we first came to Bear Island, and we mixed them. We had to keep the glue hot. It was hard work and dangerous. Hot glue could burn and Bear Tooth proved to be invaluable for he had the eyes of a hawk and could spot when Lars was about to do something which might result in injury. It was painstaking work to attach the strakes. We had inverted the hull so that we could start at what would be the gunwale and work our way up to the keel. Each strake had to overlap the others in exactly the same way. We used a mixture of hair and glue to do so. I had Ada cut some of my own hair to be used with the animal hair. It was always good to have something of the shipbuilder in the heart of the drekar. There was already blood from the time we had carved the keel and fitted the wooden pegs. Each trenail and peg was soaked in the glue before we hammered them home and after the tops had been smoothed, we added a coat of pine resin. If we fitted four strakes in a day then that was a good day.

My daughter, Ýrr, was born and she came into the world screaming and red-faced but, amazingly, when Gytha picked her from Ada's breast and gave her to me, she stopped. I put my mouth close to her ear, "I may not always be here in body, Ýrr, my daughter, but I will always be in your heart and head. When you sleep, I will be there and I will watch over you, wherever you are and whatever you do." She closed her eyes and she slept. I saw Gytha smile. I kissed the babe and then handed her back to Ada.

Ada and Gytha looked at each other. Ada nodded and said, "It is *wyrd* and I am content." The four volvas spent many hours with each other and I knew they had no secrets from each other. They had, however, many secrets they kept from us!

The days grew shorter as the winter solstice approached. Gytha left her bed and, although much thinner and looking gaunt, she showed herself to the clan. She spent part of each day at the drekar which we would name in her honour. She cut a hank of her thin grey hair and we put that in with the glue so that part of our vǫlva was in the heart of the drekar. I knew that we were doing all that we could to make a powerful drekar. Her visits helped us to work better and soon the hull began to look like a drekar as the strakes grew and filled the sides.

The longer nights meant I could not work in the yard as much and I spent more time at home with Lars and Ýrr. My daughter spent half the day sleeping and the other half screaming but Lars was growing and could now hold conversations. I began to talk to him about sailing. Fótr would be the one who would teach him but I could impart my knowledge now while his mind was receptive. Those were the good times as we stayed within our turf lined walls and listened to the winter storms rage outside. We ate well and we laughed. Ebbe and Bear Tooth got on well and Bear Tooth fitted in well with the young men of the clan. It was after we had celebrated the shortest day with a feast that the last strake was hammered home. Ebbe and the younger shipbuilders were all keen to turn her over. "No, we have to seal her and we do not have enough pine tar. There are pines on Horse Deer Island and although this is the wrong time of year to do so, soon we will take the snekke and we will collect some. We will be away for one night."

We waited for almost half a month as the weather was too rough for the short voyage we would make. When we went, I took just Ebbe, Lars and Bear Tooth. Fótr would have come but he knew how to collect pine tar and he needed to be with his family for Reginleif was with child again.

We would be away for one night and we took furs, I had had three bjorr fur given to me by Arne and Ada had sewn them into one fur which would be perfect for Lars to use as his bed. We had food and we took our bows in case we needed to hunt. The Skraeling had not returned to the island since they had slaughtered the horse deer and we had seen no fires. Nonetheless, I would be wary. We had clay pots we had made from some clay we had found on the island to collect the pine tar. I wore my new deerskin boots which Ada had made for me. They were not waterproof but they were tough and comfortable. They would do until I could hunt the seal once more.

We landed on a small beach close to a good stand of pines. This would be easier than in the land of ice and fire when we had been forced to climb up a small mountain. Here we could work on the beach. It was cold but not as cold as in the land of ice and fire. We even had a flurry of sleet and snow as we sailed across to the island but it appeared not to lay and we would not suffer. While I lit the fire, using dried kindling we had brought, Ebbe and Bear Tooth set up our camp, by hollowing out some soil to give us protection from the wind. They then set about collecting stones. We would need quite a few and while Lars found the smaller stones which were little larger than pebbles, the other two found the largest rocks that they could manage.

When the fire was going and we had some water boiling, I took the wood axe and headed for the pines. I chose a smallish pine tree and cut it down. The wood would not be wasted for it would be towed back to Bear Island and used on the drekar. Then the three of us began to dig the roots and the stump from the ground. If this had been the mainland it might have been impossible for the ground would be frozen. Here on the island, the sea made the ground slightly warmer. Lars helped by clearing away the debris. The water behind us was bubbling by the time the roots were all exposed and we put some dried meat in to cook. While it cooked, I chopped the pine root up into the smallest pieces I could. It took some time and the food was cooked by the time we had cut half of the stump and some of the roots. I set the others to add to our rock collection while I cut down a second pine. We were lucky. The island had many rocks and while they were not as hard as those on the land of ice and fire, they would do. I laid down the second pine and began to hack at the roots.

"We have the rocks, foster father."

"Good, now I will show you how to make a kiln." I began to make the kiln. I piled the rocks around the fire. I packed soil and sand in the gaps as I did so. "Collect the pine cones for they will get the fire hotter more quickly."

When the kiln wall was high enough, I resumed clearing the soil from the second pine. I stopped when the others returned, and we put the pine cones in the bottom of the kiln and added kindling. There was a small gap at the bottom and I dug a channel to the barrel which lay in the shallows and lined the channel with an old piece of leather. I used flames from our fire to start the new fire. When the fire took hold, we put the stump and roots on the top and then covered the top of the kiln with the larger, fatter, flatter stones. I used more soil and sand and then we added a second layer of stones. That done, we began work on the second pine. This time was easier for the others knew what they were doing and we soon had the second kiln finished and fired. This time the channel we dug led to the first channel. I had learned much when we had made our first pine tar in the land of ice and fire. It would take the rest of the day and the night for the wood to be burned and the tar to be released. As the tar was made, it would trickle down the leather-lined channel and settle in the bottom of the barrel. Finally, we laid the two pine trunks next to the kilns to make a windbreak.

"Now we eat for I could eat a whole horse deer, with the skin on!"

That made them laugh. We had worked hard and the boys had managed to get a sweat on. Now they would get colder and I made Lars drape his bjorr fur around his back. We ate and all felt much better. After washing it down with ale, I decided that we would strip the lower branches from the pine trees. We could burn the wood and it would be easier to tow them back to Bear Island. That done, I made the decision to see what animals now lived on the island. I let Bear Tooth lead for he was of this land. Ebbe brought up the rear and Lars walked between Ebbe and me. All of us wore thick hide vests and had hats made from the fur of the long-eared animals. They were warmer than any hat I had ever owned. I also wore my sealskin cloak. Ebbe and Lars wore two old ones. We needed a seal hunt so that we could make new ones.

Bear Tooth did not know the island well but he recognised the trail made by his people and he followed one up the slope and into the woods. I knew that there had to be water on the island for the horse deer had needed it to survive. I had never found it but Bear Tooth led us unerringly to it. It was less than five hundred paces from our beach. I realised why I had not seen it. When we had landed, it had been on the opposite side of the island. Bear Tooth knelt down. The flurries of snow were falling thicker and it was fortunate that we had come when we did. He put his hand down to some tracks, "White-tailed deer." He nodded and stood. "When the horse deer were here the white-tailed deer shunned it. See, all around are tracks. They have come to take it over."

Ebbe asked, "How did they get here?"

"Deer can swim and the two swims they would need to make from the mainland are not far."

I stored that information. Looking up at the skies, I saw that it was getting dark early. "Come, we will go back and prepare for a cold and wet night."

After checking that the tar was flowing into the barrel, I fetched an old tattered piece of snekke sail we used on the boat and laid it over the channels. It would not do to have the pine tar polluted with snow. We then took down the sail from the snekke and, after fashioning some supports from the oars, made ourselves a sleeping area. I had the boys lay stones and sand over one end and faced the open end towards the nearby fires. There would be constant heat. We had brought bread and I poured the stew into their bowls and divided the bread evenly. By the time darkness fell, we had eaten and were satisfied. Ebbe brought forth a treat packed in leaves. He handed us one each. They were his mother's honey and oatcakes. It was a treat made all the more delicious by the unexpected nature of it.

After making water and checking the pine tar, the four of us lay down beneath the bjorr fur and the bear fur. Lars was exhausted, for he was young, and he soon fell asleep. The other two were not ready yet for sleep and they talked.

"Foster father, what does the future hold?"

I laughed but clutched at my hammer of Thor as I did so, "Am I a volva or Verðandi that I can tell the future?"

"I mean our family for what you do will affect what happens to us."

"We will stay on Bear Island. How long the clan will live here I know not. The jarl has a plan to bring settlers over and make us strong. I am not sure that will work. What I know is that when half of the clan leave and return east then the ones who remain will be weaker because we are fewer. Lars and the other children will grow and become warriors but we need blood from outside." I took a breath. "Perhaps, Bear Tooth, your arrival and membership of the clan might be a hint of our future. Perhaps you might take a Norse bride and your children would be the first to be born to a clan which was changing."

"I am a slave. How can I be a father?"

"You are not a slave."

"Then I can leave the island any time I like?"

The Savage Wilderness

That was a hard question to answer and showed me how clever Bear Tooth was. I was not sure that Arne would approve but I gave Bear Tooth an honest answer for he deserved one. "If you wish to leave then, when we return to Bear Island, I will tell Arne and Gytha that you wish to leave and I will sail you back to the mainland."

There was silence and then Bear Tooth broke the silence, "I thought I was a slave. Now that I know I am not then I do not wish to leave. I like the clan and I like your people. There is nothing left for me amongst the Mi'kmaq. And now I can answer your question. If I am not a slave then when it is time, I may choose a woman and father a child!"

Ebbe laughed, "Then you do not know Norse women, Bear Tooth. They know their own minds and they will only take a man if they like him, but do not worry. I know that many of the girls like you."

"Good, for I like some of them."

This was *wyrd*. The Norns had spun the threads and made a knot which would take some cataclysmic event to break.

The snow flurry became a snowfall which became a storm. It was fortunate that I had put the barrel in the sea for it kept the temperature of the tar higher than it would otherwise have been. We were as warm as could be beneath the sail and the furs. I woke first and I slipped out from beneath the warmth and comfort and stepped into an icy, white world. The snow had stopped but it had draped everything with white. The pinewood had all burned and released its tar but the last had settled on the leather. I would take it back with us and see if we could recover it. The fire we had used to cook our food had almost gone out despite the fact that, when I had made water in the middle of the night, I had added more firewood. I rekindled it and watched the flames rise. I would add fresh water to the remains of the stew and it would give us some sustenance. We would eat better when we reached Bear Island. I knew that Ada would be fretting about us and, having seen the snow, would have a large meal waiting for us.

"It is time to wake! Bear Tooth, Ebbe, fix the sail to the yard. Lars, go and make water and collect your fur."

I folded the bear fur and placed it in the snekke and then helped Ebbe and Bear Tooth shake off the snow and then carry the sail to the snekke. Once we had attached it to the yard, they had the task of fixing the sheets and stays. I used the water to move the barrel of pine tar to the snekke. Lifting it proved harder than I had expected and that was a sign that it was full. I was pleased.

"Ebbe, Bear Tooth, the food will be ready. When the three of you have eaten then we will sail home." While they ate, I dragged the two pine trunks to the water and attached them to the prow. I tied them on either side of the snekke. I had never towed that way but we did not have far to travel. I used some stale bread to clean out the pot we had used for cooking and then rinsed it in the sea. The fire would burn itself out and I left it.

"Let us get aboard. Lars, sit by the prow and watch the two lines we use to tow the pine. Ebbe and Bear Tooth, you are in for a wetting. You must push us off and then clamber aboard."

"Aye, Captain!"

I pushed the snekke away from the snow-covered sand and hauled myself aboard. Already the wind, which was from the west, was pushing us a little and it did not take much effort from the crew to get us going and then they jumped on board. The snekke did not mind the two pine outriggers and we skated across the icy water to Bear Island. As we turned into the bay, just before noon, I saw that the new drekar was covered in snow. No-one had thought to protect it from the storm. We would lose a day, at least, of work when we need not have. After two good days with Lars, Bear Tooth and Ebbe, it was disappointing.

As I had expected there was a good meal awaiting us and I smiled as I saw Ada examine our son for any injury. She was a mother and you could not change that. Lars was full of the adventure and he barely took a breath as he ate and told his mother what we had done. I realised it was the first time he had slept away from his mother. I should have known that and been aware that he might be afraid. Perhaps I did the right thing without knowing it.

The next day was spent clearing the snow from the shipyard and storing the pine tar somewhere warm. We put the pine logs in the dry. They would be slower to season but it was useful to have them. No-one bothered to come to speak to me, neither Arne nor Siggi. I had not expected Gytha and her husband to venture forth and when we had finished work for the day, I went to see them. I did not need to say a word for Gytha had either read my mind or the situation. She addressed the issue of the snow-covered drekar.

"They see the drekar as your responsibility and it is something they will not worry about. Take that as a compliment for they think, nay they know, that you will do a good job. They should have cleared the snow but even if they had, you would have managed little work today, would you?" I shook my head. "It is just that you feel you are used by the clan and that is true." She shrugged, "Accept it as I do. The clan, with a few exceptions, only speak to my husband and me when they need something from us. You are the only one who visits us because you enjoy speaking to us. Do not let it worry you."

Snorri coughed and I worried that he too had an illness. He smiled when he saw the concern on my face. "A winter cough is all this is. "I have almost finished the figurehead. When you have coated the hull, it will be ready." I nodded and my beaming face made him smile. "What did you find on the island?"

I said, "That the white-tailed deer have now taken over from the horse deer. Is that not strange?"

Gytha answered me, "It is nature, Erik, and I think we have more in common with these Skraelings than some people think. Like us, they do not build in stone and when we are gone, all that will remain will be our spirits wandering the land for the trees, bushes and grass will reclaim our farms and our land. Our bones will feed the worms. It is as the Allfather intended."

I spent an hour with them before I returned to my home. I had much to ponder.

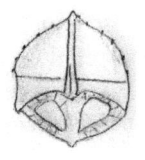

Chapter 11

I rigged the sail from *'Njörðr'* as an awning so that we could work without interference from the elements. We set to work, after heating the pine tar, and coating the strakes and the keel. We would do it once more before we inverted her and coated the insides. We let it dry and we split the two pine trees. They would season. The other pine trees had already been split and now we further split them to make the decks. This was a crucial stage for a mistake undid hard work and I did not want that. It took many days and we then coated the hull with the second coat of pine tar. We spent more days working on the sternpost. It would be ornately decorated but I needed to see the prow first.

I called upon the whole clan to turn the drekar. It was not ready for the water yet but it looked like a drekar and when it was turned the right side up, the whole clan cheered. The cheers became ecstatic when Snorri unveiled the prow. He had cleverly used many of Gytha's features and incorporated them into a dragon. It was beautiful.

"Of course, it needs paint but you can do that." Snorri was a modest man but I knew that he had put his heart and soul into the carving and when he was in the Otherworld, his wife would sail the seas. It was typical of the man I was proud to call uncle.

Once all had gone, I could begin to carve the sternpost to match the prow. Since we had returned from Horse Deer Island, I had spent more time at the shipyard. I wanted the sternpost to do justice to the work which Snorri had completed. Before I began work on the sternpost, I marked out the hole we would need in the keel to fit the prow. "Fótr, you and Ebbe can make the hole for the figurehead. Take your time and be as careful as you can."

"Am I ready for this?"

"This will be the drekar you sail east and you should know every piece of her. When I have finished the sternpost then you will be able to fit that too. Building a ship means you have to use your hands and your mind as well as your eyes."

He nodded. Bear Tooth said, "What if he makes a mistake?"

"Then the ship will be ruined and Snorri will have to make another. It will not be as good and it will add to the time it takes to build the drekar but it could happen." I saw his eyes go to Fótr who was still examining the keel.

Fótr smiled, "Do not worry, Bear Tooth, this work I do is tricky and I will stop frequently and watch my brother's progress."

In truth, I needed to reference the prow to copy the symmetrical diagonal lines which Snorri had carved. They looked simple but he had made them identical and replicating the symmetry was not easy. By the end of the day, neither of us had finished or even come close to the end of the work. Walking back to our homes, Fótr said, "It is a great deal of work we have taken on, brother, and, for you, it is wasted work. You will stay here and the drekar will belong to another."

"I know but it is for the clan and Ada, Lars and Ebbe may well be aboard her when she sails."

Ebbe said, "My mother will not go for she has you and Lars as well as my sister, Ýrr!"

"And you have a sister, Egilleif. What if she marries and the man she chooses takes her east? What then? Your mother would be torn. What if you choose a girl for yours and she has a family who wishes to go east? This decision, made by the Thing, is a complicated one. The clan will be split and divided as will their loyalties. When we left the land of ice and fire it was an easy decision. People either headed east or west for none wished to stay in the land of ice and fire. This is different. There are families who genuinely wish to stay. I make the ship as best I can for it is for the clan and I wish all of the clan to survive and to prosper. That is why I put so much effort into making this the finest of drekar."

Ebbe was thoughtful as we ate but he had listened to my words, "Foster father, the hull we have built does not look identical to *'Njörðr'*, why is that?"

"You have a good eye and a sharp mind. That is because it will not be a true drekar. It will have some of the qualities of a knarr. *'Gytha'* will be broader in the beam than *'Njörðr'* and will be slightly deeper. She will be fast but not as fast as the hunter that is *'Njörðr'*. She will be longer. When we built *'Njörðr'*, we did not have the wood we have here. The Allfather guided us to a mighty tree and that determined the length. *'Gytha'* will need to carry people rather than to fight." I drank some of the new ale which Ada had brewed. It was good. "The new ship will also handle the mighty ocean better. When the whale almost pulled *'Njörðr'* beneath the waves, I saw then that the very qualities which made her a good hunter, her narrow hull and sharp bow, also made her vulnerable. When I began this new ship, I thought of her purpose. When she is in Larswick, if Fótr wishes to raid with her, he can do so, but she will not be as good as *'Njörðr'*."

By Þorri, the sternpost and the prow were finished. We had fitted both and I was satisfied, but we removed the figurehead. That would be the last thing to be fitted before she was launched. It was then that the work slowed for everyone worked in their fields to till, fertilise and to sow their land. It was just Bear Tooth, Lars and I who worked on the drekar. We worked on the steering board for that did not require numbers of workers but it did need skill. It was slow work but rewarding for, beneath my fingers, I felt the drekar come to life and I was happy. It was while the clan was working their fields that Mikel cast his eye upon Egilleif and she returned his gaze. Ada told me as we lay together. Ýrr had finally drifted off to sleep.

"Mikel and my daughter saw each other today. She is ready to be a woman."

"Mikel is a good man. I am surprised he has not married before."

"He did not see a woman he liked before now. The winter has seen my daughter bloom and blossom."

I knew why she mentioned this to me. I was her foster father and had to give my approval. I had a responsibility and I would not ignore it. "Mikel is close to Arne and that means he would stay here on Bear Island and in the new world. The Thing will be held at Einmánuður. That is two moons away. I will speak with Mikel. When you work the fields tomorrow, ask him to come and speak with me."

The Savage Wilderness

As I lay in the dark, I realised that I was changing. I wished the clan to stay here but I would not use my position as The Navigator to do so. I wanted Egilleif married before the Thing for that would be more people who might vote to stay. It was no longer just the maid and the waterfall which held me. I was now close to Bear Tooth and that was strange for when we met, we had tried to hurt each other and yet I now saw the Allfather's hand and the Norns' threads in all of this. Bear Tooth and his people were more like our clan than the Saxons and the Franks. Those people wished to have power and to impose order upon the land. Neither the Mi'kmaq nor our clan wanted that. We cleared just enough trees to grow crops and we left the rest. I knew that there were vast areas of Saxon land where every tree had been hewn down. I was meant to come here, to this new world, and my work here was not yet done.

Mikel was the son of Finnbjǫrn. His mother and father had returned to the east on the knarr when we had left the land of ice and fire. Part of the reason he had come was that Arne had saved his life in the battle with the men on the land of ice and fire. Such matters were important to a Viking; more important than family. I wondered if the wound he had received at the bjorr dam had made him realise that life was moving along and he should sire a child. I would look into his eyes and his heart when I spoke with him.

We had just begun work on the decking when he came. "How is the wound now, Mikel Finnbjǫrnsson?"

"It does not bother me but, I confess, that it made me wonder if I was meant to die in this land."

"And that is why you wish to marry my foster daughter?"

He looked up guiltily and nodded, "That is part of the reason but, until I saw her again, after the winter, I did not know she was a woman grown. I knew her as a girl." I nodded and waited for him to continue. "I have a farm. There are two fields but we could clear another. Two fields produce all that I need and I have a goat for milk."

He was almost desperate in his attempts to persuade me that he could provide for Egilleif. I was not worried about clearing new fields. When half or more of the clan left then there would be many vacant fields.

"If my foster daughter agrees, then you may marry. If she does, it should be sooner rather than later. I know how young men are."

He looked relieved, "Do not worry, Erik the Navigator, she will agree for I have spoken with her and we are happy to be wed tomorrow if it could be arranged."

He had, of course, been wrong to speak to Egilleif without speaking to me first but I understood. "I will speak with Ada this evening but I need to speak to my foster daughter first. Bear Tooth, fetch Egilleif."

"Yes, Captain!"

He ran off and Mikel stood grinning. I gave him my sternest of looks, "Have you not fields to tend?"

"Aye, Erik the Navigator!" He hurtled off, almost tripping over some timber in his haste.

Fótr was laughing. I silenced him by saying, "As I recall, Fótr Larsson, it was not that long ago that you were the same with Reginleif."

My barb took the laughter from his voice. We resumed the decking. It was a fiddly task for we had to have two sections which could be removed to access the hold. Only the section around the mast fish and the very edge of the drekar would be permanent. We had completed the permanent section and were measuring the removable parts when he said, "The voyage east, you will not be making it with me but, of all of us, you know it best."

I nodded, "What do you need to know?"

"When you sailed back, you came to the land of ice and fire first. Should we do that?"

I shook my head, "I would not and there are two reasons. Firstly, you have to sail north more than you need to reach Larswick and both the seas and the weather are worse the further north you go. Secondly, the winds are from the west and south. If you sail due west it will be the shortest route and the quickest. Of course, you might have to risk the Isles of Syllingar and the witch who lives there but there is plenty of land to hit."

"And how long will it take, brother?"

The Savage Wilderness

I hammered a wooden peg into the hole I had drilled. It gave me time to think. "I would take provisions for two months but you can fish as you go, we did and there will be rain. Collect it."

"Two months!"

"It might well be less but tell your passengers and crew that it will take two months and they have less chance to be disappointed. Whatever length of time you say, they will expect to be there sooner. You will find people who do not like the storms the wild sea can throw at you and will swear they want to return here to Bear Island. It is in the nature of people but you will command the drekar!"

"There will be others aboard who will back me."

"Perhaps, but they are more likely to be those who dislike our brother and it may be that they feel the same about you. You cannot worry about that until you leave and that will not be for a long time if we do not get this ship finished."

"And how long for that?"

I laughed and shook my head, "Questions, always questions! We will have the whale hunt and then the Thing. It will be finished after that. It may be that some wish to leave after the harvest is gathered in, but I feel that will be too late for you would be sailing in the shortest days of the year. You are the captain."

"If you were the captain, what would you do?"

"Then I would travel as close to the longest day as I could. You have more chance of a sun sight and the weather will be as good as it is going to get."

"What if some wish to leave earlier than that?"

I shrugged, "That I cannot answer for it has troubled me too." The clan was not the same clan that had left Larswick.

Surprisingly, most of the men in the clan were happy to hunt the whale again. After we had lost Danr to the Skraeling, I thought that some would wish to stay close to their families until they could return home. I discovered that Arne had been clever. He had invited those who opposed him to be the hunters this time. It was a clever move for Arne and Siggi had killed a huge whale and those who wished to return to Larswick would wish to outdo him. It made no difference to me. I knew I still had the same job; sail the drekar.

Arne also wished to sail to the hunting grounds without camping on an island. He told me that the men could sleep while we sailed. Of course, that meant I would have to do without sleep but my clever brother had already thought of that. "This will be a good opportunity to see how Fótr can command the drekar. It will be just for one watch of eight hours and it can be during the day. Let us give our little brother a chance."

When I approached Fótr, he seemed quite happy to do so. "After all, I will only be risking the warriors and not our families. Besides, you will be there and I know that you sleep with one eye open. So long as Erik the Navigator is aboard then I am content."

Everyone seemed to believe in me and I felt the weight of responsibility upon my shoulders. I visited Gytha every couple of days. I said I was reporting on the progress of the ship but I just wanted to see how she was. Ada, Helga and Gefn saw her every day. She worsened each hour but not by as much as she had told us. Snorri told me that she was using potions and spells to fight the worm. While she was making water, he confided in me, "She wishes to be present at the Thing. She thinks she can persuade others to stay."

"Snorri, it is my dream and something within me which seeks to look west that keeps me here. I do not agree with those who desire treasure and gold for what do men spend it on? Things they do not need. We have all we need here but we made a bad start with the Skraeling."

He gave me a shrewd look, "You would have done things differently?"

I nodded, "I would have sailed the snekke up one of their rivers and approached the tribes peacefully. I know that they made the first attack but they are a primitive people. Bear Tooth has shown us that. Had I gone with just one or two others we might have spoken with them or communicated at least. When Bear Tooth first came here you used signs, did you not? I could have done that."

"And if they had attacked you?"

I smiled, "I would have used magic."

"Magic?"

"If I wore my mail beneath my tunic and my helmet on my head, I could have allowed them to stab at me with their weapons. The bone would have shattered. I could have made fire with my steel. I could have flourished my bear teeth!"

Gytha's voice came from behind me, "And you only know to do these things because of Bear Tooth. You cannot change the past by using the present. Even the Norns cannot do that. They sent Bear Tooth to us so that we could understand these people. It would be possible to do as you say now but it would take great courage and would need to be undertaken by the jarl. Arne will not do this. We need time here to grow and to understand the Skraeling. Snorri and I will not be here and it will be up to you and the three volvas." She put her thin hand, with the veins showing clearly through the translucent skin, on my hand, "You cannot seek this maid and the waterfall until we have an understanding with the Skraeling." She saw my face fall and smiled, "I read your mind and know that you are disappointed but you have a good woman and two children. A delay of a year or so will not hurt, will it?"

I shook my head for I could see that she was right but the Norns were spinning and others were making plans which would change our world forever.

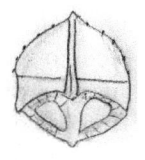

Chapter 12

We left the bay before dawn and I steered us clear of the islands and headed well out to sea. I had my map, as did Fótr who watched my every move. He was my brother and I explained to him what I would be doing.

"When we sailed the drekar on the last voyage, we sailed east and then northeast. That took time. We know where the behemoths will hunt and we will sail directly there. It will be easier for you when you steer for it is north by east. The Allfather has sent us the sun and we will use it. I will steer for an hour, watch you for an hour and then I will sleep. You can wake me when we sight the whale. Your sleep will come on the way home."

He nodded and laughed, "That seems like a fair trade!"

I know that I was a more sympathetic and gentler teacher than Ulf North Star had been but Fótr was my brother and, when he returned to Larswick, it was unlikely that I would ever see him again in this world.

As I had told Fótr, in the spring and summer the winds were, largely, from the west and it meant our men did not need to row. I let him watch me for an hour and we conferred about our position and then he sailed for an hour. He was slightly out with our position but not by much and when I had explained his error to him, I wrapped myself in my bear fur and slept. It was a dreamless sleep and a deep one. A drekar did that to me. Ebbe and Bear Tooth were close by and they would warn me of any danger before Fótr. I knew that he would try to impress me and would advise my brother when he should wake me. My two ship's boys were insurance for me.

In the end, they were not needed for Fótr had me woken when the herd of whales was spotted. This time there were more of them but they were a different type to the one we had hunted before. The whales were smaller but there were more of them and they appeared to move a little slower than the huge beast we had slain the first time. It took me a few moments to get accustomed to the sea and the wind, not to mention the speed and movement of the whales. While Fótr had the steering board, I cupped my hands and shouted, "Rowers to your oars! Spearmen to the prow!"

Arne might be jarl ashore but I was captain of this drekar and my word was law. I took the steering board and nodded to Fótr who went to the prow to help me steer. We had refined some signals for we did not want to waste effort. Fótr would signal when we needed the extra speed and only then would I begin to use the oars. It was a bright sunny day and the sea shone a deep and dark blue. The shiny black flesh of the whales was sprinkled with white foam as they dived and then rose to the surface. Fótr gave the signal and I shouted, "Let us sing the whale song and remember Danr!" It was the right thing to say and they sang and rowed with all of their might. We surged forward as though the drekar was alive.

Lars and Snorri had five fine heirs
They hunted enemies in all their lairs
Wolf or fish, dragon or bears
They could not be taken unawares
From Bear Island the five set sail
Hunting the monstrous big black whale
The whale that came from Ran's deep home
Rose like a monster through sea and foam.
The clan feared no black-skinned beast
On its flesh, the clan would feast
Njörðr flew like a hunting bird
Waiting for Ebbe to give the word
Lars and Snorri had five fine heirs
They hunted enemies in all their lairs
Wolf or fish, dragon or bears
They could not be taken unawares
Longer than a drekar and foiled with teeth
The whale was like a black-skinned reef
None was dismayed as the creatures rose

The Savage Wilderness

Arne and Siggi were the hunters chose
And two spears hung in mid-air
Waiting to strike at flesh laid bare
Arne hurt first and struck down fast
While Siggi's spear made a hole so vast
The beast it dived down to Ran's sea bed
Erik Navigator kept his head
As Njörðr fought her own hard battle
The whale rose and gave a deadly rattle
The clan had fought and the clan had won
Their great sea battle was over and won.
Lars and Snorri had five fine heirs
They hunted enemies in all their lairs
Wolf or fish, dragon or bears
They could not be taken unawares

I saw Kalman, one of the spearmen, say something to Fótr. They had identified their target and Fótr signalled me to move to steerboard. I did so gently and then Fótr held up both arms. We were on target and now it was a matter of time. We had reached the end of the song when Kalman hurled his whale spear and Ǫlmóðr copied him. The drekar surged forward as the whale dived and I shouted, "Raise oars and prepare to back water." I had thought about our first attack and decided that, when the whale dived, if we pulled back on the oars it would be harder for him to dive. We had helped him the last time by continuing to row. Fótr sent me the signal that the whale had dived and I shouted, "Back water!" This time the water which spilt over the prow was little more than we might expect in a storm and within a short time the whale had stopped and we had won. Two spears had killed our prey.

When we had hunted the first time, we had noticed that the whales floated. Kalman turned and shouted, "Let us take another!"

I shouted down the drekar, "The one we have will suffice."

Kalman shouted back, "Is this who makes decisions for us now, Jarl, a Navigator?"

Arne was seated not far from me and I saw his face. It was a mixture of anger and embarrassment, "We will try for one more if you wish, Kalman."

"I do! They have slowed and we need not row hard!"

Arne shouted, "Then let us row."

The ropes holding the whale spears were cut leaving the dead whale to drift. We now had just two whale spears left and Kalman and Qlmóðr would have to make a perfect strike. The oarsmen were tiring but Arne kept a steady beat. The fact that the men did not sing was ominous. Fótr signalled to me and he quickly raised his hands as Kalman was correct and the herd was slowing. This time it was Qlmóðr who made the first thrust and when the whale was hit it surged forward. I watched Kalman become a little unbalanced and he went to the prow to steady himself. He hurled his spear and I saw his right arm raised in exultation then something struck us a mighty blow at the bow. The oars became disrupted and I barely kept my feet. I watched Kalman pitch into the sea. The dying whale was still pulling us and unless I did something the drekar would crush Kalman.

"Back water!"

We were hit again and I feared for the rowers. I assumed it was a whale which was hitting us and if it continued to do so then there was a chance that oars might be shattered and our men hurt.

"Withdraw oars!"

Fótr shouted, "Sharks have taken Kalman! His body is being ripped to shreds before my eyes!" His voice carried along the shocked ship. In the silence of the drekar, everyone heard his words. This had been Kalman's choice and the Jarl's decision.

"Haul in the whale and we will return to the first, and this time, the captain of the drekar will be obeyed!" I saw Arne flash me a look of anger but I did not care. While at sea I commanded. I should have refused to obey my brother but that would have caused dissension. Instead, we had lost a warrior.

It was when we tied the two whales to our hull that we saw why we had been attacked. One was a very young whale. Its mother had attacked us to stop the hunt and that also explained why the herd had slowed. The mother and calf had been separated. The Norns had, indeed, been spinning. With the two animals secured to the drekar, we headed west to find land. Our plan to sail directly home was now put into disarray and we needed land and a camp. We had to be quick for the sharks, attracted to the hunt, were trying to bite chunks off our whales. The ship's boys were kept busy discouraging them and it was dark when we found a rocky island which offered us the chance to land and to butcher the animals.

This time we had come prepared and when we had tied up, half of the crew went ashore to light fires while the other half hauled the beasts ashore. The ship's boys and Fótr joined me and laid small pine branches over the deck to minimise the blood which would soak in to the decks. It had taken a great deal of work to clean them and it would take me away from shipbuilding.

We had just finished when Arne clambered up the sides. He said to the ship's boys, "Go ashore and help the men."

I was proud of my crew for they looked to me before obeying the jarl. It was a pivotal moment. I nodded, "Go, you have all done well."

They all left except for Fótr. Arne said, "Go too, little brother, I need words with Erik."

"I will stay." The division between my brothers resurfaced.

Arne turned angrily, "Are you two both against me? Obey me, Fótr, or I will hurl you over the side!"

"Fótr, do as Arne says for I would not like to spill the blood of the jarl!" I saw the anger on Arne's face.

Fótr's face, too, was infused with anger but he nodded and left. As I heard him splash into the shallows, I said, "This was not well done, brother."

He was still angry and I made certain that my hand was nowhere near the dagger in my belt. I walked to my chest and sat down. I would allow Arne to have the opportunity to be above me and to chastise me.

"What was not well done was to tell the jarl that he had to obey another."

I shook my head, "The captain of *'Njörðr'* told his crew to obey him. That is the way we do things, is it not? Or perhaps you would change it? If so then bring it up at the Thing we will soon hold and the clan can decide."

"So, you join those who are against me? Freja is right, there are few that I can trust in the clan!"

"Arne, I swore an oath with you and Siggi over Karl the Lame's body, as I held King Raedwulf's dagger. I will not break an oath and if you think so then your mind has been poisoned."

His hand went to his sword, "Do not disparage the wife of the jarl."

"Listen to yourself, Arne. I tell you what, when we return to Bear Island let us speak with Gytha and Snorri. They can settle this for I have done nothing wrong but I will not fight you. I see you wish me to draw a blade so that you can punish me and I will not give you the satisfaction. If you wish then slay me and then who will be the navigator?!"

He sneered, "Allow Gytha to arbitrate? You are her little pet, brother. She thinks to set your woman and her daughter above the wife of the jarl. I will heed your advice and I will put it to the Thing that the jarl's word and decisions are not to be questioned!"

With that, he went ashore. Fótr and my ship's boys returned a little while later with some freshly cooked whale meat from the calf. I was not hungry but I thanked them anyway and ate. Fótr must have spoken to them ashore for they all went to the prow to allow Fótr to speak with me. I knew this was a mistake for Arne would be ashore and seeing plots and conspiracies in our meeting on the drekar. That could not be helped.

"What did he say? His face looked as though he was ready to fight an army!"

I told him all for Fótr was my brother and he was the next navigator. He shook his head, "Freja has changed him."

"Perhaps, or it may be that this is the work of the Norns. I can see that the next Thing will decide much of our future and I can see now why Gytha is so determined to stay alive and to speak at it. The new drekar becomes ever more crucial. When we return to Bear Island, we will spend every waking hour to finish her. The future of the clan depends upon it."

The next day, after butchering the animals, we loaded the drekar and headed home. It was not a happy drekar. Kalman's death and the obvious rift between Arne and us meant there was neither singing nor banter. The hunt had been successful but it had cast a cloud over the warriors. I saw Siggi casting glances over at me. If Arne had spoken of Gytha, Siggi's mother, to Siggi the way he had to me then there might be another row developing there. Why had we left Larswick? When we had been there, we had had a home we could defend and we had allies around us. I stared east as we sailed.

Gytha's voice came into my head, '*This was meant to be, Erik the Navigator! This is wyrd and you must not doubt yourself.*'

I knew not how Gytha communicated with me but I clearly heard her words. She was the one who spoke with the spirits and best understood the Norns. I would have to trust her for my brother and I were no longer of one mind.

Kalman had a wife and two children. Qlmóðr Ragnarsson was his friend and he became a foster father to his children and protector to his widow. As we unloaded the drekar, he went to speak with Marta to tell her of her loss. As he was first ashore and the word of the death quickly spread, so a pall fell upon what should have been a time of celebration. Neither Gytha nor Snorri were there and, more alarmingly nor were Ada, Gefn and Helga.

Once we had tied up and while the whale meat was being carried ashore, I went to Gytha's hall. The three volvas were all there, as was Snorri. Gytha looked pale, almost translucent and I feared that she was dead. She opened her eyes and smiled, "No, Erik the Navigator, I am not yet in the Otherworld although I came close. My three acolytes saved me although I know it took all of their power to do so. I will recover in time for the Thing but after that..." she closed her eyes, "It is in the hands of the Allfather!"

Snorri said, "I thank you, the volvas of the clan, for you have saved my wife now I bid you leave us alone. Your families will need you and there will be much to say. I counsel you to choose words wisely. Our jarl teeters on the edge of madness. Let us not drive him over."

It was then I remembered all the times we had gone into battle. I had seen the joy of battle in Arne's eyes and often I had seen a little of the berserker there. What if that seed had grown and taken over my brother? What if Loki had taken Arne for one of his own? The clan was in great danger.

The Savage Wilderness

I spoke not to the others, and Ada and I hurried to our home where we spoke. I learned that Gytha had dreamed of the danger and summoned the three volvas to help her communicate with me. They had all seen the argument and it had been the power of the four of them which had allowed Gytha to speak with me.

As much as I wished to stay and speak further with Ada, I knew my place was on the drekar. I hurried back as the last of the whale bones and the meat was taken ashore. The pine branches had saved some of the deck but we would still have much work to do. We landed the pine branches which would dry out for kindling and then hauled buckets of sand and seawater up. I had five ship's boys and Bear Tooth. We began at the prow and the seven of us scrubbed and sluiced our way to the steering board. It was hard work but the deck, when we had finished, was cleansed.

I stood, "You have all done well on this voyage but we have more work to complete tomorrow. We must step the mast and then raise the deck so that the hull can dry out and I can examine *'Njörðr'* for damage."

Although the whale had only hit the side of the drekar and not the bow or stern, it was still possible that the strakes might have been sprung. We still had pine tar and horse deer glue; this would be a good time to repair the drekar and then I could return to work on the new one. By the time we had held the Thing, it would be time for our sea trials; that would be a test of my skills. We would have to sail her to Deer Island and back. If that was successful then we would sail into open waters and return. Only then would I hand her over to Fótr. Then **'Gytha'** would be his drekar.

It was dark when Ebbe, Bear Tooth and I headed to my hall. We passed the salted whale meat which had been cut into usable pieces. Four women stirred the blubber which would be rendered down for oil. By the morning there would be crispy pieces of whale crackling for us to enjoy; a rare treat.

We had to pass Arne's hall before we reached mine and he stepped from the shadows, "Brother, a word. Ebbe and Bear Tooth, tell Ada that my brother will be along shortly."

Both Ebbe and Bear Tooth looked to me for approval before obeying. I nodded and they left. I could see that Arne was not pleased with their reaction. "The jarl should be obeyed instantly and this is not right, Erik. Do you wish to be the jarl of the Clan of the Fox?"

I sighed and shook my head, "In your heart you know I do not and I have never done anything to undermine you."

"Yet you countermanded my command and sided with Fótr."

"Fótr? Do you mean our brother? Listen to yourself, Arne. We come from the same mother and father. Their spirits watch over the three of us. Do you think they would approve of the way you threatened Fótr?"

His eyes narrowed, "Now you invoke the spirits of our dead parents to chastise me too?"

"No, but I would have you rid yourself of these fears that others wish to take over the clan for none do. The voices which were against you at the Thing did not wish to usurp you but they wanted to return to the east. I can understand that. You have changed, Arne, for you happily let those who wished to return to Larswick leave in the knarr from the land of ice and fire. Yet here you see it as a threat to your authority. It is not and I have made them a drekar so that they can return across the seas."

"But they are members of the Clan of the Fox and they should stay with the clan!"

I said, quietly, "The reason we left our home in the east was because we wanted the freedom of making our own choices without worrying about a king telling us we could not."

I saw realisation in his eyes. Arne was not a stupid man but he always acted and spoke quickly, almost rashly. Sometimes that was necessary but this was not a time for rash decisions. He nodded, "We have time before the Thing to reflect on our words and our decisions. All I ask is that you do not argue with me in public."

I smiled, "Then that is easy, ask and do not command. Ask implies I have a choice and can give my opinion. Command suggests that I am your inferior."

I saw that he was about to say that I was and thought better of it. He nodded and said, "I will choose my words carefully then." He held out his right arm, "All is good between us."

I clasped it and nodded, "All is good."

I meant it and, I think, so did Arne but the Norns were spinning and the web was becoming more complicated with each passing day.

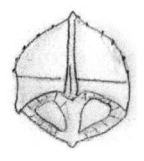

Chapter 13

It took a week to ready the drekar for the sea trials. Gytha had improved enough to come to the shipyard to see her figurehead fitted and the crew aboard for the first sea trial; she was also there to give her blessing. Gefn, Helga and Ada stood close by so that the four of them could spin their spell which would protect the drekar when she sailed the seas. Arne, pointedly, remained in his hall with his wife and sons and daughter. Perhaps he thought to allow Fótr and me the opportunity to command without his presence or it may have been he wished to distance himself from the new ship and its purpose, to return east. It was as the crew took to their oars that I realised he had done little to help us build the drekar. He had helped to fetch the wood but there was not a drop of his sweat on the deck. I wondered at that. Siggi took the leading oar and I was pleased that nothing had changed between my cousin and me. I dare say he did not like the conflict between us but he would never side with one over the other. Æimundr Loud Voice took the other oar and I was content.

I turned to Fótr and said, "Let us fit the figurehead together."

The prow of the drekar looked almost disfigured without a figurehead. The one carved by Snorri and painted by Fótr, the ship's boys and me, lay waiting to be fitted into the smoothed slot. I waved the ship's boys with us and we went to the prow. Those waiting on the shore were silent as they watched this most powerful of events. Until the figurehead was fitted, this was just a ship. When it was attached, it would become a drekar, a dragonship. It would be a shark of the sea and become a living thing. I handed the hammer to Ebbe and the peg to Bear Tooth. They had both sweated and bled in the making of this ship. Bear Tooth and Lars' weather vane stood on the masthead as a symbol of that effort.

Fótr and I took the weight of the figurehead but the other ship's boys, led by Stig, supported it, too, for they wanted their hands to touch the magical figure. We knew that it would fit but this final fitting had to be without mistakes or the ship would be cursed. We lifted it carefully, as though it was a wounded warrior or a new-born babe. It slid into the hole perfectly as we knew it would. There was just enough resistance for us to have to force it down.

Ebbe said, "Clear!" once he saw daylight through the hole. He put the peg in and Bear Tooth hammered it through. Once it was through, Ebbe took a second peg and Bear Tooth secured the first peg in place. As Fótr and I stepped back, those on the side cheered and I saw Gytha give a wave of approval.

As we headed back to the steering board, I said, "Ship's boys prepare to free us from the land. Bear Tooth, you can have the honour of climbing the mast and becoming the lookout." Poor Lars had been desperately upset that he would not be allowed to participate in the trial, and allowing Bear Tooth the honour of being the first up the mast was my way of assuaging his hurt for Lars was close to Bear Tooth. "Fótr, I will steer us to Deer Island and, when we have sailed around it, you can have the helm and take her out to sea. This is your drekar now but she needs to speak to me before I give her to you."

He smiled, "Brother, you and I are as one. Fear not that you will upset me for I know you are not Arne. This is good."

I nodded, "Cast off! Let fly the sail!" The sail was made from deer hide. It was a tough and hardy material but until the drekar returned to the lands in the east and a more functional sail was added, then **'Gytha'** would never sail as fast as she ought to. Speed was not necessary for the voyage east and so we were content. On the sail, we had painted a red fox and I heard the gasp from those watching as the wind caught it and it billowed. It was a good sign.

I nodded to Siggi who said, "Clan of the Fox, row!" He and Æimundr Loud Voice pulled on their oars and like waves rippling along the shore, each pair behind copied them. It made for a gentle, almost regal departure and we sailed slowly from the bay. As I turned to head north, the wind, which came from the west, caught us and I said, "Stop oars!" Every oar was raised and run in. The rowers would not leave their benches for this was a sea trial and before we headed to the open sea, we would test the dragonship as much as we could.

This first voyage was important and I closed my mind to everything but the ship and how it moved. It was wider and longer than *'Njörðr'* and that affected the way it sailed; it was slower to turn but there was less risk of water coming over the freeboard and that would be important when it transported animals and families east. There were no large waves in the sheltered bay but it cut through the ones we found rather than riding over them as *'Njörðr'* did. I knew she would not be as fast but she was faster than I had expected. The first real test I gave her was when I sailed through the narrow channel between Deer Island and Little Deer Island. I had sailed the snekke there and knew that the channel was deep enough, wide enough, and I had the necessary skill to navigate, but I realised that Fótr was worried when he saw that there were rocks an oar's length away. It was why I had not asked him to sail this course. I was testing **'Gytha's'** limits. She handled the turn well and we sped through the gap as the full force of the wind caught us and I felt the drekar surge like a fine stallion. Satisfied with her handling abilities in tight situations, I headed out beyond the islands. Bear Tooth's weather vane told me that the wind was behind us and **'Gytha'** seemed eager to show us what she could do.

With open water before us, I was almost ready to hand over to Fótr but I kept hold of the steering board for just a little while longer. I moved the steering board a marginally small fraction to larboard, I doubted that any of those aboard would have known I had made a movement but I felt the extra speed the move generated.

I did not turn as I spoke; a good captain kept his eyes on the sea and the course he was navigating, "Fótr, this drekar is very responsive. It will take you time to learn how to get the most out of her but she is a good ship. Take her now for the shipbuilder hands her over to her new captain. May the Allfather watch over you."

I waited until he had the steering board in his hand before I stepped to the side. I saw the nods of approval from Siggi and the senior warriors. It had been well done.

The Savage Wilderness

Fótr said, "I am honoured, Erik, that you have put so much into this ship and I swear that I will try to live up to the high standards which you have set." He raised his voice, "Clan of the Fox, I am young to be a navigator but so was my brother and there is no greater navigator than Erik. Let us see what **'Gytha'** will do. We will sail east for an hour and then turn to head home. It will mean the rowers will have the opportunity to get to know this fine lady who will carry the hopes of the clan in the future."

I stood aside to watch Fótr and to feel the ship. She was a deep-water vessel for unlike **'Njörðr'** she was not as affected by the larger swells which came in from the east. True, we did not have to endure the huge troughs and crest we had experienced heading west but I was confident that she would handle them well. When we had to row for the last few miles, the rowers found the experience easier than on **'Njörðr'**. Much of that was down to my design and that had been determined by the wood we had used. It was *wyrd*.

Fótr showed how much he had grown for he chose a chant to make the crew and ship one. He picked the Clan of the Fox chant and that was good for it honoured our father.

The Clan of the Fox has no king
We will not bow nor kiss a ring
We fled our home to start anew
We are strong in heart though we are few

Lars the jarl fears no foe
He sailed the ship from Finehair's woe
Drekar came to end our quest
Erik the Navigator proved the best
When Danes appeared to thwart our start
The Clan of the Fox showed their heart
While we healed the sad and the sick
We built our home, Larswick

The Clan of the Fox has no king
We will not bow nor kiss a ring
We fled our home to start anew
We are strong in heart though we are few

The Savage Wilderness

When Halfdan came with warriors armed
The Clan of the Fox was not alarmed
We had our jarl, a mighty man
But the Norns they spun they had a plan
When the jarl slew Halfdan the Dane
His last few blows caused great pain
With heart and arm, he raised his hand
'The Clan of the Fox is a mighty band!'

The Clan of the Fox has no king
We will not bow nor kiss a ring
We fled our home to start anew
We are strong in heart though we are few

It was the first time I had heard the words when I was not steering and I seemed to hear them for the first time. They brought a lump to my throat.

As we sailed into the bay and moored next to '*Njörðr*', I knew that this was the end of one era and the start of another. We now had two drekar and that gave the clan choices. When we held the Thing, warriors could speak their true feelings and I wondered how that most crucial of gatherings would go.

Snorri was interested in how the ship sailed and I went to speak to him when we landed. I let Fótr and the ship's boys attend to its mooring. It was no longer my ship. Gytha tried to rise but I waved her to her bed and I sat on the chair next to the bed as Snorri questioned me, "Well, nephew, how does our drekar sail?"

"She will make a better trader than a warship, uncle, but, having said that, she will be able to hold her own against any ship which tries to take her. For what we intend, I would say she is perfect. The passengers will be more comfortable on the voyage east and she will ride the storms and huge seas easier."

He looked pleased. He would never sail east and would not travel on her but he had been instrumental in her construction. I had consulted him each day. It had been mainly to confirm that what I did was right but at others, he had gently pointed me in the right direction.

When I had finished, they both looked at me and Gytha said, "And Arne?"

"You know already."

"Perhaps, but I would hear it from your lips for the words you choose will tell me much."

"Arne sees enemies everywhere. He fears conspiracies and plots." I shook my head, "I am loyal to him and yet his words encourage me to betray him. He did not come to see the ship sail nor sail with us. He did not come to speak to either Fótr or me when we landed. It is as though we are no longer brothers."

Snorri gave me a sharp look, "But you will not betray him, will you?"

"I will not."

"Brothers often have differences."

"Not you and my father, surely."

He nodded, "I am sorry to say, aye, but none were as dangerous as the one which divided the three of you. Your father resented Gytha and the influence she had on the clan. He wanted your mother to be the matriarch of the clan and she never was. I had to swallow many insults but I did so for the good of the clan. You have done the same. Poor Fótr does not deserve this."

"There is more, is there not, Erik?" Gytha was, once more, reading my mind.

I nodded, "I believe he has some plan for the Thing. I cannot divine what it is but he is desperate for the clan to remain in the west, the new world, and he will do all in his power to achieve that end."

"And that is why I cannot understand his treatment of you. You are an ally who wishes to stay here. Snorri and I also wish that but Arne has yet to cross the threshold of our home. Do you know that? In all the time we have been here, he has never once stepped into our home to consult or to ask how I am. I am sadly disappointed in him."

Snorri said, "He has much to occupy his mind."

Gytha shook her head, "It is Freja. He changed when he married her. She wishes to be a queen. She wants others to fawn all over her. The word shallow does not even begin to describe her."

I hid my smile. Gytha was accurate in her description. I had thought Freja just to be a pretty face but she was not; she was vindictive, and worse, she could smile with her mouth as she was plotting. She was shallow and measured success in clothes and jewels. I wondered if she wished to return east too. That might explain Arne's short temper.

She said, "And now you should leave us for this conversation has tired me. I will speak at the Thing, even though I know it will take much out of me."

I left and felt sad for Gytha would shorten her days on this earth by trying to save the clan. Ebbe and Bear Tooth had already reached the hall by the time I had made my way from Snorri's home. Lars greeted me with a running hug which almost knocked me from my feet. "Bear Tooth told us how you made the new drekar fly and that you sailed her through a gap little larger than that of a birch bark boat."

I looked at Bear Tooth who shrugged and gave an apologetic grin, "Captain, you are a shaman for no other could have done that which you did."

Ada shook her head, "Showing off again, Erik?"

"I was just testing the drekar to see her limits," I said, defensively.

"Sit and eat. You will not have to sail now until after the Thing. You can get to know your son and daughter a little more!"

Arne came to see me early the next morning. "The drekar is ready?"

"Aye. If the clan decides it wishes to make its home in the east then it can take many of them. At a push, it could take most of them but I hope that will not be the case."

He gave me a strange smile, "That will not happen. Come, walk with me to the water." We headed towards the two drekar, "And Fótr, he can make the journey?"

"No one has ever made that journey, not even me, but I believe he can."

"Could you make it?"

"I just told you that I believe that Fótr could."

"But you know that you could?"

I did not understand the direction that this conversation was taking. Did he want me to go? "Aye, I could but I will not for I do not wish to upset the Norns and Fótr can do this."

"Of course." He pointed to the three ships, the snekke and two drekar. "Who would have thought when we boarded our first ship that one day you and I would have three such vessels? If Karl and the others could see us now... eh?" I nodded as I did not know what he wished me to say. "And I have your support at the Thing?"

"Of course, although I had not planned on speaking."

He looked relieved, "Good! You have done much for the clan and now you can enjoy time with your family."

I obeyed my brother and Ada. It was easy. I could play with Ýrr and it took little to amuse her. Lars and I carved bone. I wanted my own whale spear, not to hunt whales but the design was one which would make a kill on a horse deer more certain. I wondered why the Mi'kmaq had not used them. Bear Tooth was helping Lars and me to carve them and he shrugged, "We use the same methods used by our forefathers; bone spears and dogs. It works and we do not like to change what worked in the past."

I said nothing but I knew that new things had to be tried.

We also made fish hooks from the smaller bones. Finally, we began to make a set of chess pieces from some of the bone we could not use for any other purpose. After we had made the first four pieces, Bear Tooth became quite agitated, "You are a shaman, Captain, for this is what our medicine men do. They make figures of our enemies and then use them for spells!"

I laughed, "This is a game. This piece," I held one up, "is the king and the object of the game is to capture him. When we have made it, I will show you and Lars. It will be good in the long winter nights to do something which occupies our minds."

He said, shrewdly, "Then you will still be here in winter, Captain?"

I could not answer him for I did not know. It was the Norns and their webs which would decide that. I had to accept my fate for I was in their power.

Lars was growing and so we took one of the hides from the white-tailed deer and made him a tunic and pair of breeks. This land was less tamed and cultivated than where we had lived in the east. He needed something robust. Bear Tooth showed us how to make wooden beads which he painstakingly drilled with a piece of bone and then, after staining them, attached them to the tunic. Lars was delighted and it drew Bear Tooth and him even closer. Ýrr also changed as she ceased to be a mewling babe forever seeking milk to one who would take note of what you did. She could laugh and she could use her tiny fingers now with purpose. She could grab my increasingly unruly hair and giggle as she tugged it. It was a good time and I was truly happy, and then we held the Thing.

The clan had agreed a time but the sight of the newly finished drekar bobbing in the bay made those who wished to return home, impatient. The day arrived and the Allfather showed his favour by sending bright, warm sunshine even though the day was so cold, with a wind from the east and north, that some needed a fur. Two chairs were brought out for Gytha and Snorri, and while Snorri managed to walk from the hall unaided, Siggi and I carried Gytha. Her skin was even more translucent than it had been and I felt as though I could almost see her bones beneath the skin, yet her eyes were bright and her mind was still sharp. She chuckled as we sat her down. "That I am still alive will upset Freja!"

Siggi, Tostig, Fótr and I stood together and we waited for Arne, Freja and their children to emerge. They kept us waiting. I said nothing but Fótr shook his head and said, "This will be Freja. She will have someone braiding her hair and using the juice of the beetle to make her lips red."

Siggi laughed, "You know her too well. Arne will be chafing to get out here!"

I thought that Siggi was wrong and that the new Arne would be happy about the delay as it would increase what he perceived as his power. They came out and Freja stood with the women who fawned around her. Ironically, most of them were the wives of the men who wished to return to Larswick. I saw that she had, indeed, braided her hair and made her lips red. She wore a deer cloak trimmed with bjorr fur and I saw that she had rings upon her fingers made from some of the jet we had brought from Larswick. She was emulating a queen.

The Savage Wilderness

This time there was no need to demand silence for all were eager for it to start. Arne looked around the clan. When he saw me, his gaze stopped as though he was trying to read my mind. Then he moved on but he did not risk looking into the eyes of Gytha. Eventually he spoke, "The clan asked for a year to allow Erik the Navigator to build a drekar and for all members of the clan to search their hearts and decide if this was what they wished for the clan, this new world of regular crops, plentiful fish and game and no enemies who can threaten us."

My hand went to my hammer of Thor. It did not do to provoke the Norns. I saw Gytha shake her head and some of the older warriors also clutch their amulets. It was not a good start and I wondered why Arne had chosen those words.

"I too have had a year to think. Erik the Navigator has built the drekar and we have lost one of my oathsworn. We have hunted the whale and another of our warriors died." He had not spoken of me as a brother and he was dwelling on the disasters. I wondered why. "I am not a jarl who shuts himself away in his hall and does not listen to the words of his people."

I saw Gytha and Snorri start at those words. We were not his people; we were the Clan of the Fox and belonged to no-one.

"Some families wish to return east and I have come to see that is a good thing. I do not think that we should divide the clan but those who wish to return are right in a number of things: we do not need those to live with us if they do not wish to be here and we need more people to live here for with greater numbers we can conquer the lands to the west. We have seen nothing there to daunt us save the sheer weight of numbers of Skraeling. That is why we need more warriors."

I saw his words having the desired effect. Those who wished to return home, including Harold of Dyroy, were nodding. Gytha frowned; was she reading my brother's mind? I could not and I thought I knew him better than any.

"Let us do both; let us allow those families who wish to return to the east to do so but let us also send Erik the Navigator with the new drekar, to return here with more warriors and families." My mouth almost dropped open. I now understood his questions. "But I do not propose to send just the families who wish to return back. We hunted the bjorr and the horse deer.

There are other animals who live over here which have fine fur. I say let us trap those animals and send back the furs. The families who wish to return to Larswick would have the silver the furs brought to make a start again and Erik the Navigator could use the rest of the coins to buy iron. Harold of Dyroy is quite right, until we find where the iron lies in this new world, we are reliant on the old world to furnish it. With warriors and families of a stronger heart and more courage, we can begin to take the land to the west. We can build a stronghold that will be superior to Larswick. I propose we spend a season hunting and, in the spring, send the new drekar and Erik the Navigator back to the east. That is all I have to say."

His words had taken all by surprise and no-one stepped forward. Gytha held up her hand. Siggi shouted, "Silence, the mother of the clan wishes to speak."

All became silent and when Gytha spoke I was amazed at the strength of her voice. She looked frail and yet her words carried even to those at the rear of the circle. "The jarl has made a reasonable proposal and he is right; we do need more warriors for I agree, this land has much potential, but he is making a decision for another. Erik the Navigator has done more for this clan than any other warrior but he is being asked to sail back across the wide ocean with men he does not know. When we came west, there were doubters but the clan held firm and we persevered. When **'*Gytha*'** strikes those walls of water and those maelstroms, will these new warriors, who are not of our clan, have the courage to go on? We need to hear the words of Erik the Navigator."

Gytha did not use the words '*that is all I have to say*' yet all eyes turned to me and I was forced to step into the centre of the circle. I was in an impossible position. Gytha was right and so was Arne. I owed it to the clan to do their bidding but it would defer the fulfilment of my dream and I would be in a perilous position sailing the ocean with a crew I neither knew nor, in all likelihood, could trust.

"I am here to serve the clan but all who are present know of my dream. I could return to Larswick if folk wished to return but the seas are wide and the drekar could be lost. It has happened." I saw Arne about to step forward and I knew that he would suggest that I was afraid and I was not. "I am not afraid of going to the Otherworld, although I would like to see my son and daughter grow a little first if I did not return the clan would have a long period when they would not know. Also, my brother," I deliberately called him that rather than his title of jarl for I wished the clan to know I still thought of him as family, even if the feeling was not reciprocated, "assumes that the Skraeling will allow us to hunt. Why do we not, instead, try to speak peace with the Mi'kmaq? I would be quite happy to travel into their lands to speak with them. That way we could negotiate hunting and trapping rights. Who knows, it might even give us the chance to live on the mainland. That is all I have to say."

This time my words, which had surprised me for I knew not where they came from, created a hubbub. I saw Gytha smile and then she caught Siggi's eyes. He forgot himself for he simply said, "My mother wishes to speak."

All eyes turned to Gytha, "I apologise to the clan for I forgot the conventions. I had not yet finished but I am pleased that my nephew spoke for his words show wisdom beyond his years. I think an embassy of peace is a good idea. That is all I have to say."

Gytha had given me her approval and I knew that Freja and her cronies apart, it would have swayed the women of the clan and that was a victory. More, she had given my words credibility in the eyes of many men.

Harold of Dyroy stepped forward, "I wished to leave but my reason was the lack of iron. There is none on these islands, I can see that, but there must be some on the mainland. If Erik can negotiate a peace then I am happy to stay for I could wander the land and search for iron. That is all I have to say."

Arne's face was a mask of anger. I knew not whom his anger was directed at but his eyes burned. It was Fótr who stepped forward. "I, too, wish to sail home, but I am happy to wait until my brother Erik has made this embassy of peace. All know that I wish to return home but I would not return east and leave the clan in danger. I am content to sail with him should he wish to do so. That is all I have to say."

Eidel stepped forward, "I, too, wish to sail home and, like Fótr, I am willing to wait, but there is a time limit for we would have to sail before the storms of Haustmánuður. Erik and Fótr would have to sail and return before then or we would be committed to another year here. That is all I have to say."

Arne finally got to enter the conversation, "I have heard the words of the clan, all of them, and they are wise although, in my view, dangerous. If our two navigators sailed to make peace and did not return then I would have lost two brothers but more importantly, we would have lost our two navigators." He smiled, "But it would be the decision of the clan. That is all I have to say."

My brother was clever. Was he trying to ensure that the clan was forced to stay here by allowing Fótr and me to risk our lives? I would tell Fótr that he had to stay if the clan sanctioned the peace mission.

Gytha raised her hand and all murmured conversations ceased. "I have been in the spirit world and dreamed more than I have not of late." She shrugged, "Soon I will be in the Otherworld but I have yet to dream the death of either Erik or his brother. If they were to leave within the week, I can promise the clan that they will not die. That is all I have to say."

No one else spoke and so Arne stepped forward, "Erik and Fótr, you have chosen this task yourself. It is brave, not to say foolhardy, and the clan risks having the only two men who can sail them home leave but it seems that the will of the clan is for you to go. You must leave within five days and when you return," he paused, "if you return, then we will hold another Thing to consider your words. That is all I have to say and the Thing is over."

When all had gone, Siggi and Fótr came to me as I headed to speak with Gytha. Siggi shook his head, "Arne is right, this is brave and foolhardy. When did you come up with the idea?"

"As I stood there, and as for where the idea came from? I have no idea."

Gytha had not risen and looked even frailer, "They came from the world of the Spirits for they spoke to me at the same time. The Norns have spun. This is right and I have faith in the two brothers. They will succeed but there are so many dangers that I cannot say that they will return without hurt."

Tostig and Siggi carried their mother back and Snorri clasped my arm, "There are heroes and then there are those who climb higher than a hero can ever dream and that is you and your legacy, Erik the Navigator. When I am in the Otherworld, I look forward to watching your adventures!"

Bear Tooth, Ebbe and Ada had been at the back of the gathering and had only heard the words. When I returned from Gytha's home they stood there looking at me. Ada said, "I am worried that they may kill you, Erik. Why go?"

"Because it is the one chance we have of living in peace here in the new world and Gytha does not think that I will die."

"She is not as powerful as she once was."

"Yet she used what power she had to visit the spirits. I will trust her. Bear Tooth, is there a sign for peace we could take?"

He shook his head, "There is but you do not have one. It is a woven piece of deer hide with the story of the clan. It is called wapapyaki."

I smiled, "We have deer hide and we can make pictures. Why cannot we make it?"

Ada said, "Because, as I understand it, you have but five days before you have to leave."

"Then five days will be enough. Bear Tooth, I want you to find deer hide of the right size and shape. I will draw the pictures but you must tell me the form I should use. Do you think that this might work?"

"It might get you close enough to talk but they still might try to kill you when they see you are of the clan who killed our warriors."

An idea came to me, "And how would they do that?"

"Kill you?" I nodded. He looked confused but he answered me, "If they were being kind then they would smash in your skull with a club to give you a quick death but if they wished you to suffer then they would use a knife or a spear to rip open your stomach so that you would take days to die."

I nodded, "You believed I was a medicine man when you first saw me?"

"I still do."

"Then your people would as well. Ada, I want the bear fur making into a cloak but leave on the head. I would ask you to use Helga and Gefn for I would have the power of the volvas in their needlework."

"If it is for you then we will use the most powerful spell that we can."

We made our way back to my hall and my arm was around Ada. "I think that this was meant to be. It is summer and the tribes live on the coast. We do not have to travel deep into their lands. Bear Tooth can take us to his home. All of his family died so when they see him, he will appear like a ghost. The last time he was seen he was about to be slain by me, a shaman."

When the words had come to me, they had terrified me but no longer for I saw hope where there had been despair. If I could make this peace work then I could live in the new world and I could find the maid and the waterfall and put my mind at rest. I could live with my children and Ada, happily, but first I had to make a peace.

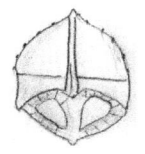

Chapter 14

The next day, while Bear Tooth prepared the deer hide, I spoke with Fótr to explain my plan. Reginleif was terrified but, by the time I had left, she was happier. I also spoke with Snorri. Gytha was asleep as the Thing had taken much out of her but he approved of the plan and clapped me on the back. "By the Allfather but you have some of the qualities of my father. He was clever and we managed to have victories through his cunning. You are the same. He would be proud of you. Lars and I were a mixture of my father but I see him reborn in you." When I left them, I felt hopeful.

My son, Lars, and Ebbe wished to come and were most upset when I said they could not. Ebbe was a clever boy and had learned to argue well, "You said it was safe and so I cannot see why I cannot come with you."

Lars was growing and within a year or so he would be able to come to sea with me as a ship's boy but he was not ready yet. "Gytha said she had not dreamed my death nor that of Fótr. Gytha's dream means that whilst we might be hurt, we will survive. But Bear Tooth was not mentioned and he could be in danger too."

"Yet you take him." He was like a dog with a bone and would not let it go.

"He is willing to take the risk and we need him for this meeting to work. Neither of you is coming and that is an end of it."

I saw the relief on Ada's face. I felt like a bad father yet I knew that I was right. To make it easier for them I allowed them to help with the painted deer hide. I drew the shapes and they used our natural dyes to colour them. Bear Tooth had made some painted wooden beads which he sewed on to the hide. It added to the authenticity of the wapapyaki. We just had to get close enough to them to speak. By holding the hide, Bear Tooth told us that his tribe called it wapapyaki and that any tribe would allow the bearer to speak upon its production in negotiations. That was all that we needed. While Ebbe and Lars coloured the wapapyaki, I went through with Fótr and Bear Tooth what would be said. We were making a performance for I was attempting to deceive the Mi'kmaq. I did not like to do so but the future of the clan was at stake and I would do anything for the clan.

It did not take us long to make something which Bear Tooth assured me looked enough like a wapapyaki to ensure we could talk. We knew where we would land for Bear Tooth's clan had once buried an ancestor close by and the place was sacred to his clan. When the bear cloak was finished, we prepared to sail. All but Arne and Freja came to see us off. Even Gytha left what seemed increasingly like her deathbed to embrace me with her blue-veined arms and to kiss me.

I wondered if she would be alive when I returned but she said. "I will be here when you sail back. Come to see me first when you return, for my days are to be counted on my fingers."

"I will, I swear."

The snekke seemed tiny and vulnerable after the two drekar I had sailed but, somehow, I felt more comfortable and at ease for it was also cosy. Fótr and Bear Tooth would be the crew and I had the helm. *'Jötnar'* preferred it that way. With the wind from the southwest, we had to tack and turn to sail to the small bay and tiny stream which marked the summer home of Bear Tooth's clan. I think that the Allfather sent the adverse wind to make our progress as slow as possible. It allowed the Skraeling to gather at the beach and watch our approach. Bear Tooth bravely stood at the prow in his loincloth clutching the wapapyaki. We had a few spare bear teeth and we had strung them about his neck. He was nervous until Gytha told him that she had worked her magic on them and they would protect Bear Tooth. The bear teeth and the wapapyaki would make the warriors wonder at our purpose and be less likely to use violence.

The closer we came to the beach, the more foolish and ridiculous I felt. I was very hot for I had a bear fur as a cloak and the skull was over the top of my head. My whole plan seemed nonsense and yet all those I respected had thought it good. I touched my hammer of Thor and prayed to the Allfather to help me. I saw that the warriors were armed but Bear Tooth had told me that if they intended war then they used paint on their faces to make themselves fiercer. Some even cut themselves before they fought a battle and a warrior with many such cuts was one to be feared for each one marked a victory. A wall of spears and hide shields closed with the water's edge.

"Fótr, take down the sail and then jump into the sea and pull us ashore."

"Aye, Brother, and I will hold my sword's hilt as I do so that I may meet you in Valhalla!" He was terrified and I heard it in his voice.

"Trust in me, Fótr, for I know what I am about. I was given a skill in navigation and in languages. Today sees both come to fruition. Remember, until I speak, we feign any knowledge of their words. We trust to Bear Tooth." I knew this would be the hardest part. I had to show no emotion no matter what they said.

The sail came down and I felt the keel slide up on to shingle and sand. Fótr showed more courage than I had ever seen and he jumped into the water with a rope and struggled up through the surf to hammer a peg into the earth which lay beyond the sand and to tie the rope to it. Warriors ran up to him and roared but he did not flinch. I was proud of him. Bear Tooth stepped from the snekke and waded ashore. I waited until he was on the sand before I followed. Fótr took a second rope and peg and marched up above the first stake where he hammered a second peg in. When he headed back to me, I saw the relief on his face.

I heard the warrior address Bear Tooth using the name I still could not pronounce.

Bear Tooth said, "I am now Bear Tooth for this shaman who steers the devil boat used a spell to enchant me and I am now his servant."

"But you were dead! I saw you die!"

"And this shaman, with the bearskin, brought me back. I am happy to be his servant for I was dead and now I am alive."

I saw the Skraeling look at the wapapyaki. "And what is this?"

"The story of his clan. He wishes to speak with Chief Wandering Moos."

The Savage Wilderness

"He is not here. He is at the camp in the woods by the stream."

"Then we should go. I would have his devil boat watched for it is enchanted and it would not do to have it harmed. The shaman has great power."

I kept a straight face as four young boys were told to guard the snekke. I knew that the eyes of our clan would be on us. We would be dots in the distance but my bear cloak would mark me and, therefore, the others. When they saw us heading up the path with spears all around us, they would fear for our safety. Fótr obeyed my commands and said not a word. Ahead of us, the warrior whose name was Long Sight spoke with Bear Tooth assuming that we could not speak their language.

"We have lost many warriors to these devils from the sea. You were lucky to be saved and now you can tell us how to defeat them."

"They have great power and magic, Long Sight. They have witches who can read men's minds and see beyond the seas."

"Are you certain?"

"I have lived with them since I came back from the dead and I can tell you that they can do all that I say."

"And why are they here?"

"To make peace for while they are strong, they also believe in peace."

There was silence as we followed the narrow stream up a steep-sided valley then Long Sight said, "That makes sense for, apart from the fight on Moos Island and when they stole the trees, they have not attempted to fight us and we know they have powerful weapons. How can that be?"

"I told you that they use magic but they also come from across the eastern sea. They travelled for more than a moon across the sea to reach us."

"More than a moon? Then they are powerful. Perhaps we should kill these two while they are in our power."

Bear Tooth's voice remained as calm as ever as he said, "I would not recommend it. This is a shaman. See the bear teeth and cloak; they are a sign of his power and this one is the one who sailed across the endless sea. He sailed with clouds and at night when the stars and the sun were hidden. Could any of our people do that?"

The question silenced our guide or perhaps he knew we were close to the summer camp for we came upon a huge number of the wigwams Bear Tooth had told us of. We were led through the encampment in the midst of yapping dogs and women, the widows I assumed of the men we had killed, hurling insults at us. It was hard to do so but I kept the same pace and the same expression. We were surrounded by a wall of hate. Ahead I saw their leaders, or what I believed to be their leaders. They were waiting in a line before a large tent. I saw the tribe's shaman. He, too, had an animal skin covering his back. It was a skin made from bjorr skins. I knew that he would assume that, as I was wearing a bear's head, I was a bear shaman and I would have more power.

The chief, Wandering Moos, neither looked at me nor addressed me. He spoke to Bear Tooth. While he did so, I studied the men around him. I was looking for the headstrong one, the warrior who wished to challenge me. I saw him straight away. He was standing next to the chief and he had angry eyes. More, he kept his hand upon a stone knife. He would be the one.

When Wandering Moos spoke, it confirmed that he was the chief, "Your return is a miracle but why have you brought these killers of our young men to our camp?"

Before Bear Tooth could speak, the angry young man said, "It matters not, let us kill them!"

"Eyes of Fire, know your place or leave this gathering. They have brought with them the wapapyaki and that means we guarantee their safety. I am sorry, continue."

"I was on the raid which killed my family, Chief Wandering Moos, and I was dead. The shaman of the bear brought me back to life and made me his servant. I have sailed the seas in their dragonship and I have hunted the whale. I was with them when they sailed the River of Peace and slew the Penobscot." As we had expected, that drew a murmur from those who were close enough to hear. Even Eyes of Fire looked subdued after the comment.

"Then why are they here?"

"It is simple. They wish peace and want to trade and to live in our land, here, this side of the sea, in peace."

"You speak for them?"

"I speak for them."

The chief turned and looked at his advisers. All except Eyes of Fire nodded, "And you swear that they wish peace?"

"So far they have not tried to take our land. None live on the island they took and Moos Island was just used for hunting."

Eyes of Fire suddenly said, "I have had enough of this! Let me kill them, father, and begin to avenge our warriors who were slain."

This was the moment and, when I spoke, I made my voice as deep as I could. Bear Tooth and I had practised the words I would say and I had it word perfect. When I spoke, they all physically recoiled. "Eyes of Fire, if you wish to try to kill me then do so. Take your knife and rip out my guts. I will not try to stop you for Bear Tooth is correct, we are powerful but we wish only peace. Do it now so that we can speak without anger and without blood boiling in our heads and hands."

I had hoped that the bluff would work but Eyes of Fire was scared and he just reacted; he slashed his stone knife across my middle. The blow would have hurt had I not tightened my stomach but the mail I wore beneath my bear cloak and tunic broke the blade which fell at his feet. He physically recoiled. I heard a shocked murmur from all those watching. As Bear Tooth had advised, it was a clear sign of our power.

I spoke to the chief, "You cannot hurt us. Now, Chief Wandering Moos, can we talk as men and not as headstrong boys who wish to prove themselves?"

Wandering Moos nodded, "You have embarrassed me, Eyes of Fire, go and join the women!"

The young man rose and, after glaring at me, flung away the remains of the broken stone knife. Folding his arms across his chest, he stormed away from the council.

Chief Wandering Moos waited until his son had gone before he said, "You speak our words?" I nodded. "Then we will speak directly. What is it that you wish, Shaman of the Bear?"

"My clan is the Clan of the Fox and, as Bear Tooth told you, we travelled across the huge ocean from the land of the rising sun. We wish to make a new home here. We come in peace but we are men of the sword."

The looks of puzzlement told me that I had not thought this through properly. "Sword?"

I turned to Fótr, "Show him, Fótr."

We had sharpened and polished our swords before leaving and when Fótr stood and drew his sword the sunlight caught it and it shone so brightly that some of the council had to shield their eyes from the flashing shafts of sunlight.

"Aieee, it is magic! Tell your man to cover it, Shaman of the Bear!"

"Sheath it, Fótr."

The council were more shocked by the sword than even my feat of surviving a knife thrust. "You all have such magic?"

"We do." I saw them look at each other and I did not need to be a volva to read their minds. They had nothing to counter this magic. The chief looked at their shaman and said, "Stalking Bear, have you some magic to destroy their magic?"

He shook his head, "I will have to visit the spirits and ask them. They may have powers they can give to me but I can do nothing about them now."

The chief nodded, "You have powerful magic; what is it that you wish?"

"We would live here on the mainland." The word I used was not '*mainland*' for Bear Tooth had told me that the tribe had no concept of the world outside their tribal lands. "We would build homes of wood, hunt and trap, fish and trade."

"You trade?"

I nodded, "We do and we have a gift for you." I nodded to Fótr. "Fótr."

He stood and unslung the ale skin from around him. After his performance with the sword, I saw the fear on the faces of the council. Bear Tooth took two horn beakers from his satchel and held them out. Fótr poured ale into the horns and gave them to me.

"We brew a beer which is like your pine beer but we think better. We would trade this and other goods with you. The skin of ale is a gift." I handed one horn to the Chief and then drank from the other. The Chief was no coward but he was speaking with someone he thought had magical powers and when he drank, he did not know if he would die or not. The Council also watched in fearful dread as the Chief took a tentative sip. Then he nodded and drank half of the brew. "It is good. You would trade?"

"We would trade and we would search your land for the iron to make our swords."

The word sword was a Norse word and the Mi'kmaq chief did not understand it although I had used it before. I tapped my sheathed sword and he nodded, "Then you will waste your time. If we had found this," he made an attempt to say iron and failed although I knew what he meant, "then we too would have your magic."

I pointed west, "Somewhere in this land will be iron but it will be buried deep and men would have to dig for it in the soil and make a fire as hot as the sun to change it from stone to metal. If we found it, we would share our magic with you."

I had already thought we were winning but that moment guaranteed it. Bear Tooth had told us that the Penobscot, although a smaller tribe, were more aggressive and won more battles against the Mi'kmaq than they lost. Having iron would ensure victory.

"We will need to speak further on this matter. We will retire to our lodge." He looked at Bear Tooth. "You will stay here?"

It was an imperative but couched in such gentle terms that it made me smile. Bear Tooth nodded, "Aye, Chief Wandering Moos."

The council disappeared into the large lodge. I spoke in Norse, "That went better than I had hoped."

Bear Tooth shook his head, "Eyes of Fire is an angry man and he has support amongst the young men of the tribe."

"Yet," I said, "he either did not come on the two raids or he was very lucky."

I saw Bear Tooth consider my words, "You are right. He said he was unwell on the first raid when my brothers died and that he did not wish his illness to risk the warriors."

"I have seen men like him before, Bear Tooth. We had some in our clan. The danger from Eyes of Fire is a blade in the back."

The fact that we were talking amongst ourselves had gradually encouraged the women and some of the other warriors to come closer to us to gain a better view of us.

Fótr chuckled, "If I had thought that polishing a sword would bring such an easy victory then I would have done that before." He stopped and then said, "Why did that not stop them on Horse Deer island or when they slew Benni and his family?"

"Both times the battles were fought on cloudy days in forests. The sun did not shine upon them and, in the heat of battle, they must have seen them as clubs." I looked at Bear Tooth.

He said, "You are right. We thought they were bone weapons which were coloured like our faces. The ones who found out they were not, realised it too late."

"I will be glad to take off this cloak and this mail shirt. I am unused to both and the heat is oppressive."

Bear Tooth nodded, "And here it is cooler than our winter home."

I realised that this was a vast land for back in Orkneyjar and Larswick there was no such difference. If we had walked from Larswick to Hwitebi across the whole of the land of Dane, there would have been such little difference in the temperature that the clothes we wore would have made no difference. Here the whole tribe had to move for comfort. I looked around at the village and saw that the homes, the wigwams, were larger than I would have expected. I saw that the saplings could be bound together for ease of transport. They were cleverly designed. I also saw furs. These people trapped other animals; it was not just the bjorr. It suggested a richer land away from the coast. That made sense for we had only spent a few days in the land of the Penobscot and yet we had seen many tracks I did not recognise. We had not seen sheep and we had not seen cattle. Were they further west or had the Allfather not sent them to this land? Perhaps we were meant to bring them. Had we sailed here from Larswick we might have brought more sheep. I wondered, then, at Arne's idea to trade. If we did then we could bring out a couple of rams and some ewes. Ideas buzzed around my head like bees.

The flap on the hide lodge was opened and the council came out. We had heard no raised voices from within, just a murmur like bees around a hive. This time the villagers moved closer to us as the chief spoke, "We have heard your words and they were reasonable. You are right, you did not strike the first blow, we did and we are thankful that you are happy to bury the hurt. We are content for you to live on this side of the sea but this is not our decision only. We cannot give permission without we speak to the other clans of the tribe. We will have to convene a gathering of all of the chiefs and put your proposal to them."

I nodded. It was a reasonable request and would be like our Thing. "And when will that be, Chief Wandering Moos?"

"When the new grass grows and the blossom returns, we will travel to the great water and there we will meet. If you return when the clan does, we will have an answer."

That was not so bad; from what we had observed that would be at Einmánuður. It still might mean that some of the clan returned east but it might be that it delayed that journey. I had an answer.

I stood and held out my arm. The Chief frowned and then copied me, I clasped his forearm and he held my gaze and nodded, "You are a warrior, Shaman of the Bear. This has been good. We will not raid you and I hope, that you will not raid us."

"You have my word on that."

"Then all is good."

Bear Tooth hung the wapapyaki around my neck and followed Long Sight from the camp. Fótr followed and then me. The clan formed two lines to watch us go and I saw the looks which had been of hatred were now of curiosity. We could sleep easier at night on Bear Island.

Leaving the village, we had just begun to descend through the trees and were headed towards the beach when I heard footsteps pounding behind me. The mail and the bear fur were tiring me and I was slow to turn. That saved my life. Fótr, Bear Tooth and Long Sight turned and then I felt great pain as something struck me on the back of the head. I almost stumbled but did not. I drew my sword and turned as Fótr raced past me with his blade drawn. I saw Eyes of Fire looking in horror. Fótr did not hesitate. He swung his sword and hacked through to the backbone. The angry young warrior lay dead in a pool of his own blood. Fótr had undone all of the good work we had begun. I had been safe. I saw the stone-headed spear lying on the ground. A combination of the bear fur and the mail hood I had borrowed from Qlmóðr Ragnarsson had kept me safe although I felt blood trickling down my neck. Now, as the village ran up, I wondered what would happen to us.

Chief Wandering Moos stopped when he saw his son and Fótr with the bloody blade in his hand. He knelt and stroked his son's head. He said some words quietly and then rose. He walked over to me and I pointedly sheathed my sword. I did not want more blood on our hands. The Chief said, "I am sorry, Shaman of the Bear, that my headstrong son forgot the rules of the wapapyaki. He has paid a terrible price. Let that be an end to it and do not visit your wrath upon us for his foolish action."

I could not believe it; he was asking our forgiveness even though his son had died. The Norns were spinning, "Chief Wandering Moos, our two people are more important than the actions of one misguided man." I held out my arm, "We are friends."

He clasped my arm and said, "We are friends but I will have my warriors escort you to your boat in case any of my son's friends are as foolish as he."

Long Sight walked next to me and he kept glancing at me as we headed towards the beach. I desperately wanted to take off the fur, mail and hood and examine the wound but that would ruin the illusion. My head felt as though a swarm of bees had taken it over.

Long Sight said, "It is good that you wish peace, Shaman of the Bear, for Eyes of Fire's blow would have killed any other man yet you walk and talk as though nothing happened. Are you immortal?"

"Let us say, Long Sight, that we have great powers."

The snekke was as we had left it and we boarded. I sat at the steering board while Bear Tooth raised the sail and Fótr untied us. The sun was setting behind us but the wind which had slowed us heading west now aided us as we sped east. We would be home shortly after dark. I could see that someone had lit a fire at the entrance to our bay and the smoke was rising like a beacon. When darkness fell, I would keep the fire to larboard.

"You almost undid all the good work there, Fótr."

"I am sorry, but when he ran at you and threw the spear, the blood came into my head and I did not think."

Bear Tooth shook his head, "No, Captain, Fótr did the right thing. Eyes of Fire was a danger for he had been insulted. He would have come after us just to break the peace. It also demonstrated the power of the sword. I have never seen a body almost cut in two. I saw the faces of my tribe and they were terrified. We have won and I am confident that when the new grass comes, we will live on the mainland and we will have peace."

It was much later when I realised that Bear Tooth had become a Viking for his words stirred the Norns and they spun once more. I did not know it then but his words were like the crack of doom for the plans of the clan. We headed for the bay and our home. The fire drew us towards safety. I took off the bear cloak, metal coif and padded helmet liner. My hand came away sticky with blood but it was not flowing. My precautions had worked and certainly saved my life.

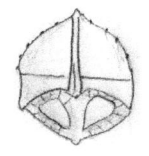

Chapter 15

Padraig and Aed, along with Ebbe and my son, awaited us as we came slowly into the bay. We sailed passed the two drekar and slid up on the shingle and sand beach. Padraig and Aed secured it. "Well?"

I nodded and regretted it immediately for my head hurt, "We have a peace, of sorts, but we have to wait until we have a new year before we will know if we can move to the mainland."

They both looked relieved. Padraig said, "I am pleased for although I earned a wound for my troubles, I liked the land we explored."

Fótr said, "Ebbe, take my brother to your mother. He has a wound. We will see to the snekke."

Aed looked concerned, "You said we had peace."

I gave him a wry smile, "I did not say that the peace came without cost. My brother has saved me from worse injury than a bloody scalp!"

Ada fanned the flames of the fire to give her enough light to see the wound. She washed it and then rubbed it with vinegar. "It will not need stitches and I have a salve to seal it. What happened?"

While she tended my wound, I told her. Bear Tooth returned halfway through. "The snekke is secured, Captain."

I continued with my tale. When I finished, I added, "And the clan owes you a great deal Bear Tooth. You should be rewarded."

"I have been, Captain, for I am now part of your family. Lars is like a brother to me. It is good."

Later, as I lay in Ada's arms, she said, "Had you not worn the metal hood then you would be dead."

I said, "The helmet liner would have saved my life. I might have needed stitches but I would have lived. The stone spears are effective against bare flesh but any kind of covering renders them less efficient. Why the Skraeling do not wear hide, I do not know."

That was not quite true. From the way I had seen them fight, the Skraelings relied on their stone spears and arrows to create small wounds and then use their stone clubs and axes to break bones and batter their enemies to death. It was something to bear in mind, although if we had peace then we would not need to fight them again.

I went, the next morning, to visit with Arne. I was not annoyed that he had not come to see me. I now expected it. Freja had changed him so that instead of being the brother of Arne, I was now the brother of the jarl and, as such, subservient. When I told him my news, I could not tell if he was disappointed or not. His eyes were closed to me. He did not seem concerned that I had been wounded, more that Fótr, who was the least skilled of us, had managed to chop a warrior almost in two.

"And you say that when Fótr whirled his sword they thought the flashing blade was magic?"

"Aye. They all recoiled. It was a sunny day and the Allfather sent the rays of his orb to aid us."

He nodded, almost absentmindedly, "Then if we were to polish our helmets and our mail think of the effect we could have. We would have to choose a sunny day but…"

"Did you not hear me, brother? I said we had peace. Even if the whole tribe do not agree, we will not be attacked."

He waved a hand, "I was not thinking of the Mi'kmaq. Thanks to your embassy they are as good as defeated anyway."

I looked at him. "I told their chief that we had no ambitions to take over their land."

"But you are not the jarl, besides you have done all that I could have expected and more. Fótr has done well too for he has slain the one who might have opposed us."

"I told you that they will not oppose us!"

"Now we know they fear shiny swords then it matters not. You have done well. I will speak of this at the Thing."

"No brother, I will speak of it and then I know that the words which are spoken are the truth and not your version of it."

"Erik, you are speaking of the jarl! Do not impugn his honour!" The harpy at his side spat her words out like arrows.

"And he was my brother long before he met you, Freja, and we swore an oath in blood, did we not, brother?"

The anger in his eyes dissipated a little as I reminded him of the oath, we two and Siggi had sworn on King Raedwulf's dagger which was in my belt. "True, but do not push your luck. You think I would twist your words?"

"I know not, but I do know that you have changed and others have noticed it too." I saw his eyes widen, "And before you speak of conspiracies, there are none. It is Gytha and Snorri who have seen the change, and Fótr. We are your first family and we have known you the longest. Look into your heart and you will see that I speak true, Arne. I will speak of the embassy and what happened because only I know what truly happened. The words are in my heart and my memory. If you reported this tale to Siggi it would not be exactly the same for some of what I said was not important to you. You selected the information about the swords as being the most important. Others may not. There are those in the clan who might be happy that we may be able to trade and that there is a possibility of searching for iron."

In his eyes, I saw that I had spoken true. He had not even heard those words. He shrugged, "Very well but after your words, I will make the proposal of what the clan should do."

I nodded, "And ask the clan to vote."

His eyes narrowed, "And ask the clan to vote but do not oppose me, brother. Like me, you wish to stay in the new world."

"True, but I fear our motives are different."

I had the last word and I headed for Gytha and Snorri's hall.

Although it had only been a couple of days since I had seen her, Gytha was worse and I could barely see any flesh on her bones. Snorri too, for the first time, looked more emaciated than he had. However, when they looked up and saw it was me who had arrived, I saw the joy in their eyes. I was touched. Unlike my brother, their first thoughts were for me and my crew. "I see you are whole and how are Fótr and Bear Tooth?"

"They have not a scratch. I will tell you all for you will see the threads of the Norns run through the tale.

I told them everything that had occurred, leaving nothing out and then I told them, word for word, the conversation with Arne.

Gytha shook her head, "Had I half the powers I once had then I would have seen all of this but I am coming to the end of my time and I am lucky that I still breathe. Come, let me look at the wound. I doubt not Ada's skill but..."

I knelt and felt her fingers pick amongst my matted hair. Snorri said, "I fear that Arne has another plan for the Thing and I am not certain that Gytha will be up to attending."

Gytha snorted, "I will be there. If I am to die then where better than in the heart of the clan stopping Arne and Freja from getting their way. I will be there. The wound is fine. Tell Ada that I could not have done better." Ada would be delighted for that was rare praise indeed. "And you, Erik, have done better than any could have predicted when you set sail in your snekke to discover this new world. Arne fears you for you should be jarl. You are wise and you are courageous, more, you see into the future and know that the old ways will not work here. That is why Arne fears you. You are right to speak first and Fótr can back you up." She closed her eyes and laid back on her bed. "Go now for I need to gather strength for the Thing. Snorri is right, this will be my last appearance in this life." Her eyes were closed but an elfin like smile came over her face. "As for the next life? Who knows?"

I went to Fótr's home in the woods. He and Reginleif were with their son, Erik. Reginleif looked larger than when I had last seen her but that had been before the whale hunt. "You are well, foster daughter?"

"I am, Erik the Navigator, and all the more pleased that my husband returned without a wound, and how is your injury?"

"It is nothing and was worth it to get the result we did. Fótr, I have seen our brother and Gytha." I told them both all. Fótr, like me, was angry with Arne for his words and saddened that we would soon see Gytha no more. "Gytha thinks it is important that the clan hears the truth of my words and that you are there to support me. I believe that Arne would not have mentioned the trading and the permission to seek iron. Nor would he have dwelt upon the fact that this agreement needs the approval of the whole of the Mi'kmaq people."

The Savage Wilderness

"What does he want?"

"I think he wants those who oppose him to be sent to the east and he hopes that they will be replaced by warriors who will allow him to carve out a kingdom here in the west."

Fótr nodded, "He wants to be rid of me."

"And yet he pays you a compliment for he thinks you will survive and be able to send back warriors."

"Sadly, brother, that is not true for you will have to be on the drekar to sail it back here. Reginleif and I are happy that the clan will have peace but we want to live close to the Land of the Wolf. Unlike others, I am realistic enough to know that Larswick may now be Norse and the people there will follow the King. There will never be a king in the Land of the Wolf and that is where I will go."

"And that is wise." I smiled, "Who knows, when I have found the waterfall then I may join you there."

The look on his face told me that he did not believe me. Siggi and Tostig came to see me later in the day. After visiting Fótr I had spent the rest of the day with my family. Ýrr changed day by day and she appeared to be less wild. I needed to spend as much time as I could with them.

"We have come from our mother. She has just hours left in this world, you know?"

I nodded, "She will speak at the Thing and that will suck all of her life from her. She need not speak, Siggi. It might only give her a few more hours of life but it is not necessary for her to lose those hours. You can stop it."

He looked at the ground before he answered, "How?"

"Arne is lost now to Fótr and to me. He sees us as rivals at best and enemies at worst. We are neither but he does not see that." I held his gaze, "Do you?"

He shook his head, "It is a nonsense and I know it but he will not listen to me. You are right for he ceased to speak to me after we won our first battle."

I was relieved for I had thought that Siggi, too, was of the same mind as Arne. The problem was that Arne was the best warrior in the clan and he knew it. The younger ones who wished for glory would follow him and none would threaten his position for he was not like my father, nor Snorri, and he would fight to keep hold of the title.

"Do you know what he plans to say at the Thing? I know it will involve a war of one kind or another as he seeks glory."

"He has not said but I think you are right. My father told me of the peace you brokered and it is good but Arne will see it as weakness on the part of the Mi'kmaq."

"And that would be a mistake." Ada had brought freshly brewed beer and we each finished half a horn before I spoke again. "It may be that he has no support for his ideas. That is my hope."

"I hope this does not break up the clan, Erik. When we swore the oath on the dagger my hope was that we three would be the rock on which the clan would stand."

"If we had been at Larswick then the clan would have been destroyed for many would already have left; Fótr for one. Here, even though we have two drekar, it is a momentous decision if we were to sail east. This Thing is as important as the one which brought us west." I turned to Tostig, "What is it that you wish?"

"My mother and father to be well, the clan at peace and a wife; in that order."

It was then I realised that was what had made Fótr decide to leave. His only ties were to me and Arne. If I went west then he would be alone. He was not abandoning me, he thought that I was leaving him."

I got to the Thing early for I wanted to help bring Gytha forth. Tostig, Siggi and Fótr were there at Gytha's home already. Snorri looked ancient and his body was wracked by a coughing fit as I entered. It was not a good sign. Siggi shook his head, "I tried to persuade her to stay indoors but she refuses. My father told me that she will speak to no one until the Thing. She will speak after Arne."

I nodded. To the end, Gytha, the matriarch of the clan, was doing all in her power to hold us together. If we fell apart then it would not be her doing. We carried out a bed stuffed with goose and hen feathers and placed it at one end of the circle. The four of us carried her out, reverently, although, in truth, anyone of us could have managed it. She seemed to have shrunk. The warriors who had arrived early clutched their hammers of Thor when they saw her. I saw that the senior warriors, Harold of Dyroy, Æimundr Loud Voice, Gandálfr, Halsten Haakensson, had all gathered close to where Gytha and I would be. It was a statement that they were behind me. As others came, they filled the side close to us until Arne, his son Lars, Folkman, Faramir, and Galmr arrived. Lars Arneson was close enough to manhood to attend. His younger brothers were not and they stayed with their mother.

Arne gave a wry smile when he saw that Siggi was close to me and his mother. This was the first Thing where he had abandoned Arne. I hoped that the move would make Arne reconsider his ways. He stepped to the middle. "Erik the Navigator and Fótr have travelled west and met with the Skraelings. Erik would like you to hear what happened in his own words. When he has spoken then I have something to say. Erik…"

I stepped forward and began to speak. I made certain that my voice was neither angry nor excited and I just gave a detailed account of what was said. Fótr kept nodding as I did so to confirm that I spoke the truth. "That is all I have to say."

Arne had made certain that all knew he intended to speak second and I saw him become angry as men began to talk with their neighbours. Fótr, Siggi, Tostig and I kept silent. I did not want to give Arne the chance to say we were plotting.

He shouted, "Are we civilised or is this a Skraeling camp?"

It was an unfair thing to say for, from what I had seen, the Mi'kmaq were both polite and civilised. It had the desired effect, however, and men stopped speaking.

"There are still those here, I believe, who wish to return east across the wide and dangerous ocean. At the last Thing, before Erik the Navigator offered to seek peace, I suggested that we trap the bjorr and the other animals which live in this verdant land. I think that if we do divide the clan then we still do this. For those who wish to leave there are two clear choices. The people who wish to return to Larswick either do so now or wait until the new grass. You all know what I wish. I want the clan to stay here. That is all I have to say."

I was surprised at Arne; I had expected something different.

Before any could speak or step forward Siggi said, "My mother wishes to speak."

Every eye went to Gytha. Her eyes were closed as though she was dead already but, when she spoke, her voice was clear and, as always, commanding. "I have heard the words of the two brothers, Erik and Arne. Arne is right; if a ship is to return, it must travel soon. That means the clan has to divide the animals we brought. Those who stay will have to become closer for there will be less for them to share. There can be no divisions. The clan is of one blood." She was silent and I wondered if she had passed over. She laughed, "I am like Erik the Navigator, he is a man I admire as much as my husband, Snorri, for he is true to his word and the clan. I am like Erik because I have helped to steer this clan. When Lars, my husband's brother, died fighting the Danes the brothers were young and unformed. Now they are men. I leave the clan now and hope that the clan knows who is best suited to steer the clan into the future. That is all I have to say."

The word 'say' seemed to become a sigh and her head lolled to one side. Snorri had been kneeling next to her and holding her hand. He bowed his head and kissed her forehead. Silence hung like a sword above the Thing. Even Freja and Arne seemed unable or unwilling to speak and break the spell. Eventually, Snorri rose.

"Gytha the volva, my wife, is dead but her spirit is above us and she watches and she listens. The three volvas of the clan, do you feel her presence?"

I looked around and saw that Gefn, Helga and Ada held hands and their heads were bowed. Helga said, "Aye, my mother is close and my father is right. Let the Thing decide for she wishes it so and then we will bury the Queen of the Clan of the Fox."

It was only later that I thought about those words for I was still thinking of the woman who had guided me since before my father had died. Those were not Helga's words, they were Gytha's and they were intended as a barb for Freja.

Every eye went to Arne. He had heard the words but, as with me, they had not sunk in; Gytha had openly questioned Arne's right to be jarl. He spoke, "We must honour Gytha's wishes. Who else wishes to speak? That is all I have to say."

Fótr stepped forward, "Reginleif and I still wish to take our family home. I will sail *'Gytha'* this day if the clan wishes it. We have peace with the Skraeling but I do not think they are the only enemy. I think that this land changes men and I would return east before I am changed. That is all I have to say."

Fótr had been reckless. He was speaking of Arne and most of the men understood that. Arne's face was a stone mask and he showed no emotion.

Eidel Eidelsson stepped forward, "I, too, wish to return home but Gytha's words have made me think. Do we take the animals which the clan needs to live, back to the east? I would not return as a pauper. Perhaps Arne and Gytha are right and we need to reflect on the life back in the east. That is all I have to say."

Halsten was the next to speak, "I, too, wish to return east. I think this land is rich but my wife's sister's son was bitten by one of the creatures which fly in the night and died. I have been lucky thus far but I would not lose a child to an insect. Fótr, if you wish to return now then I will come with you. That is all I have to say."

Qlmóðr Ragnarsson stepped forward, "I would stay for this land owes me weregeld for my friend Kalman was slain by the whale. I say we fight for what we have. Erik the Navigator has bought us a precious peace with the Skraeling and a few months is not long to wait. That is all I have to say."

Before anyone else could speak, Siggi stepped forward, "Enough of this. We can talk and we can talk but my mother lies here waiting to be buried. Her spirit watches us. Let us choose now. I have listened to all of the words that men have spoken and it seems to me that there are three choices: we all stay here and make this our home, we let those who wish to return home soon or, finally, we wait until we hear from the Skraeling. Jarl, give the warriors those choices. That is all I have to say."

Arne had no choice for it was obvious that all had been said that needed to be said. He stepped forward. "Who wishes to stay regardless of any peace?" I raised my hand, Qlmóðr Ragnarsson, Siggi, Tostig and Arne's supporters did so. I saw that Arne was less than happy for he had expected more support, "Who wishes to wait until the peace is confirmed?" This time only four warriors did not raise their hands. I saw the smile return to

Arne's face. "And who wishes to return home now?" Fótr and the other three were the only ones who raised their hands. "Then we stay another season and we can trap the bjorr and produce as many more animals as we can. That is all I have to say!"

The victory for Arne was a hollow one for all attention was on Gytha's body. The three volvas hurried to the hall and the four of us who had brought the living matriarch carried her back within. Snorri came with us. We laid her in the hall and then stood outside. None of us said a word. This would have been the opportunity for Arne to join us and heal the rift but, instead, he was with his few supporters and showed me just how much he had changed.

Snorri came out and spoke to us, "My wife, Gytha, wished to be burned and her ashes scattered here on Bear Island." He gave a wan smile to Siggi and Tostig, "When it is my turn, I will join my wife in a fiery end and our spirits will wander together. The volvas prepare her for death. Go and build a pyre where the drekar are moored. The rocky headland above the bay will be perfect for the clan can all watch."

I was just pleased to have something to do and we gathered the men of the clan to build a pyre. With all of us working we managed to make one as high as our chest. The top was perfectly flat. We soaked the wood in whale oil. While the other warriors gathered the clan, we returned to the hall and fetched Gytha's body. She was dressed in a gown which was rich with decoration. Her thin grey hair had been combed about her shoulders. She was wrapped in a wolf cloak we had brought from Larswick. Her body was bedecked in wild summer flowers. She looked at peace. We lifted her and carried her body towards the sea. The rock upon which she would be burned was the highest point in the bay and the clan were all gathered to look at the pyre. With her body on the wood, we each said our goodbyes. Siggi and Tostig had faces covered in their tears. As I kissed her dead hand, I felt a surge of power from above me and I was not sad, for Gytha's body might be dead but not her spirit. We returned to our families and it was left to Snorri to use his steel and set the flames.

The fire roared up the sides as the oil was ignited and Gytha's body disappeared in flames. Snorri smiled as he descended, "A good fire, Siggi. It almost took my eyebrows." Snorri, like me, was not sad for he knew this was a beginning. Some of the clan swore they saw her spirit rise from the flames. They did not for that was smoke. Her spirit had left when she had ceased to speak. It was now above Bear Island and I for one felt safer.

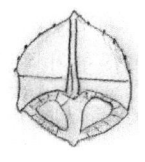

Chapter 16

Ada waited until we were in bed before she spoke of the death. "The spirit of Gytha came into my head, Erik. It was as though she was in the same room. I now have some of her power. I spoke with Gefn and Helga and they are of the same view. Perhaps I will be able to speak with you when you are far away."

I kissed her forehead and shook my head, "Gytha did that at great cost and she died before her time. I would not have that fate for you."

She closed her eyes and kissed my chest, "Is Fótr angry that his suggestion was rejected?"

"You do not know my brother. He knew that the clan would never agree to such a short time elapsing. He said what he did as a challenge to my brother and he wished to send Arne a message. He was telling Arne that Arne had changed. It was a dangerous thing to do and yet I wonder." Even as I said it, I realised that Fótr was being clever. Arne wished to send for more men and that required Fótr and me to return to the east. His anger might be vented on others but we two were safe for he wished Fótr gone and he needed me to serve him. The Norns were spinning.

Snorri gathered the ashes and he put them in a clay jar. He spoke with Helga and, later, Ada told me that he wished his ashes and those of Gytha to be mixed and he wanted his children to scatter them after he died.

The Thing had not settled anything and each family seemed to withdraw within their homes. There was less laughter and there was less sense of the clan. Gytha's death had created a void which needed to be filled. Arne came to see me a month after Gytha had died. Snorri was growing close to the end of his life and I spoke with him each day, as did Tostig and Siggi. Arne came to speak to me about him, "How is Snorri, our uncle?"

The Savage Wilderness

"He is dying and you should ask him yourself."

"He does not like me."

I shook my head, "Arne, you are a fool!" His eyes flashed. "Our uncle is of our family. No matter what we do, we are in his heart. Whoever planted this seed in you has changed you. I will speak openly for I have to; I am your brother and we swore an oath. You are estranged from all those who care for you. Siggi, Fótr, Snorri, all of us see the man you were and that is not the man we see before us. Freja has changed you."

"Brother, do not push me." I saw the anger flare in his eyes and his hand was perilously close to his sword hilt.

"Or what? You will draw a sword and slay me? Aye, you could, but who would bring back your warriors? You need me, Arne Larsson, and you will hear my words. No one wishes to usurp you but you are not the jarl you were. Speak with Snorri and make your peace. Heal the rift with Fótr and remember the oath we three swore. I promise that I have no wish to take the clan from you. I am not a warrior; I am a navigator."

He nodded, "You are a fool but an honest fool and I will think on your words, but do not speak to me like this before the clan or there will be consequences."

He left but I saw that my words had made a change for he went to speak with Snorri and spent an hour with him. He did not speak with Fótr but he had made peace with Snorri and that was good. Perhaps Snorri had been waiting for such a meeting for after he took to his bed, and Siggi fetched me one evening in early Tvímánuður.

"My father is dying and he has asked for you and Bear Tooth."

We hurried to the hall. Helga left as we arrived. She smiled at me, "I have said my goodbyes and now I must spin so that his journey to the otherworld is smooth."

Despite the fact that he was dying, Snorri Long Fingers looked content. Tostig knelt next to him. I saw that Snorri's sword lay along his body for he was ready to go to Valhalla. He smiled and held out his hand before speaking in Mi'kmaq, "Come, Bear Tooth, for I would say farewell to you." Bear Tooth understood the arm clasp and he gripped Snorri's forearm, "You taught me much about your world and my own. We were a bridge between our two people and I hope that Erik can continue this. Farewell."

"Farewell, Snorri, father, I hope your spirit and Gytha, mother, are joined in the Otherworld. I learned much from you." He stepped back and I took his place.

He spoke Norse to me, "There are no words, Erik, save to say that you are the Clan of the Fox. Know that your family will always be protected and held in high esteem regardless of what happens to you. You have a long journey; I am no galdramenn but I can see that far ahead. Thank you for watching over my sons. Farewell."

"Farewell, Snorri Long Fingers, and I will try to live up to the high standards you have set."

I stepped back and, holding his sword in his right hand, he held up his left hand. Tostig and Siggi grasped it; Tostig still wept for he was younger than Siggi. Siggi had seen death many times and knew that his father would walk in the Otherworld and meet up with his brother in Valhalla. "Watch over each other. Farewell!"

It was as though he had chosen his own moment of death. His eyes closed and a smile came over his face, there was a soft sigh and Siggi said, "He has gone." We four waited, each lost in our own thoughts. I could actually feel his spirit as it rose and headed for the skies. My cousin turned to me, "We will prepare my father, Erik, would you have the men make the pyre? I am anxious to send him to my mother as soon as I can. My sister is spinning and we must play our part."

The men who lived close by knew that something was happening and they joined us to build the pyre for Snorri had not an enemy in the world. Arne did not dirty his hands nor make an appearance. Fótr arrived and we went to the hall to help Tostig and Siggi carry their father on the last journey. I did not know then that day meant the end of something; we could not know that for you can only see the end when it has passed. I thought that we were burning a great man. It was only later that I realised that the last of the generation who had brought us into the world was now gone and we were the older generation. We were the elders of the clan and the young would look to us; it was a sobering thought.

As Snorri was a warrior, we celebrated by getting drunk and telling tales of the past. We sat around the pyre long after the flames had consumed the body and the wood, and we each told a story of Snorri. Even Bear Tooth told a story but he did not drink as much as the rest of us. It should have been a perfect end to the life of Snorri but for one thing; the only warrior who was missing was the jarl. He and his family kept within their hall. Fótr and Tostig became drunker and drunker and as they became consumed by the beer so their anger with Arne grew. Siggi and I were saddened rather than angered at his absence but our two younger brothers allowed their anger to spew forth. They cursed Arne for being thoughtless and heartless. They questioned his leadership. It was when they began to talk of me as the next jarl that Siggi and I acted.

"Come Bear Tooth, let us take Fótr to his wife and then we will return for Tostig."

Fótr tried to shake us off, "Leave me alone, I am not a child!"

"I know but you have a family now. Come with us for Reginleif is what you need now."

Fótr began to cry, "Why does the Allfather take the good and leave that which is rotten? Why?"

"Because, little brother, it is the Norns who spin the threads and not the Allfather. You do not think the Allfather would have chosen to take Snorri, do you? It is the Norns and you should accept it."

He suddenly passed out. It was good that both Bear Tooth and I were strong or he would have fallen to the ground. Reginleif was alerted by the noise of our steps. "What has happened?"

I smiled, "He has drunk too much ale. It will pass."

"Thank you, foster father. Once more I am in your debt."

By the time we had returned to the fire, all had left save Siggi. "We took Tostig soon after you departed. This is a bad business for word of their anger will reach Arne and he will not be happy."

"It is Tostig who should fear his wrath for Arne needs Fótr to sail the drekar. The Norns have indeed spun for Arne now needs Fótr more than anyone else save me. I believe he wishes he did not but he does."

The Savage Wilderness

Surprisingly nothing was said the next day nor the next month. Arne had to know of the angry words but he did nothing. Instead, he spent the time preparing the men for the journey to Fox Water. He had decided to use that vast expanse of river to trap and to hunt. That way he could use the drekar as a weapon. He had listened to my words about the birch bark boats and planned for them. The men of the clan spent each day making traps for the bjorr and the other animals Bear Tooth had told us of. He sent for Fótr and me one day, a week or so before we were due to leave.

"We will take *'Njörðr'* to Fox Water. Our new drekar is bigger and slower." I nodded for it made perfect sense and I was more comfortable with the old ship. "Fótr, we do not need you. You can stay and protect the women and *'Gytha'* if you wish."

I knew then that this was the punishment for his outburst. Fótr would have none of it, "I am coming on this hunt for I have still much to learn about navigation and I do not wish to be parted from my brother. Erik is wise." It was an insult by omission and I saw Arne wince, although he shrugged as though it did not matter.

"Very well. I will find another to stay."

It was Tostig who was chosen and I saw a vindictive side in Arne which had not been there before Freja. Arne decided we would go at Gormánuður. It was a little later than when we had last travelled to Bjorr Beck. As we would only be travelling as far as Fox Water and that lay on the River of Peace, I hoped we would not run the risk of conflict.

My son, Lars, wished to come on the hunt but I told him he could not, nor did I allow Ebbe. I asked Bear Tooth to stay at home and to watch over my family. "Will you not need me, Captain?"

"Perhaps, but my family and the clan need you more. You will stay here." The decision made me feel better and Bear Tooth was happy to be given the responsibility. Lars was unhappy with my decision because my nephew Lars Arneson was allowed to go. My son did not accept the argument that Lars Arneson was older but then my son was still young. Ebbe was just angry. I explained as patiently as I could, "When I went to sea before there was always Gytha and Snorri to watch over the clan. They had Gytha's magic. Both are gone and there is now Ýrr as well as your mother. You two are warriors." I took my sword and scabbard, "Here Ebbe, wear this until I return and then when I have sailed east and returned, I will see if we can get one for Bear Tooth and Lars too." The last argument and the sword swayed it.

Bear Tooth said, "What about you, Captain? Will you not need a sword?"

"We go hunting and I am captain. I will take my bow. It is not a Saami bow but it is a good one and made from yew. It will do and I have my bone plated hide. I will be safe."

Perhaps it was because I had taken the mail byrnie to the Skraeling camp and had not placed it in the chest was the reason that when we did set sail I went without mail. Although it may have been the Norns spinning for, before we left, I went through the chest to ensure that my hourglass and compass were there along with my maps. I should have seen it was not there. My helmet was but, for some reason, I did not see it. I let Ebbe, Bear Tooth and Lars take my chest to the drekar. They would secure it well and I said farewell to Ýrr and Ada. That morning I saw more than recognition on Ýrr's face for she put her arms out to hug me. Her tiny arms gripped my neck and I felt a lump rise and I sensed tears were close.

Ada too was upset, "I fear that this will be the last time I see you, Erik the Navigator."

I shook my head, "Do not say that. You feared when I went to the Mi'kmaq camp and when I scouted. I always returned." I laughed, "I do not say that I will not have lumps and bumps but here," I tapped my chest, "I do not think I will die."

She kissed me and took Ýrr from me, "I dreamed last night. Since Gytha died I have dreamed each night. I have seen Larswick and the Land of the Wolf. I have seen Lars a man grown and I have seen Bear Tooth with children."

"There you are!"

"But I have not seen you and last night's dream was of *'Njörðr'* sailing into the bay and Fótr was at the steering board."

"That should not worry you for I often give him the practice; soon he will sail across the wide ocean and he needs as much experience as he can get."

She nodded but I saw in her eyes that she was not convinced. "Then when you return, I shall be joyous but until then I will pray for you. Know that I have loved you more than any other man. I thought Dreng's father was the love of my life but it is you."

"And I love you."

"Yet you see the maid and the waterfall." She held her hand to my mouth, "You need not speak for I know that you love me and I am content. I knew that I might only have you for a short time and already I have had two children by you and a third is now within me." She smiled, "This one will be a surprise for there is no Gytha to tell me if it is to be a boy or a girl. Be safe and I will watch for your return."

I bent down to kiss her and, in that moment of time, I wished to tell Arne to sail without me. I did not and the moment passed and in that moment my future changed beyond all recognition. I headed to the drekar with a heavier heart than before. I would have another child. I knew then that, when I returned, I would marry Ada. My dream was just that. I had met the maid and I had seen a waterfall before. Now that I was an elder, I would behave as one.

Half of the crew were there before me. Ebbe was checking the ropes which held my chest to the cleats. I nodded, "You have done a good job, now watch your mother for me and I shall see you before you know it. We may be away a month but your mother has dreamed the return of the drekar."

Bear Tooth nodded, "Come Ebbe, Lars, let us go to the burning place and we can watch *'Njörðr'* for the longest time."

As they went, I heard Lars say, "Can I carry the sword?"

Ebbe said, "You are not tall enough but I will let you hold the scabbard." That pleased my son and the three of them headed to the place we had burned Gytha and Snorri. I knew their spirits would watch over my family while I was at sea and in the land of the Penobscot.

Reginleif and his children accompanied Fótr and he looked as thoughtful as I knew I must. The rest of the warriors were in good humour for we would be, hopefully, bringing back furs which would make us rich men and provide the money to buy animals when the ones who wished, returned to Larswick.

The Savage Wilderness

After taking my hourglass and compass from the chest I sat upon it, "Remember, Fótr, that while Arne and the rest want furs, we need as many deer of any kind as we can manage. If all goes well, we will make pine tar too."

Fótr seemed distracted and I put it down to leaving his family but he suddenly said, "Arne means to make war on the Penobscot."

"What? Surely not? We have just made peace with one tribe so why should he risk a war with another?"

"Tostig told me. He was speaking with Lars Arneson and Arne's son boasted that he would be making his first kill when we trap the bjorr."

"It may be Lars is being boastful; do not judge yet and besides, we two can stay aboard the drekar. If they are foolish enough to risk a war then we are not."

My answer seemed to please Fótr and soon Arne and his son, along with his oathsworn arrived. We had many young men taking an oar for the first time. Stig Eidelsson who had been ship's boy now sat across from his father. Every oar would be manned but that did not mean a smooth passage. The new rowers would have to learn. It was good for this was a safe place to practise while the wide ocean needed men who had skill. As was usual at this time of the year, the wind was from the south and west which meant the men would have to row.

Arne waved to those watching us and then sat at his oar with his son on the chest next to him. He smiled at me, "Well brothers, your nephew takes an oar for the first time. This is a great day!"

I was pleased for Arne, "Aye, it is. Ship's boys, loose the ropes. Rowers prepare to row. Steerboard, on my command, push us from the quay." The boys untied the ropes and leapt aboard. I had chosen when the tide was on the turn and it helped to move us. "Steerboard, push!" They pushed us away and then I shouted, "Oars, in! And row!"

I chose a simple chant which would help the new rowers get into the rhythm quickly. It was one we had used when we had left Larswick.

Clan of the Fox, from Orkneyjar's shores

The Savage Wilderness

Clan of the Fox, take to your oars
Clan of the Fox, we row as one
Clan of the Fox, heading west to the setting sun
Clan of the Fox, from Orkneyjar's shores
Clan of the Fox, take to your oars
Clan of the Fox, we row as one
Clan of the Fox, heading west to the setting sun
Clan of the Fox, from Orkneyjar's shores
Clan of the Fox, take to your oars
Clan of the Fox, we row as one
Clan of the Fox, heading west to the setting sun

By the third verse, the odd badly handled oar had ceased to be noticeable and the new rowers were learning to twist the blade of the oar when it was withdrawn from the water and to use both legs and arms. *'Njörðr'* was moving well. I had spent some time clearing weed from her hull but, in truth, there was little to worry about. It was a little disconcerting to have Fótr watch my every move but I understood why. He would soon be at the steering board of his own drekar. I had watched Ulf North Star and my father and followed what they had done. Once we had cleared the islands which lay close to Bear Island and we headed into the wind to allow us to turn west and save the rowers, I said, "Take her for a while and head into the wind. I will walk down the drekar and see how the new warriors fare."

Lars was the image of his father and although not yet fully grown, when he was, he would be a giant. There was enough excitement about the voyage for him to forget that his father and I had fallen out. I smiled at him, "You are doing well, nephew, but soon your back and your legs will burn." He did not stop nor speak but nodded and I saw the sweat pouring down his back. Stig was trying to copy his father but he was struggling. "Stig, use your body when you lean into the stroke; do not try to simply pull." He nodded. I spoke to each new rower to offer advice. I reached the prow and touched it for luck then I walked down the centre. As I looked to steerboard, I saw that it was time to make the turn.

I reached Fótr and shouted, "Ship's boys, prepare to loose the sail!" Some quickly ran to the sheets and stays while four of them clambered up to the yard. We had spent five days practising. Young Snorri Siggison had fallen but not broken anything. I remembered when that had been his father, Siggi and Karl had called him the Clumsy. My ship's boys were just concerned that Snorri was not hurt.

"Let fly!" As the sail came tumbling down, the boys on the sheets and stays hauled and tightened them on the cleats. I put the steering board over and waited until the sail billowed before I shouted, "In oars! Well done, Clan of the Fox!"

It had been a good start and we had had no disasters. We could sail north and west and use the wind to take us to the coast, avoiding the islands and rocks which lay to the east of it and then we would row, once more, down to the River of Peace. We reached the coast towards evening. This time we would camp at the island at the mouth of the river. Now our course changed for the coast ran south and west and we followed it. The ship's boys kept an eye out for fires. There were none but we were still on the Mi'kmaq side of the river. When I saw the sun beginning to set, I had the rowers increase their speed and we used our first chant again.

Clan of the Fox, from Orkneyjar's shores
Clan of the Fox, take to your oars
Clan of the Fox, we row as one
Clan of the Fox, heading west to the setting sun
Clan of the Fox, from Orkneyjar's shores
Clan of the Fox, take to your oars
Clan of the Fox, we row as one
Clan of the Fox, heading west to the setting sun

Harald Gandálfrson was on the yard and it was he spied the island and the beach. There was just enough light to allow us to reach it, run in the oars and tie us to a pair of rocks. Then the sun dropped behind the cliffs and all went dark. Æimundr Loud Voice shouted, "Get kindling and light a fire!"

Arne should have given the orders but he did not. The crew poured over the side. We had rowed as much in one day as we had when on a whale hunt and the men were both tired and hungry. We also needed a fire for heat. The nights were cooler

The Savage Wilderness

now. My bear cloak would prove to be useful during the day as well as at night. Fótr and I were the last ones ashore. Normally I would be alone but I wanted to teach my brother what to do. We checked all the sheets and stays. We examined the sail to make certain it would not flap open should a wind suddenly arise, finally we went, first, to the prow and then the stern to ensure that there was nothing which might damage those two most important parts of the drekar. That done, we went ashore.

Siggi and Tostig had saved us a place by the fire and handed us an ale skin. The first ale of the day always tasted best and I knew not why. The ship's boys had been set to collect shellfish as soon as we had landed and they would add a naturally salty flavour to the horse deer stew we would eat. We also had bread and this would be the last time we would eat it for up to a month. I still hoped that we might find cattle or sheep ashore for I missed cheese. We had so few animals that Arne was the only one who had his fill of cheese, and butter was used sparingly.

Siggi looked west, "The land is so empty and yet it is so vast."

I nodded, "I think that the Allfather sent us here to fill it with our people. We have much in common with the Skraeling but we also have far more we could give to them."

"When we first met them, I thought they were savages who were little better than animals but Bear Tooth has shown me something different. I was wrong."

"Aye, Tostig, and when Erik and I saw their village I was amazed at how civilised they were. I know one tried to kill Erik but who wouldn't?" My little brother laughed, as did the others.

Siggi had been listening to our words and he said, "But the Penobscot have not yet been offered peace."

I said, "Aye, but now we know the trick and I have the deer hide with the story on it, the wapapyaki. If I approach them with it then they may not fight."

Siggi was sceptical, "You are certain?"

Fótr nodded, "That is what we were told before we met the Mi'kmaq and it should work with the Penobscot, too."

Siggi smiled, "Then we might have a peaceful hunt and if we see the Penobscot then we can talk."

A wind came from the east and I was sure it was the sigh of the Norns, "Perhaps."

It took two days to head up the river to Fox Water. That was partly my fault for I wanted to ensure that Fótr knew why I did all that I did. Arne became impatient. As we camped at the large island just before Fox Water, he said, "Erik, are you deliberately trying to delay us?"

"No, Arne, I am just being careful. If we damaged the drekar it is a long walk home and, besides, the longer it takes us the less likely we are to find Skraeling."

He laughed and turned to his son, Lars, "We fear no half-dressed savage who is terrified of a boy with a shiny sword!" The insult was intended for Fótr and the arrow struck. Fótr coloured and then went to speak with Siggi and Tostig.

"Brother, why do you insult him?"

He shrugged, "He annoys me for he is weak."

"Do not disparage the Skraeling for they are as fierce as berserkers. I thought you would have seen that the last time."

"The last time we were unprepared. This time we will hunt armed and mailed. You see, Erik, I have listened and listened well. We will march with burnished helmets and mail when we go to trap. That was where they caught us. If they try and attack us while we hunt the horse deer then we will be alerted by the animals." He beamed, "You see, I have thought all of this through. I would not have risked my son had I thought there was danger."

And that was the trouble; this was a wild land and a savage one. Danger could be just around the corner. I slept aboard the drekar, along with Fótr. I wrapped myself in my bear cloak but I was woken in the dark of night by a rainstorm. I took my sealskin cape and fashioned a shelter between my chest and the steering board and I was dry. Ada had made me a potion to help me to sleep and to take away pain if I was hurt. I had decided not to take it but as I tried to get back to sleep, I had no choice but to take a mouthful, washed down with ale. It had the desired effect and I was soon in a sleep that was so deep that I dreamed.

Gytha came to me but she was not the emaciated Gytha I had known for the last year of her life. She was the beautiful woman whom I had known on Orkneyjar. She took me by the

hand and we walked across the water from the drekar to the western shore. She took me to a Skraeling village. It was not Mi'kmaq and I guessed it was Penobscot. Just beyond the village, in a small clearing, I saw the maid but she was crying and she tended what I took to be a grave. I tried to speak to her but could not. She rose and walked to a small stream where she took off her hide shift and stepped into the water. She began to bathe and I averted my eyes. Gytha's lips did not move but I heard her voice in my head, "You must watch, Erik, and you must remember." When I looked back, she had emerged from the water and she began to dry herself. She had hung her hide shift on a branch of a stunted, lightning struck oak. The tree looked to me like a dwarf. I saw two arms and a helmet atop his head. I wondered if some other Viking had come and been transformed into a tree. The maid stood and walked back towards the village. The journey back seemed much longer. When she reached it, a Penobscot woman shouted something and then began to beat her with a stick. I tried to shout but no words came out. I tried to move but it was as though I was stuck in quicksand. Then I realised that I was in quicksand and I was sinking. I flailed my arms as I tried to escape but I could not and I could not breathe.

"Erik! Erik! Wake, you are dreaming!"

When I opened my eyes, I was back on the drekar. Fótr pointed to the cloak, "That was wrapped around your head and it was as though you were trying to fight it. Come, food is ready and Arne is keen to get to Fox Water."

As I put the cloak back into the chest, I wondered if Ada had known I would dream. It would not surprise me. I was happy that day for I had seen the maid and I had seen Gytha. Was my first dream to be realised?

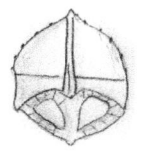

Chapter 17

We only had a few miles to travel and we entered the huge expanse of water a couple of hours before noon. We could have chosen anywhere to camp and to trap but Arne wished to use the western bank. He pointed to a spot halfway along the Water. He said it was because there were rivers and streams and that some of the rivers looked large enough for the drekar. I knew different. He wanted to be as close to the Penobscot as he could for he wanted a war. We rowed slowly across and I aimed for the thinnest patch of trees I could. We needed a camp and I wanted minimal work. The ship's boys tied us to the two largest trees while our lookouts peered west to seek danger.

He and half of the crew, including Siggi and his oathsworn, donned mail and waded ashore. I had moored the drekar close to the side of the huge expanse of water and a stream which fed it. It was too small for us to sail but it would be a way into the land. I had the sail secured. I was tempted to step the mast but if we had to make a hasty retreat then the sail could make all the difference. While Arne and the scouts were out, I had the rest of the warriors go ashore and clear a camp by the river bank. There were just a few trees with overhanging branches and the rest were berry bushes. I set the ship's boys to clearing the bushes of berries and then we would clear away the bushes. I knew that the berries would be a temptation for bears and I wanted to avoid that sort of confrontation. In the absence of Arne, I took charge and when the berries were stripped, I had the bushes pulled up and made into a barrier around the outside of the camp. We could improve it with stakes later but we had a fence of sorts. We had brought some kindling with us and when the men had hewn down a couple of saplings, I lit a fire. We needed dry wood for thick smoke would be seen for miles. As it was, I expected to

The Savage Wilderness

be seen by the Penobscot but I hoped that my deer hide would gain me the time to talk to them before blood was shed.

It was some time before Arne and the men returned. I saw that they had hunted. They carried two white-tailed deer. "We saw no sign of Skraeling but we did see a couple of streams which looked like they might be bjorr rivers. The game is plentiful and I have high hopes that this will be the making of the clan." I nodded. "You and Fótr will stay close to the drekar. I would not risk losing our navigators."

I shook my head, "I will explore the waters close to the drekar for I wish to know the land and to look for signs of Penobscot scouts. You are right to go mailed for you will be protected, even if you are ambushed, but *'Njörðr'* is vulnerable."

I thought he might argue but he agreed, "You make a good point. We have grown apart, Erik, and that is not right. I feel that Siggi, too, is not the blood brother he once was. When we return to Bear Island, we can repair the damage, eh?"

It was typical of the new Arne; he was putting the blame on Siggi and me. I pushed his words from my mind. "Fótr, Arne wishes us to stay aboard but I wish to explore. I will make a camp on the land and leave you on the drekar. Are you comfortable with that?"

He nodded, "If it means I have less to do with Arne then, aye, but will you be safe?"

"I wish to explore the land around here to ensure that we are not attacked. When last we came it was my foray that spotted the Penobscot. Perhaps it was a message." I did not tell Fótr of my dream. If I could find the lightning struck tree then I might understand my dream better.

I went to my chest and took out all that I would need in this wild land. I took out my old seal skin boots, seal skin cape and fur. I packed my satchel with my steel, flint, Ada's salve, honey and vinegar. I do not know why but I also took my spear and shield as well as the bow and my arrow bag.

The men were arranging their own camps with oar brothers. Arne, his son and his oathsworn were the closest to the fire. Siggi, Tostig, Æimundr Loud Voice and Gandálfr were with the more senior men while the younger ones had a camp together. I went to the very edge of the camp. As I had expected, the ship's boys and young warriors who had made the tangled barrier had left a gap by the river. It was a gap through which an enemy could creep. I would make it safer by camping here, and laying down my war gear and satchel I took off my deer hide boots. The river had a muddy bottom but when I stepped in, I did not sink far. I waded down the Water until I found some pieces of driftwood and I dragged them back to my gear. Using the wood I had brought and some smaller branches from the hewn saplings, I made a natural-looking barrier. I used my shield as a roof and I had a dry den as my personal home for the next month. Any Penobscot coming towards the camp from the south would find a natural log jam and head further inland or try to wade past the obstruction. I might be furthest from the fire but I would be dry and safe should we have a night-time attack.

The smell of food drew me to the fire once I had made my camp as comfortable as I could. I turned and looked at my den; it could barely be seen. Siggi smiled when he saw me approach, "We wondered where you were." He pointed to Fótr who was filling his bowl at the pot. "Fótr said you were ashore. Why not camp here with us?"

Siggi was a blood brother and that made him closer than Fótr. "I dreamed and saw somewhere I think might be close. Your mother's spirit guided me. I need to be able to slip in and out of the camp like a ghost."

Siggi shook his head, "You and your dreams." His son came from the drekar. "Here is Snorri. Did his fall not remind you of mine that first voyage?"

I nodded, "It did but did you notice that none mocked him? We have no Karl with us."

He lowered his voice, "Perhaps it is a new Karl who leads us."

"Siggi, if we can avoid a war and return laden with furs then it may be that Arne will revert to the blood brother we both knew."

"You would do as he asks and sail the ocean again?"

"I think it may be my destiny. If I find the tree and the waterfall now then I will have satisfied my curiosity and the dreams will have served their purpose."

Fótr and Snorri Siggison joined us. Siggi said, quietly, "The Norns, Erik, the Norns."

I clutched my hammer of Thor and my fingers touched the bear teeth. Siggi was right, the dream had another purpose and I was deceiving myself.

Arne divided the men into two groups. Æimundr Loud Voice led the hunters. I saw that Siggi, along with Snorri Siggison, went with Æimundr. It was a smaller party who took the traps. Both parties went armed for war but only Arne's trappers wore mail. I saw that he and his trappers had polished their helmets and mail. I wondered at that. It was a cloudy day but all that it needed was for one shaft of sunlight to strike a helmet and it would be like a beacon which could be seen many miles away.

Arne and his trappers followed the stream and I headed south. I had to use the Water to get around the tangle of undergrowth before I found the animal and hunters' trail which skirted the water. None of the human footprints was recent but I was wary. I had my bow, arrows and satchel. I only had ten metal headed arrows but the other ten flint arrows could stop any game I found. I had gone just half a mile when I found a larger trail heading south and west. The trail along the river became wider and I guessed that the trail heading south and west would take me closer to the Penobscot. I followed that trail for I needed to find out if there were any Penobscot close by. We were hunting and trapping later in the year than the last time but then there had been a hunting camp and, there had been the maid! It was a risk taking the trail which would take me further from the camp and closer to Skraelings but it had to be explored. The trail climbed through trees which became increasingly thinner. It did not go to the top of the ridge but followed its contours. A path led to the top but I ignored it and kept along the larger trail which descended to the valley floor. I saw, on the top of the ridge, a stand of pines.

I spied the Penobscot camp not long before noon. I could see that it was deserted for there were no homes and no fires. Even so, I went along the edge of it and as I circumnavigated it, I saw that it was a large one. There had to have been at least forty homes and that meant upwards of four hundred people. That number of warriors could overwhelm us. Having found it, I descended to the valley bottom to confirm my theory that there was water nearby. I reached the small river. It was thirty paces wide and I saw stones below the surface which suggested that the Skraeling could ford it. I drank some of the water for it bubbled and did not smell bad. Finding a place beneath an overhanging tree branch, I ate some dried horse deer where I could not be seen and I contemplated my options. Perhaps the Norns were spinning or maybe the Allfather took a hand but I had a whiff of an animal. The water bubbled before me and the breeze was in my face. I strung my yew bow and took out a good arrow.

Sure enough, there were deer; a small herd of a deer I had not seen before wandered down to the water. They looked to be the size of a large dog, almost a dwarf deer. I nocked the stone-tipped arrow and waited for them to come to drink. The male came first and sniffed the air. He had stubby antlers and his fur was darker than the white-tailed deer. He seemed satisfied and drank. The four females and five young joined him. I saw that one of the females was larger than the others but had a leg which did not move easily. I aimed at her. I pulled back and the arrow flew. As soon as it left the bow it hummed and that was enough of a noise to startle the herd which fled north, away from danger. I hit the female in the side. It was not a killing strike but she had a bad leg. Grabbing my bow and nocking another arrow, I raced across the river where the water came up to my waist and slowed me down but the blood trail was clear to see. The wounded female managed almost a mile before she succumbed to her wound. After checking that the rest had fled, I put my arrow back in my arrow bag and slung my bow. I slung the carcass over my shoulder and headed back to the river.

The river twisted and turned, finally emerging half a mile north of the stream Arne had followed. As I walked down it, I saw the pink-fleshed fish which were so good to eat. We could use fish traps for them. I also saw some stoat and ferret-like creatures as well as the long-eared animals which were so easy to catch. This was a paradise and a man would never go hungry, but there was still no iron. Until we found it then the clan would never be happy on this side of the sea. When I reached the camp, Arne and the trappers were already back.

Eidel Eidelsson began to cheer when I walked into the camp, "It is good to see that Erik the Navigator has not been idle. Let me take that off your hands. I will prepare it for Æimundr Loud Voice and his hunters are not yet returned."

Arne had taken off his mail and helmet, "Well, brother, where did you find this?"

"There is a river north of this stream and it teems with fish as well as these tiny deer. Did you have success?"

He nodded, "We had to walk a long way but we found bjorr. Perhaps we will follow your river tomorrow for the colony we found was small. Did you see any sign of Skraeling?"

I nodded, "I found their summer village." Every ear in the camp heard my words and turned expectantly. "It was empty but it was large and held more than four hundred Penobscot." I saw Arne coming to the same conclusion as me but I explained it for Lars and the other young warriors, "That means it could have contained more than a hundred warriors."

"But you saw no sign of them now?"

"No. They will have gone to their winter homes but this smoke will tell them that someone is here and they will investigate."

"And this time we will be ready. I intend to take some of Æimundr Loud Voice's hunters when we go to your river on the morrow. They can set the traps while we keep watch for the Skraeling."

When Æimundr Loud Voice and his hunters returned, they had four horse deer with them. It had been a success. The senior warriors held a meeting and Arne explained what he wanted to do. Æimundr nodded, "Those who will not hunt tomorrow will prepare the meat and begin to render down the hooves. If we are here for a moon then we can have cured hides to take home with us. This is a good land, jarl."

"And I will have my ship's boys make fish traps and then we will head for some pines I saw. It is close to the Penobscot village but as it is deserted, we can make pine tar. As Æimundr said, if we are here for a month then we have time to gather as much as we can from this verdant land."

Arne was silent and I knew that he was disappointed that he could not show his son how the great Arne Larsson could fight.

The Savage Wilderness

The traps were easy to make and we had all of them laid before noon. I then led Fótr and my boys to the village and thence to the pines. By dark we had the kilns burning away and the natural slope helped us to collect pine tar, not in barrels, for we had used them all, but in clay jugs we had made on Bear Island. I had seen, at the mouth of the river, some river clay and I thought to make some crude jugs just to carry more tar home with us. There were enough pines to keep my boys and me occupied for seven days at least. We could use the kilns after they had made the pine tar to fire the clay pots. We left before dark, leaving the kilns to do their work.

Arne had found more bjorr and this time it was a huge colony but he was still unhappy that he had not seen Skraeling. And so, the first seven nights passed peacefully. Each day we collected great numbers of fish who were unused to fish traps. We made twenty jugs and fired them. Eight survived the process and by the end of the seven days, we had burned all the pine roots and made our tar.

I went alone on the eighth day to collect the last of the tar. There were just two clay jugs but they were like gold. I was going to head back to the camp when I saw a hunting bird, a hawk of some type, and it swooped down towards the river. I was intrigued and, as I had plenty of time to return to camp before dark, I investigated. It was as I neared the stream that my heart skipped a beat and I stopped in shock. I spied the grave I had seen in my dream. There were dead flowers upon it. I looked at the ground and saw footprints. They were either made by a child or a small woman. To confirm it, I headed to the stream and saw the lightning-struck tree. It looked like a dwarf and my dream had been accurate. I saw that the reason the stream was wide enough to bathe was that a small colony of bjorr had built a dam. Selfishly I decided not to share this news with Arne. I would return alone, each day, in the hope that I saw signs of the maid. I knew that it was unlikely for she was a slave and would be close to the main camp but it was a chance and I would take it. Of course, if Laughing Deer was close enough to visit the grave then it meant there could be a Penobscot camp close by too. I had a dilemma; did I tell Arne or not?

Arne and the rest of the warriors were in camp when I returned. "The day after tomorrow we go further afield. I will head west and north for we have trapped all the bjorr and the horse deer herds have moved on."

Although the other warriors, Siggi and Fótr apart, nodded, I knew that his real reason was to provoke a confrontation with the Penobscot. Each day, when I had ventured forth, I had brought the wapapyaki with me. Now I saw that it was even more vital.

While the rest of the warriors spent the day preparing to go into a more dangerous country, I went back to the grave. Before I reached it, I had a feeling that I was being watched and I nocked an arrow. I had become complacent and I was walking in the land as though it was safe and it was not. As I passed the lightning-struck tree and headed towards the grave, I saw that there were more prints leading from the stream. Sniffing the air, I could smell Skraeling. When first he had come to us, Bear Tooth had smelled differently but, as he ate our food and drank our ale, his smell became that of the clan. There were Skraeling close by and I wondered if I should run back to Arne and tell him. Gytha's voice came into my head and just said, *'Peace, Erik the Navigator.'* I walked towards the grave and when I saw it, I stopped. There were fresh flowers upon the grave. It had been tended and the prints I had seen were those of the maid's feet. She had been here and I had missed her.

I headed back to the stream and this time I examined the prints more carefully. I could see the fresh ones and they led from the stream towards the grave and they did not return. Was there another crossing? I thought not and I could still smell Skraeling.

When I reached the grave, I laid down my bow and said, "Laughing Deer, I will not harm you. I am the devil of whom you dreamed." I peered around the trees trying to see her but Skraeling had darker skins than we did and they blended in, especially at this time of year.

Then her voice came from ahead but I could not see her, "You are 'captain'?" She mispronounced the word but I recognised it and remembered that Bear Tooth had called me that.

"Yes, I am. Let me see you for I will not hurt you."

She stepped from the trees and I saw that she had grown in the time that had elapsed since the last time I had seen her. She spoke urgently, "You are in great danger. The Penobscot are close by and they are hunting your men who came in the ship with the snake's head." I picked up my bow and looked frantically around. She laughed, "Not that close. They have made a camp close to the roaring water half a day from here."

I looked from her to the grave, "This is your mother and you brought the flowers?"

She nodded, "She was beaten when you slew so many of their warriors for they blamed us both and she died from a wound to her head."

"But not you?"

She shook her head, "I was given a worse punishment. The warriors took me and that is why I am here with the warriors who come for war. Young females like me, those taken from other tribes and clans, are brought so that when the warriors have victory, they can spill their seed and make new warriors."

"You are Mi'kmaq?"

She nodded, "How did you know?"

"Bear Tooth is of your tribe but a different clan. Come with me to our snake-headed boat and I will take you to Bear Tooth's clan. They will take you back to your family."

She shook her head, "I would give anything to do that but I have a little sister. I cannot leave her."

"Then fetch her." Now I knew the purpose of the dream; I was here to save two slaves and reunite them with their families. "I pointed downstream, "We are moored at the large piece of water where the rivers and streams end."

She nodded, "I will come but it may be too late. The warriors plan an attack on your camp tomorrow."

"They know where it is?"

"The smoke rising from your fires tells them." She looked pleadingly at me, "We can come with you but I pray that you speak truly for if you are a spirit who toys with us then the warriors will use my sister and me until we are dead."

I held the bear teeth, "I swear by this and," I took out my dagger, "and by this, that I will take you to your home."

She smiled and kissed my hand, "Thank you. I know not your name for I saw when I used that word before that it was wrong. What do I call you?"

"I am Erik of the Clan of the Fox."

She said the name a couple of times, almost rolling it around her mouth as though she was tasting it. "It is a good name, I like it. And now I must return before I am missed. They think I collect wood." She turned and was gone so quickly that I thought that she was a sprite or an aelfe. Pausing only long enough to pick up the pine tar I had left by the stream, I ran, for Arne would have his wish; war was coming.

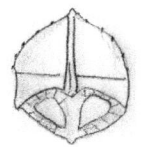

Chapter 18

I burst into the camp so hurriedly that every hand went to a weapon. Arne's eyes narrowed, "What is amiss, brother?"

"The Penobscot know where we are and they plan to attack tomorrow. I know not the time but they will come." I suddenly realised that I had failed to ask Laughing Deer how many warriors there were.

Arne said, "Are you galdramenn that you know this?"

I had to tell him how I knew but I also understood that he would be angry. "The maid from my dream, I met her and she is a slave of the Penobscot. It was she told me."

"And you did not bring her back here? What if she tells the warriors where we are to be found?"

"I told you that they already know that and she has to fetch someone from their camp."

"You know where they have a war camp?"

"By the roaring waters." I shrugged for that was all that I knew.

Gandálfr said, "That sounds to me like a waterfall and if they are close enough to attack then we follow the largest river we can and head for higher ground."

Arne nodded, "But first we prepare for these warriors. We know that they are coming and we can give them a warm welcome. Then we can follow them as they head to the camp and end this. We eat well tonight for tomorrow we go to war! I want a palisade and a ditch surrounding the camp. We will show them how Vikings fight!" As the warriors rushed off, he said, "But you should have brought her and forgotten this ridiculous dream!"

I laughed, "Arne, listen to yourself. It was a dream and it is coming true. Nothing I do or say will change this for it is the Norns. We are in their hands."

I went aboard the drekar, "Fótr, Arne sees tomorrow as an easy battle and it may be but, just in case it is not, let us have the ship's boys prepare to sail if it does not go well. It would be as well to have the barrels of meat and jugs of pine tar loaded anyway for we do not want them damaged by the battle."

He nodded, "Aye, Erik. You spoke to the maid?"

"And she has a younger sister. Now I know why the dream came to me and I know my purpose. I am here to save two slaves."

"Two slaves? Do the Norns care about slaves?"

"Do you remember the story about the Dragonheart?"

"Aye, the warrior with the god touched sword whose spirit guards the Land of the Wolf, what of it?"

"He was taken as a slave by Vikings. He was not Norse. The Norns had plans for him so do not ask why the Norns would worry about a slave. They do." He nodded and went to begin loading the drekar. I would help him but first I went to my chest and took out my helmet. I would be using my bow but I knew how effective stone clubs could be and I needed my head protecting. I still had the helmet liner and I would wear that too. I put all of my weapons in my den and then helped to load the drekar.

Arne was busy supervising the defences but when he saw us loading the barrels he came over, "What is it that you do, Erik?"

"There will be a battle here tomorrow and I do not want the fruits of our labours destroyed. They will be out of the way and safer on the drekar."

He grinned, "I forget sometimes how clever you are. That would have been something Snorri Long Fingers would have done."

"And tomorrow I will command the boys with bows and slings. I brought no mail."

"That is good for you will keep them calm. You should know what I intend. We let them attack us and you will use your bone and stone arrows. When we have blunted their attack and we have bloodied them then we will pursue them back to their camp and we will destroy them. That way we can spend months here rather than weeks."

"The drekar is almost full as it is."

"Aye, we should have brought the snekke too. Next time."

With the defences made, we ate and then half rested while the others watched, I shared a watch with Fótr. All of the warriors were up before dawn. Bear Tooth had said that Skraeling did not like to fight at night but that did not mean they could not move and be ready to fight when the sun rose. I realised that, unless we were very lucky, there would be no shaft of sunlight to shine off a burnished helmet and terrify the enemy. Men made plans but the Norns decided the outcome.

The night was cold and it was damp. I wore my sealskin cloak. I had Harald Gandálfrson with me. I sensed that he was nervous, "Harald, it is unlikely that they will come at night. The jarl is just being cautious."

"I know, Captain, but I will fight tomorrow and will have to kill. What if I am killed?"

"If you are killed then you will have a weapon in your hand and you will go to Valhalla but I do not think you will die, for Arne is a good leader and our camp is well defended but, should the unthinkable happen and the jarl and his warriors are killed, then we have the means to escape on *'Njörðr'*."

"There is no honour in running."

"And to die without living is foolish too. Trust in the shield wall for they will trust that you and your bow can slay as many Skraeling before they reach our wall." That seemed to satisfy him and we watched until it was time to wake the warriors. Dawn was not far away and we would be ready when the barbarians came at us."

We had two very young ships boys with us, Leif Mikelsson and Danr Gandálfrson. Both had seen just seven summers and only had slings. As they were roused and joined me and the other ship's boys, I said, "You two will be on the yard today. From there your slings will send the stones further and you can watch for an attack on the drekar." The fact that they had an important job to do eased the pain of not standing with Erik the Navigator and fighting. Harald's words had made me remember what I had felt when I had been a ship's boy.

It was the sound of disturbed birds which heralded not only the dawn but also the attack. Arne was a canny leader and as soon as the birds flew up with a frightened cacophony of screeches and flapping wings, he ordered the horn sounded. We knew from Bear Tooth that the sound frightened the Skraeling.

Fótr and I were at the two ends of the bowmen and slingers. When I left, he would continue to lead them. "Nock an arrow and prepare a stone. We aim blindly over our shield wall. We keep sending arrows and stones until the stone arrows have all been spent. Then you will all use slings and river stones until we have won."

As the last note of the horn died, we heard screams from the grey light of a western dawn. Arne began to bang his shield with his spear and he began a chant. I knew why he did it. The terrifying screams which rent the air would dishearten the young warriors, including his son Lars, who stood behind him. A man who is singing is not as afraid as one who is not.

Clan of the Fox, from Orkneyjar's shores
Clan of the Fox, take to your oars
Clan of the Fox, we row as one
Clan of the Fox, heading west to the setting sun
Clan of the Fox, from Orkneyjar's shores
Clan of the Fox, take to your oars
Clan of the Fox, we row as one
Clan of the Fox, heading west to the setting sun

Then I saw them. They were less than forty paces from our palisade, "Loose!"

I aimed for I knew which ones were the leaders. The half dozen arrows we sent over found marks but mine hit leaders and killed them. The Penobscot arrows rattled and cracked off mail, metal and wooden shields. It sounded like hailstones. There appeared to be no end to the mass of painted warriors who hurled themselves at the palisade. Inevitably their dead and dying bodies gave them a platform and they would come face to face with the spears of Viking warriors. It would not get any easier for them. I sent my last stone arrow and I turned to Fótr, "I will join our brother in the shield wall."

"May the Allfather be with you."

I ran to my den and, dropping my bow, I picked up my shield and my helmet. By the time I reached the shield wall, I saw that the battle had been engaged and I saw casualties on our side. Stone clubs could break limbs and render warriors unconscious. As I ran to take the place of Gandálfr, I shouted, "Take the wounded on to the drekar!"

Fótr nodded and detailed some of the larger boys to do so. Carrying a fully-grown warrior wearing mail was hard.

I found myself next to Lars Arneson, my nephew. His spearhead was unbloodied. "Uncle, there are so many of them!"

"Just kill them one at a time as your father does." A Penobscot had managed to hurl himself in the air and was descending with a stone axe towards Arne's head. I rammed my spear up and it caught the Penobscot in the centre of his chest. There was a bone there and a stone spear would have shattered. I had honed my spear and it slid in and tore through to his back. I used his momentum to throw his body behind me. Emboldened, Lars thrust between Siggi and his father. His spear struck the open screaming mouth of a warrior and the angle of Lars' thrust drove it into the warrior's brain.

"Good, now twist and withdraw."

It went on for what seemed like hours yet it could not have been. Lars and I thrust and stabbed with our spears while Siggi, Arne and the warriors used swords and axes to hew heads and tear terrible wounds into their bodies. I heard a Skraeling cry out, "Back, we are lost, back and we fight another day." They turned and ran.

Our warriors cheered until Arne shouted, "Silence, this is not over. Those without wounds follow me and we will follow them to their camp. Erik, Fótr, take charge here and dispose of the barbarians!"

Breaking down our own barrier, Arne led the first fifteen warriors in mail to pursue the broken enemy. They clambered over the dead bodies while Fótr and his boys began to shift our wounded and there were more of them than I had expected. Other warriors picked their way through the debris to follow Arne. All that remained were the Skraeling dead and our wounded. Eidel had a wounded arm. From the way it was hanging, I think it had been broken at the wrist. That there appeared to be no dead was a miracle. I began to drag the bodies across the camp and drop them into the river. I could not possibly attempt to remove the charnel house of corpses which lay beyond our barrier and in our ditch. If there had been one hundred warriors in the deserted village then most had perished for I estimated more than eighty dead.

I had just dumped the last one and the wounded were all aboard the drekar when I heard the horn sound. It was the call for help and I knew that disaster had struck; the Norns had spun. Arne had fallen foul of the three sisters. I turned to Fótr, "I will go to our brother's aid."

"Is there no other who can do this?"

I waved a hand. The camp was empty and we two were the only two unwounded warriors left, "You might have to sail back to Bear Island with just this crew. You can do this. The Norns have spun, Fótr. If I do not return then swear you will watch over my family."

"Do not say that! You will return!"

"Then you will not have to keep the oath but just to make me happy, swear on this!" I took the dagger, King Raedwulf's dagger. It bound Siggi and Arne with me and now it would bind Fótr. *Wyrd.*

"I so swear!"

He made the mistake of grabbing the blade and he cut himself, "Now there is blood on the blade and the oath is the most powerful one that a warrior can make. I am content." I sheathed my dagger, "And watch over the clan for that is the lot of our family."

I grabbed my spear and ran off down the path. I passed bodies of Skraeling who had been wounded and had been caught by Arne and our vengeful warriors. I ran harder. I was lucky for I wore no mail. Arne and the others would be exhausted. The Skraeling wore no mail and knew where they were going. It was as though I had second sight for I knew that the Penobscot would have reached their own camp long before Arne and they would have had the opportunity to prepare their own ambush. That was why the horn had been sounded and I feared that I would be too late.

The river was to my left as I ran and the sound of my padding deer hide boots was replaced by the sound of battle. I saw that there were some rapids and rocks. The water bubbled and boiled.

There was no sound of metal on metal. There were cries from the clan and from the Penobscot. There was the sound of wood cracking and stone hitting metal but it was not like a battle in the east. Then I heard, as I neared it, the roar of water from a waterfall; we were close to their camp. I hefted my spear for soon I would need it. As I came around a bend, I saw that Æimundr Loud Voice had a shield wall of men and they were blocking the path. The Skraeling could not get past but the press of the enemy was so great that they could not advance. Then I looked to my left. There was the waterfall of my dream. I would not leave this place for I would anger the Norns. I saw that my brother, Siggi and four others were fighting at the top.

"Æimundr Loud Voice, leave this place and get back to the drekar."

"But the jarl!"

"I will go to his aid. The clan cannot lose you and the others. Fótr has the ship ready to sail, get back to him. It is my command for I am the jarl's brother."

"Aye, Erik, but what will you do?"

"I will climb the other side of the fall. There are no Skraeling there." Even as I looked, Leif Leifsson, one of Arne's oathsworn, fell from the top and I heard his body crash onto the rocks. "Æimundr Loud Voice, go! Save the clan!"

"May the Allfather be with you." He then used his loud voice. "Clan of the Fox, sword foot back!" He began a monotonous chant as the clan stepped backwards. If he kept his movements slow and if the men moved together then they would reach the drekar although it would take some time. The Skraeling could not kill them but they could cause wounds and I doubted that any who returned to *'Njörðr'* would be whole.

I was not wearing mail except for my helmet and I plunged into the water which came to my chest. I forced my way across. Some Skraeling sent arrows at me which hit the water, my hide jerkin and my helmet but none of them caused any damage. When I reached the other side, I shouted, "Brothers of the blade, I come!"

Another body fell onto the rocks. I did not see who it was but I heard the crack as the warrior's spine was shattered. Using the spear as an aid, I climbed up the side of the falls; it was manageable. By the time I reached it, I saw that Siggi, Arne and Lars were the only survivors. The rest were all dead. The three stood on an island of rock in the middle of the falls. To get to it the Skraeling had to jump from rock to rock and they could not do it in numbers. Lars had no shield and his left arm hung down at his side but he still held his sword. There were four rocks I had to jump to reach them. The sound of the falls obliterated any noise I made. The first jump was the easy one for it was just a little longer than a pace. Some of the others meant I had to jump almost two paces and when I landed on their rock, Arne and Siggi whirled with blades ready to skewer me. Siggi grinned, "This is *wyrd*, the brothers of the blade together at the end."

"Who says it is the end? We can get down the way I came up. There is a path down the cliff."

Siggi smiled, "Then there is hope."

Arne asked, "What about Lars, he is wounded and I will not leave him?"

"We leave no one, brother, for we are the Clan of the Fox." I drew King Raedwulf's dagger so that I had two weapons.

The Skraeling were still hurling their clubs and spears at us. Arne and Siggi held their shields above them to protect the three of them and now me. Three Penobscot tried to emulate me using the rocks and islands which lay upstream, one did not make it for he missed his footing and he cracked his head on a stone and slipped over the falls. The other two did make it but I thrust my spear into the chest of one and, as the other landed and struck my shoulder with his axe, I ripped the dagger across his throat. It bought us a little time.

Arne said, "Siggi, jump back on to that rock and I will use my shield to protect Lars and Erik."

I stepped into the space vacated by Siggi as he turned and jumped. He barely made it. He was tired and he wore mail. He turned, grinning, and hefted his shield before him. He shouted, although I barely heard him against the sound of the roaring water, "I am ready!"

"He has made it, Arne!"

He nodded, "Thank you for coming back. I was wrong about you. Forgive me."

"What is to forgive, are we not brothers of the blade?"

The Savage Wilderness

Two more Skraeling tried the leap and they both made it. My shoulder ached from the first blow but I still had the strength to thrust with my spear and gut the Penobscot. Arne was a mighty warrior but he was tiring and although his sword slashed across the savage's head, the dying warrior still managed to ram his spear into Arne's lower leg. Blood poured.

"Lars, you need to follow Siggi. Go now!"

He nodded and, sheathing his sword, he leapt. It was at that moment that a Skraeling arrow hit his calf. Lars made the rock but the arrow was embedded in his leg and I saw the water turn pink close to the rock. Father and son had the same wound and it would slow us as we made our way down the river. Lars showed his courage for he drew his sword and faced the enemy.

Just when we thought we had a chance, a number of Skraeling all decided to make the leap across the water. My rescue attempt had shown them a way to get to us and the wounding of Arne and Lars had given them hope. Three fell into the falls and were swept over to smash upon the rocks below but three others made it. My spear took one but the dying warrior held the shaft as he plunged into the water and I was left with King Raedwulf's dagger. Arne had been attacked by two and his sword became his bane. He rammed his blade into a Skraeling but he could not withdraw it and the other Penobscot smashed his stone club into the side of my brother's head. As his head turned, I saw the light leave his eyes as he died. I rammed the dagger up into the enemy warrior's rib cage for he had killed my brother. Arne's body tumbled into the water and slipped over the falls. The jarl of the Clan of the Fox was dead. I pulled his sword from the dead Skraeling.

I heard, as though it was in the distance, a voice, it was Lars, "Father! Noooo!"

Siggi shouted, "It is now or never, Erik!" Each rock we jumped would make it harder for the Skraeling to reach us and I jumped. As I did so, something hit my back and when I landed, I was winded. The Norns were spinning for as Siggi bent to help me up a spear was hurled and hit Lars in the face. He fell backwards into the water. He was swept over the falls still holding his sword in his dead hand. He would be in Valhalla!

The Savage Wilderness

As I stood, still trying to get my breath, three Skraeling followed my path and jumped to our rock. Siggi swung his sword and connected with the side of the head of one while a second stabbed at Siggi with his stone dagger. I blocked the Penobscot club which came at my head with my dagger while forcing Arne's sword up through the rib cage and into the skull of the other. I twisted his body and two Penobscot arrows hit him. His dying body knocked the last warrior into the falls. There were just two of us left for Arne, his son and his oathsworn were all dead. I risked looking over my shoulder. I could see Æimundr Loud Voice still backing down the path. Soon they would be lost to sight but the Skraeling were not hurting them.

Siggi said, "The last blow drew blood; I am hurt. Save yourself, Erik, and I will hold them off."

"We are brothers of the blade and we swore an oath, let us keep it. Jump to the next rock for that will leave just one and then we can reach the bank for it is the shortest jump."

"You had best go first and you can pull me across. I tire."

His words made sense and I jumped, When I made it easily, I grew in confidence. I turned and said, "I am here, Siggi."

He slipped his shield over his back and sheathed his sword. He took a run and he leapt. A spear and an axe came at the same time. The spear hit his shield and did no harm but the stone club hit his helmet and unbalanced him. He missed his footing and landed in the water. I knelt and offered my right arm. He tried to grab it but missed. As he was swept over the falls, I heard him say, "Siggi the Clumsy!" I saw that behind his shield he held a dagger. He would go to Valhalla and I would see him there.

I retrieved my brother's sword and stood. I was angry and the tears which came were a mixture of anger and sadness. The Norns had toyed with me. They had given me a dream which suggested hope and yet it had ended in tragedy. I raised my sword and shouted in Mi'kmaq, "One of the Clan of the Fox remains alive. I fear no Penobscot! Come one come all and I will slay each one of you!"

Even as three of them came at me, I wondered it Fótr would take the maid and her sister to Bear Island. Perhaps that was meant to be.

The Savage Wilderness

I no longer had the advantage of a spear and the first savage did. As he rammed it at me, I twisted. He caught a piece of bone on my jerkin and the end caught and stuck. The blow still hurt but I spun around. His momentum carried him over the falls and my dagger, still in my left hand, slashed across his throat. Blood sprayed over me. The last warrior was blinded by the blood and my sword took his head in one blow. His torso stood, briefly and then toppled over the falls. I put my dagger in my sheath and I leapt to the last rock. I turned, just in time to see two more warriors come at me. I had no dagger and so I stabbed one with my sword and head-butted the other with my helmet. His dagger raked down my left arm and the blood flowed freely.

I could still escape. If I could make the last jump, I would be on the bank and I could climb down the waterfall. I sheathed my sword and prepared to jump. I was actually in the air when something, I guessed it was a stone club or axe, hit the side of my head. The last thing I saw before all went black were the rocks at the bottom of the falls. They were covered in dead men including the body of my cousin Siggi. My last thought was that I was not holding my sword and I would not go to Valhalla. I would spend the next life drifting in darkness. My last sight in this world was Arne's broken body and then all went black.

Fótr

Fótr and the Clan of the Fox

It was almost dark when Æimundr Loud Voice, leading the survivors of the disaster at the falls, made it to the drekar. I had the ships' boys on the ropes and I held my bow. The Skraeling fought all the way to the camp. When I loosed a hopeful arrow in the air and killed a large, bloody warrior they seemed to lose hope and they fell back. I did not see faces, just warriors. When they were all aboard, I said, "Are the others following?"

Æimundr Loud Voice took off his helmet. I saw blood dripping down his cheek from a scalp wound. He shook his head and said, "They are all dead, the jarl, his oathsworn, his son. Siggi and Erik."

"Not Erik, surely not the Navigator?"

"I wish it was not true but it is. Erik almost saved them. He climbed the waterfall and almost brought them to safety. We waited to watch and see if we could help but first the Jarl, then his son and finally Siggi were washed over the falls and plunged to their deaths on the rocks below. Siggi had a blade in his hand, as did Lars."

"But Erik!"

"We watched him defy all and then, as he leapt, an axe hit him in the side of the head and he joined his brother and cousin. I am sorry." They all looked at me. Æimundr Loud Voice said, "You are, until we reach Bear Island, the captain and jarl. What are your orders?"

My brother had made it quite clear what I had to do and I would obey his last orders. "We sail home! Cast off and lower the sail." I walked to the steering board and, opening Erik's chest, took out the hourglass, compass and his charts. I looked at the fresh wound in the palm of my hand. I had sworn a blood oath and I owed it to Erik to keep that oath and watch over his family. I sat on the chest and pushed the steering board over. It was dark but I knew that we had to sail down the river and reach the sea. My brother had told me how the Skraeling had tried to ambush them with boats. The longer we stayed, the more chance they had of doing so.

"Stig Eidelsson, I need you here at the steering board." My brother's ship's boy joined me. The news of Erik's death had spread and there was a pall of despair in the drekar. Arne was forgotten but Erik and Siggi would be mourned. "Stig, I need you so come back to this life and leave my dead brother behind. We mourn him when we are back at Bear Island." He nodded, "Only you have done this journey at night. I need you to be my eyes, I need you to be Erik. He would wish this. Can you do it?"

I saw steel in his eyes, "For Erik, aye. We need someone at the prow, Captain."

"Harald, get to the prow and use your eyes!"

Snorri Siggison came along the drekar, "What do I do, Captain?" He sounded as though he was in a trance. He had lost a father but I did not dare mention that in case he shattered like a piece of ice. I needed him occupied.

"I want you with Harald and you can bring any messages. The two of you will get us home and the clan will thank you."

He nodded, dully, "But not my father."

I pointed up to the sky, "He died with a sword in his hand and so he is in Valhalla."

He brightened and taking out his dagger he pointed it to the sky, "Fear not, father, I will care for my mother and my sisters, I will be the warrior of the family."

"Go and help Harald."

Stig said, "That was well done, Captain."

I shook my head, "Nothing, save Erik's sacrifice, was well done on this raid. We should have stayed on Bear Island and awaited the peace."

"We still can!"

"Can we?"

All through the night and the next morning as we headed for Bear Island, I wrestled with the events which had, to all intents and purposes, destroyed the clan. Arne's plan was in tatters but we had two drekar and a snekke. We had lost many men and the ones who were left, with one or two exceptions, were like me, the younger warriors. I did not leave the steering board for a whole day and a night. I did not need to make water and all that I had to drink was one beaker of ale. I should have been dropping but I kept going. I had the bad news to deliver to many families but the hardest would be my own, Helga and Ada were like sisters to me. I knew not what Freja would make of it all. She had two toddlers and a baby son, Arne. Her world had been destroyed more than any.

It was fortunate that we had not had to row for I am not sure that we could have done. The men had wounds but more than that they had their heart torn from them. The clan could have had no warning of the disaster for with Gytha gone we had no one to speak to the spirits. The faces which lined the quay were full of joy. I saw wives looking for husbands. The benign wind set us gently to rest and the ship's boys quickly tied us to the shore. Reginleif looked joyous but Ada and Gefn showed that they understood why Siggi and Erik were not there. Freja just kept staring along the side of the drekar as though hoping that Arne and Lars would manifest themselves. Tostig was the first to board and he looked at the faces of the crew seeking his brother and Erik.

I shook my head, "Come Tostig, I will speak with you and Helga first. I have much bad news to spread." I stepped ashore. Helga was the senior member of the family now and she walked towards me, "What happened, Fótr?"

I was aware that all the families who lived close to the bay were present and each and everyone was listening intently. I shouted, "We have warriors who have hurts but what you need to know is that the Jarl, his son, his brother Erik and Siggi their cousin, the jarl's oathsworn, all died in battle with the Skraeling. They took many enemies with them and their deaths were glorious but they are dead." I did not believe in the glory of those deaths but it was what I was expected to say.

Freja pointed an accusing finger at me, "You lie! You and your brother, Erik, have conspired with these traitors to kill my husband and my son. I curse you! I curse you! I curse you!" She ran off leaving a shocked clan.

I confess that I felt as though I had been slapped and I just stood shaking my head. Æimundr Loud Voice stepped forward,

"Freja, wife of Arne, is wrong. We did all that we could to save them. Erik need not have died. He could be here now but he saved me and most of the clan and he almost saved the jarl!"

Helga nodded, "Freja has no powers but Gefn, Ada and I will spin this night and we will speak with the Otherworld. If they are in Valhalla then we will know."

I nodded, "Have the ship unloaded and the furs stored. They cost the clan all and we owe it to the dead to save that which they gave their lives for." I wanted to speak with Ada but it was not the time. I had work to do and the three volvas had to undo a spell.

In the end, I did not speak to Ada until the next day. Unloading had taken a long time and the three healers had had much work to do. When I spoke to Ada and told her of the maid, she seemed relieved. "I had thought he would live with the maid but if he intended to bring the maid and her sister here then that is different." She looked up to the skies, "I am sorry, Erik, I misjudged you and I should have known better." She smiled, "Your promise to care for us is unnecessary. Bear Tooth is almost a man and Ebbe is not far behind."

"Nonetheless, I swore an oath!" I held up my palm. And now we need a Thing."

She shook her head, "Helga, Gefn and I spoke on this when we lifted the curse. We need a Thing for we have to have a purpose and a jarl but now is too soon for the wounds are still raw. The three of us will spin tomorrow night and speak with the dead. Until then, spend time with your family. It was what Erik would have wished." She patted her belly, "And I will have another child to remember Erik by."

I spent the rest of the day speaking with the widows of the dead and assuring them that they would have a place in the clan for as long as they would need it. I was ready to go back to my family when Gefn sought me out.

"Freja is missing!"

"How do you know?"

"She has abandoned her children. Young Arne needed milk and his sister, Maren, and brother Siggi, brought him to me for she could not find Freja. A mother does not abandon her baby!" She was angry.

The Savage Wilderness

I nodded and went to the horn. The last time it had been blown was by Æimundr Loud Voice to fetch help for the jarl was in danger and now we blew it for his wife. *Wyrd*. When the people came, I told them that we had to search the island for her. There were no dangerous animals but there were places where she could hurt herself. It took all day and it was Bear Tooth and I who found her. She was close to the bear cave and she had climbed to the top of the hill which covered it and thrown herself to the rocks below. Bear Tooth offered to climb down and fetch her body back for burial but those with us said it was the Norns and he should leave her where she had died. Even as we prepared to leave, a wild wave came and swept her body from the rock.

The three volvas communed with the spirits and discovered that of the four, only Siggi and Lars were in Valhalla. Gefn was distraught but Ada just took the news philosophically. "Erik was never a warrior; he was a sailor. When we sail east, I will listen for the seabird which has his spirit. It will talk to me."

I was sad for I hoped to die with my sword in my hand and go to Valhalla. I wanted to see my brother in the Otherworld.

We held the Thing at the Winter Solstice. It seemed right and we held it on the beach. The wind blew savagely but it was dry and none wanted to be indoors. There were less than twenty-eight men at the Thing. I began it by asking what they wanted to happen.

Harold of Dyroy said, "I want to go home and I think most of the clan do too, but first we need a jarl. I say it should be Fótr, brother of Erik, who would have been my choice had he lived. That is all I have to say."

Rather than being insulted with the title of second choice I was flattered. The clan ignored the conventions and all shouted Fótr, and in that single moment, I became jarl of the Clan of the Fox. I did not want to be jarl but I had no choice. Erik had made that quite clear. When I asked for a vote on whether to go or to stay it was unanimous. All wished to leave. They wanted to leave as soon as the winter storms had gone. We decided that would be Einmánuður. The hard work began. I thought that was ironic for Einmánuður was when we were supposed to have our answer from the Skraeling. Now that answer did not matter.

Helga's husband, Padraig, was chosen to captain *'Njörðr'* for he knew it well. Aed could sail the snekke. We would not have enough men to row, although that might not always be necessary, Erik had told me the winds would help us. Even in death, he served the clan. The lack of numbers meant we could take all of the animals as well as the valuable furs. We planned on heading to Whale Island in the Land of the Wolf. We were not enough to fight for land and the Clan of the Wolf had been, in the past, our friends. We packed the three ships at night and camped by the beach with our animals. Our homes were left standing for we had not the heart to destroy them. Who knew what the future held? Only Verðandi, and I had had enough of the Norns. Perhaps others would hear our tales and come west. I believed that the Mi'kmaq would honour the peace but the seas were wide and it took hardy men to sail them. But for the courage of my brother, we would not have done this.

Before we left, Tostig and Helga went to the place we had burned their parents and left a sacrifice. They came back to the three ships content.

As the sun rose, I ordered the animals and people to be boarded and, with *'Gytha'* leading, we left the bay to sail around the island and head out to sea. As the sun shone on to the mainland, I saw Skraeling on the beach. They had come early with their camps or perhaps it was to find out if we still wished peace. I will never know for the wind came from the west and we sped through the channel and out to sea. I could not look back as I was the navigator and I had to look forward. The Clan of the Fox returned home.

Erik

Epilogue

It was as though I was flying on a dark night. I felt as though I was high in the air and I wondered if this was the Otherworld. My sword had not been in my hand when I had died and I would be reborn as a seabird constantly sailing the seas and I thought, as I floated in the blackness, that such a life was not a bad one for a navigator. And then I plunged down to the sea. I knew it was the sea for it was cold and it was wet. I found myself choking and I wondered why for I had always been able to swim. It was at that moment that I wondered if I was dead. Did the dead feel pain, for I felt pain? I tried to open my eyes for if I could see where I was then I would know if I was dead or alive. Then I heard Gytha's voice in my head and when she spoke, I was convinced that I was in the Otherworld.
"Fight for your life! Do not surrender! You are a Viking!"

I was not in the Otherworld and I kicked and flailed my arms. Suddenly I saw the sky above me, and the water around me bubbled and boiled. I knew where I was, I was in the water downstream from the waterfall. The fall had not killed me and I was alive! If I could make the river bank then I could clamber ashore. I kicked as hard as I could but I was not certain which way I faced. Either bank would do. My hand grabbed a tuft of grass and I pulled but it slipped from my grasp and I brought my arm over and grabbed again. This time I found a branch and when I pulled it held. I tried to use my left arm but it hurt too much. I remembered that I had been stabbed there. I used one hand to haul myself up and by scrambling with my feet, I managed it. I was aware that I was in plain sight and I rolled away from the water. The Allfather helped me for there was a slight bank and I lay there, breathing heavily. I was about to try to rise when I heard voices. They were Penobscot and so I lay as still as I could. Their words were indistinct which made me think that they were on the other side of the river. When they faded, I reached down and took out my dagger. If they came again and found me, I would take as many with me as I could. I decided to wait until dusk before I moved.

I heard more voices but this time they were heading towards the still roaring falls. I lifted my head when darkness fell. I saw nothing and more importantly, I heard no one. I rose. My arm and back, not to mention my head, all hurt. The blood was still flowing and so I tied a thong from my jerkin to slow the blood and help the wound to scab. I headed down the path knowing that I would have to cross the river sometime if I was to get back to the drekar. I felt dizzy and I lurched forward into a shallow sleep. I had no idea how long I was out but I knew that I had to get across the river now before I was incapable of doing so. When I made the drekar then Fótr could heal me. I looked up and downstream. I saw a movement and I waited before I moved. I saw that it was a body floating down the river. It was the headless body of the warrior I had decapitated. I took it as a sign and I dived in the water. I used my legs to kick. It hurt my back but I managed to make progress and the current helped me by taking me towards the drekar.

Once again, getting out was harder than getting in for the sword, still sheathed in its scabbard, tried to drag me down but I managed it for I had developed a technique of using my feet to do most of the work. I managed it quicker this time but I made the mistake of standing and walking too soon. I knew I was not far from the ship. I managed barely twenty steps before I lurched forward. This time, as I slipped into oblivion, I knew I was in more danger for I had heard Penobscot on this side of the river. This time, if they caught me and killed me, I would go to Valhalla for my hand still grasped King Raedwulf's dagger.

Ada was stroking my brow with water and she was speaking to me. How could that be? The water on my head roused me and I opened my eyes. I was looking into the face of the maid, Laughing Deer. She smiled when I opened my eyes, "I thought you were dead. I have bandaged your head but we cannot stay here. The Penobscot are everywhere!"

I stood, sheathing my dagger as I did so. I did not want to hurt her by accident. "We can go to my ship." She looked puzzled and I said, "Snake headed boat."

She shook her head, "It is gone. The Penobscot wrecked your camp. Stands Alone and I went there first."

"Stands Alone?"

Laughing Deer stood to the side and I saw a little girl of perhaps five or six. "It is my sister but she has not spoken since we were taken captive four summers since."

I nodded, the Norns were still spinning, "We will go to the camp in any case. There are things there I need."

"I told you, it has been wrecked."

I smiled, "Lead me there."

When we reached it, I saw that she was right but it was the main camp they had destroyed. I went to my little den. It must have been dusk when they vented their anger on the camp and had missed my den. I put my satchel over my shoulder and donned my bear cloak. I put the seal skin cape over the satchel. I slung my shield over my back and regretted it for my back still hurt. To my delight, I found that my bow with eight arrows in my arrow bag was untouched and undamaged. I was a Viking and so long as I had weapons then I had a chance. I scrabbled around in the dark and found an ale skin I had left. It was half full. I drank some and offered some to Laughing Deer. "Drink."

She drank and said, "It tastes funny."

"Give some to your sister." Stands Alone would not drink. I could not force her. She would drink when she was thirsty. I took some dried deer from my satchel. I chewed a piece and gave one to each of the girls.

As I chewed, I noticed that they both had a hide bag slung over their backs. We had to get across the river to the Mi'kmaq side and then make our way to Bear Island. The ale and the deer had worked their magic.

"We need to get across the river. I know it is wide here but how can we do this?"

She pointed south, "Half a day from here is a birch bark boat. It is damaged and was abandoned but I think we can repair it." She looked at me, "You said you will take us home. Did you mean it?"

"I meant it when I said it and I mean it now. Let us go for the Penobscot will be back in the morning." I said, "We must walk in the river or they will follow us. Will your sister let me carry her?"

"No, Erik, but I can carry her if you carry our bags!"

And so, the three most incongruous group of people headed south down the River of Peace. We were miles away from the nearest help and so close to our enemies that if we sneezed too loudly, they would find us but, as we waded through the water in the middle of a chilly autumn night, I was content for Fótr and the ship had escaped and that meant my family would be safe and my dream had been true. I knew not what the future held. In all likelihood it was death but I was alive. My two brothers of the blade were dead but the Norns had saved me, for whatever reason, and I would take this maid and her sister back to her tribe and then walk to the coast near to Bear Island. They could not return to Larswick until the spring. I had all winter to make the journey. There was a new hope and I had the spirit of Gytha to guide me.

The End

Norse Calendar

Gormánuður October 14th - November 13th
Ýlir November 14th - December 13th
Mörsugur December 14th - January 12th
Þorri - January 13th - February 11th
Gói - February 12th - March 13th
Einmánuður - March 14th - April 13th
Harpa April 14th - May 13th
Skerpla - May 14th - June 12th
Sólmánuður - June 13th - July 12th
Heyannir - July 13th - August 14th
Tvímánuður - August 15th - September 14th
Haustmánuður September 15th-October 13th

Glossary

Afen- River Avon
Afon Hafron- River Severn in Welsh
Àird Rosain – Ardrossan (On the Clyde Estuary)
Balley Chashtal -Castleton (Isle of Man)
Bebbanburgh- Bamburgh Castle, Northumbria is also known as Din Guardi in the ancient tongue
Beck- a stream
Beinn na bhFadhla- Benbecula in the Outer Hebrides
Blót – a blood sacrifice made by a jarl
Bondi- Viking farmers who fight
Bjarnarøy –Great Bernera (Bear Island)
Bjorr – Beaver
Byrnie- a mail or leather shirt reaching down to the knees
Càrdainn Ros -Cardross (Argyll)
Chape- the tip of a scabbard
Cyninges-tūn – Coniston. It means the estate of the king (Cumbria)
Dùn Èideann –Edinburgh (Gaelic)
Drekar- a Dragon ship (a Viking warship) pl. drekar
Duboglassio –Douglas, Isle of Man
Dun Holme- Durham
Dún Lethglaise - Downpatrick (Northern Ireland)
Dyrøy –Jura (Inner Hebrides)
Dyflin- Old Norse for Dublin
Eoforwic- Saxon for York
Føroyar- Faroe Islands
Fey- having second sight
Firkin- a barrel containing eight gallons (usually beer)
Fret-a sea mist
Fyrd-the Saxon levy
Gaill- Irish for foreigners
Galdramenn- wizard
Hersey- Isle of Arran
Hersir- a Viking landowner and minor noble. It ranks below a jarl
Hí- Iona (Gaelic)
Hjáp - Shap- Cumbria (Norse for stone circle)

Hoggs or Hogging- when the pressure of the wind causes the stern or the bow to droop
Hrams-a – Ramsey, Isle of Man
Hundred- Saxon military organization. (One hundred men from an area-led by a thegn or gesith)
Hwitebi- Norse for Whitby, North Yorkshire
Jarl- Norse earl or lord
Joro-goddess of the earth
kjerringa - Old Woman- the solid block in which the mast rested
Knarr- a merchant ship or a coastal vessel
Kyrtle-woven top
Ljoðhús- Lewis
Lochlannach – Irish for Northerners (Vikings)
Lough- Irish lake
Lundenburh/Lundenburgh- the walled burh built around the old Roman fort
Lundenwic - London
Mast fish- two large racks on a ship designed to store the mast when not required
Mockasin- Algonquin for moccasin
Midden- a place where they dumped human waste
Miklagård - Constantinople
Njörðr- God of the sea
Nithing- A man without honour (Saxon)
Odin- The "All Father" God of war, also associated with wisdom, poetry, and magic (The Ruler of the gods).
Orkneyjar-Orkney
Ran- Goddess of the sea
Roof rock- slate
Saami- the people who live in what is now Northern Norway/Sweden
Samhain- a Celtic festival of the dead between 31st October and 1st November (Halloween)
Scree- loose rocks in a glacial valley
Seax – short sword
Sennight- seven nights- a week
Sheerstrake- the uppermost strake in the hull
Sheet- a rope fastened to the lower corner of a sail

Shroud- a rope from the masthead to the hull amidships
Skræling -Barbarian
Skeggox – an axe with a shorter beard on one side of the blade
Skíð -the Isle of Skye
Skreið- stockfish (any fish which is preserved)
Smoky Bay- Reykjavik
Snekke- a small warship
Stad- Norse settlement
Stays- ropes running from the mast-head to the bow
Strake- the wood on the side of a drekar
Suðreyjar – Southern Hebrides (Islay)
Syllingar Insula, Syllingar- Scilly Isles
Tarn- small lake (Norse)
The Norns- The three sisters who weave webs of intrigue for men
Thing-Norse for a parliament or a debate (Tynwald in the Isle of Man)
Thor's day- Thursday
Threttanessa- a drekar with 13 oars on each side.
Thrall- slave
Trenail- a round wooden peg used to secure strakes
Tynwald- the Parliament on the Isle of Man
Úlfarrberg- Helvellyn
Úlfarrland- Cumbria
Úlfarrston- Ulverston
Ullr-Norse God of Hunting
Ulfheonar-an elite Norse warrior who wore a wolf skin over his armour
Veisafjǫrðr – Wexford (Ireland)
Verðandi -the Norn who sees the future
Volva- a witch or healing woman in Norse culture
Waeclinga Straet- Watling Street (A5)
Walhaz -Norse for the Welsh (foreigners)
Waite- a Viking word for farm
Wapapyaki -Wampum
Withy- the mechanism connecting the steering board to the ship
Woden's day- Wednesday

The Savage Wilderness

Wulfhere-Old English for Wolf Army
Wyddfa-Snowdon
Wykinglo- Wicklow (Ireland)
Wyrd- Fate
Wyrme- Norse for Dragon
Yard- a timber from which the sail is suspended
Ynys Enlli- Bardsey Island
Ynys Môn-Anglesey

Historical Note

I use my vivid imagination to tell my stories. I am a writer and this book is very much a 'what if' sort of book. We now know that the Vikings reached further south in mainland America than we thought. Just how far is debatable. The evidence we have is from the sagas. Vinland was named after a fruit which could be brewed into wine was discovered. It does not necessarily mean grapes. King Harald Finehair did drive many Vikings west but I cannot believe that they would choose to live on a volcanic island.

I have my clan reaching Newfoundland and sailing down the coast of Nova Scotia. The island I call Bear Island is Isle Au Haut off the Maine coast. Grey Fox Island and (Horse) Deer Island can also be found there. The Indigenous people, the Mi'kmaq, inhabited the northeastern coast of America. In the summer they would migrate to the coast and in winter when there were fewer flies, they would retreat back to the hinterland. The maps are how Erik might have mapped them. Butar's deer are caribou and the horse deer are moose. Both were native to the region.

For the voyage, I used the records of single-handed sailings and rowing of the Atlantic.

The Vikings were a complicated people. Forget movies where they wear horned helmets and spend all their time pillaging. They did pillage and they could be cruel but they were also traders and explorers. The discovery of Iceland and after that Greenland and America has been put down to the attempt by King Harald Finehair to create a Viking Empire. True Vikings never liked kings. Rather than be taxed they sought new lands. Iceland was empty and bare but they made it their home.

http://www.hurstwic.org/history/articles/daily_living/text/Demographics.htm is a good website with some interesting stats. In 1000 AD 75% of Vikings were under 50 and under 15s represented half! A boy was considered a fully-grown man by the time he was 16. A man could be a judge at the age of 12. Helgi and Bergr were 10 and 12 when they avenged their father by killing his killer. We cannot imagine their world.

The compass I refer to was used in the Viking times. There is a Timewatch programme made by the BBC in which Robin Knox Johnston uses the compass to sail from Norway to Iceland. He was just half a mile out when he arrived.

A word about honey in the new world. One of my readers pointed out that the honey bee was not introduced into North America until the first Europeans came over. I found this hard to believe as honey is found on every other continent. I discovered that the Mayans used honey from a stingless bee. I will continue, therefore, to allow Gytha to brew mead from honey and for my Vikings to use it for wounds. I am working on the principle that if the Mayans had it then another tribe might have been as resourceful!

I have had to use my imagination a great deal for I am writing about a time 600 years before the next Europeans visited the New World. The tribes who were found in Northeastern America would have evolved in that six hundred years. The landscape would, largely, be the same but the people would have different alliances, tribal areas and, perhaps, organization. I have used a dwarf deer in the story as there were such dwarf deer in the rest of the world. In south-east Asia, they continue to thrive but one species, Candiacervus, became extinct in Europe after the last Ice Age and when man was first colonising the northern lands. As I say, this is a what-if book- welcome to my mind!

I used the following books for research:

- Vikings- Life and Legends -British Museum
- Saxon, Norman and Viking by Terence Wise (Osprey)
- The Vikings (Osprey) -Ian Heath
- Byzantine Armies 668-1118 (Osprey)-Ian Heath
- Romano-Byzantine Armies 4th-9th Century (Osprey) -David Nicholle
- The Walls of Constantinople AD 324-1453 (Osprey) -Stephen Turnbull
- Viking Longship (Osprey) - Keith Durham
- The Vikings in England Anglo-Danish Project

The Savage Wilderness

- Anglo Saxon Thegn AD 449-1066- Mark Harrison (Osprey)
- Viking Hersir- 793-1066 AD - Mark Harrison (Osprey)
- Hadrian's Wall- David Breeze (English Heritage)
- National Geographic- March 2017
- Time Life Seafarers-The Vikings Robert Wernick

Griff Hosker
September 2019

Other books by Griff Hosker

If you enjoyed reading this book, then why not read another one by the author?

Ancient History

The Sword of Cartimandua Series
(Germania and Britannia 50 A.D. – 128 A.D.)
Ulpius Felix- Roman Warrior (prequel)
The Sword of Cartimandua
The Horse Warriors
Invasion Caledonia
Roman Retreat
Revolt of the Red Witch
Druid's Gold
Trajan's Hunters
The Last Frontier
Hero of Rome
Roman Hawk
Roman Treachery
Roman Wall
Roman Courage

The Wolf Warrior series
(Britain in the late 6th Century)
Saxon Dawn
Saxon Revenge
Saxon England
Saxon Blood
Saxon Slayer
Saxon Slaughter
Saxon Bane
Saxon Fall: Rise of the Warlord
Saxon Throne
Saxon Sword

Medieval History

The Savage Wilderness

The Dragon Heart Series
Viking Slave
Viking Warrior
Viking Jarl
Viking Kingdom
Viking Wolf
Viking War
Viking Sword
Viking Wrath
Viking Raid
Viking Legend
Viking Vengeance
Viking Dragon
Viking Treasure
Viking Enemy
Viking Witch
Viking Blood
Viking Weregeld
Viking Storm
Viking Warband
Viking Shadow
Viking Legacy
Viking Clan
Viking Bravery

The Norman Genesis Series
Hrolf the Viking
Horseman
The Battle for a Home
Revenge of the Franks
The Land of the Northmen
Ragnvald Hrolfsson
Brothers in Blood
Lord of Rouen
Drekar in the Seine
Duke of Normandy
The Duke and the King

Danelaw

The Savage Wilderness

(England and Denmark in the 11th Century)
Dragon Sword
Oathsword
Bloodsword
Danish Sword

New World Series
Blood on the Blade
Across the Seas
The Savage Wilderness
The Bear and the Wolf
Erik The Navigator
Erik's Clan
The Last Viking

The Vengeance Trail

The Conquest Series
(Normandy and England 1050-1100)
Hastings

The Aelfraed Series
(Britain and Byzantium 1050 A.D. - 1085 A.D.)
Housecarl
Outlaw
Varangian

The Reconquista Chronicles
Castilian Knight
El Campeador
The Lord of Valencia

The Anarchy Series England 1120-1180
English Knight
Knight of the Empress
Northern Knight
Baron of the North
Earl

The Savage Wilderness

King Henry's Champion
The King is Dead
Warlord of the North
Enemy at the Gate
The Fallen Crown
Warlord's War
Kingmaker
Henry II
Crusader
The Welsh Marches
Irish War
Poisonous Plots
The Princes' Revolt
Earl Marshal
The Perfect Knight

Border Knight
1182-1300
Sword for Hire
Return of the Knight
Baron's War
Magna Carta
Welsh Wars
Henry III
The Bloody Border
Baron's Crusade
Sentinel of the North
War in the West
Debt of Honour
The Blood of the Warlord
The Fettered King
de Montfort's Crown

Sir John Hawkwood Series
France and Italy 1339- 1387
Crécy: The Age of the Archer
Man At Arms
The White Company
Leader of Men

The Savage Wilderness

Tuscan Warlord

Lord Edward's Archer
Lord Edward's Archer
King in Waiting
An Archer's Crusade
Targets of Treachery
The Great Cause
Wallace's War

**Struggle for a Crown
1360- 1485**
Blood on the Crown
To Murder a King
The Throne
King Henry IV
The Road to Agincourt
St Crispin's Day
The Battle for France
The Last Knight
Queen's Knight

Tales from the Sword I
(Short stories from the Medieval period)

**Tudor Warrior series
England and Scotland in the late 14th and early 15th century**
Tudor Warrior
Tudor Spy
Flodden

**Conquistador
England and America in the 16th Century**
Conquistador
The English Adventurer

Modern History

The Savage Wilderness

The Napoleonic Horseman Series
Chasseur à Cheval
Napoleon's Guard
British Light Dragoon
Soldier Spy
1808: The Road to Coruña
Talavera
The Lines of Torres Vedras
Bloody Badajoz
The Road to France
Waterloo

The Lucky Jack American Civil War series
Rebel Raiders
Confederate Rangers
The Road to Gettysburg

Soldier of the Queen series
Soldier of the Queen
Redcoat's Rifle

The British Ace Series
1914
1915 Fokker Scourge
1916 Angels over the Somme
1917 Eagles Fall
1918 We will remember them
From Arctic Snow to Desert Sand
Wings over Persia

Combined Operations series 1940-1945
Commando
Raider
Behind Enemy Lines
Dieppe
Toehold in Europe
Sword Beach
Breakout

The Savage Wilderness

The Battle for Antwerp
King Tiger
Beyond the Rhine
Korea
Korean Winter

Tales from the Sword II
(Short stories from the Modern period)

Other Books
Great Granny's Ghost (Aimed at 9-14-year-old young people)

For more information on all of the books then please visit the author's website at www.griffhosker.com where there is a link to contact him or visit his Facebook page: GriffHosker at Sword Books

Printed in Great Britain
by Amazon